JUST BREATHE

Also by Cammie McGovern

A Step Toward Falling
Say What You Will

JUST BREATHE

BREATHE

CAMMIE McGOVERN

HARPER TEEN

An Imprint of HarperCollinsPublishers

Library of Congress Control Number: 2019947138
ISBN 978-0-06-246335-7

Typography by Chris Kwon
19 20 21 22 23   PC/LSCH   10 9 8 7 6 5 4 3 2 1
❖
First Edition

JUST BREATHE

PART ONE

CHAPTER ONE

JAMIE

From: turnerj@northwoods.edu
To: sheinmand@northwoods.edu
Subject: Hello!

Dear David,
I just wanted to tell you that I can't really do this idea of being pen pals or whatever you're suggesting. I'm not very good at that kind of thing. I'm sorry. I hope you're feeling better soon.
Signed, Jamie

I've already wasted way too much time thinking about this response. If he writes me again, I'll probably lose the whole afternoon.

He does.

Write me again.

From: sheinmand@northwoods.edu
To: turnerj@northwoods.edu
Subject: RE: Hello!

Hi, Jamie, what are you talking about? You're great at this! I especially like the "Signed, Jamie" part. That's not strange at all.

From: turnerj@northwoods.edu
To: sheinmand@northwoods.edu
Subject: RE: Hello!

Ha ha. I warned you.

From: sheinmand@northwoods.edu
To: turnerj@northwoods.edu
Subject: RE: Hello!

Fine, we don't have to be pen pals if you don't want to. I wanted to write and thank you for what you did for me the other day. You pretty much saved my life, and I owe you.

From: turnerj@northwoods.edu
To: sheinmand@northwoods.edu
Subject: RE: Hello!

Hardly. I just went and got a nurse.

From: sheinmand@northwoods.edu
To: turnerj@northwoods.edu
Subject: RE: Hello!

I vaguely remember you laying a hand on my sweaty
back, which couldn't have been pleasant. I was in the
worst pain I've ever experienced and I'm only grateful
now that I hadn't wet the bed. My embarrassment is still
high, and my gratitude is bottomless.

From: turnerj@northwoods.edu
To: sheinmand@northwoods.edu
Subject: RE: Hello!

Don't be embarrassed. Seriously. No one should be
embarrassed for being sick.

From: sheinmand@northwoods.edu
To: turnerj@northwoods.edu
Subject: RE: Hello!

The embarrassing part isn't being sick so much as being
gross and smelling like roadkill. I'd thrown up a few hours
earlier and I still hadn't taken a shower. Aren't you glad
to know that now? Doesn't that make you want to go and
wash your hands? Like five times.

No, it doesn't make me want to wash my hands. It
makes me look at my hands and remember how he felt—

warm and a little sweaty.

I keep expecting this email thread to stop, and then I turn on the computer that I now share with my mom and find another message from him. The computer sits in our new, tiny, not-private living room, and even though my mom is on the sofa a few feet away, looking over at me with a face that says, *What are you doing over there?* I'm not leaving. I'm staying here, writing these messages and waiting for another one.

This is the problem with sharing a computer and spending all our time together. My doing anything different seems strange.

From: turnerj@northwoods.edu
To: sheinmand@northwoods.edu
Subject: RE: Hello!

Maybe you've forgotten that I volunteer on the pediatric floor of the hospital. I've seen a lot of gross things.

From: sheinmand@northwoods.edu
To: turnerj@northwoods.edu
Subject: RE: Hello!

Oh, tell me the grossest! Please. It'll make me feel better.

From: turnerj@northwoods.edu
To: sheinmand@northwoods.edu
Subject: Gross things

There was once a boy who threw up into a nebulizer mask. Those are machines that you use to breathe medicine if you have asthma. That was fairly unpleasant.

From: sheinmand@northwoods.edu
To: turnerj@northwoods.edu
Subject: RE: Gross things

I know what a nebulizer is (all too well) and I make a big point of only ever throwing up on myself and my own clothes. I just think there have to be some rules. By the way, when you said you're bad at these things, what did you mean? Emailing? So far, I'd say you're fine.

I didn't mean emailing exactly. I meant talking casually and seeming normal over email. Even though I'm pretty sure my mom is still watching, I type and delete a few different answers as quickly as I can:

I have a bad track record with friends.
I had a few friendships last year that blew up spectacularly.
Right now I have no friends unless I count my mom, which I do, but I'm not going to tell you that because even I know how pathetic that makes me sound.

Finally, I give up and write:

From: turnerj@northwoods.edu
To: sheinmand@northwoods.edu
Subject: RE: Gross things

I'm shy.

From: sheinmand@northwoods.edu
To: turnerj@northwoods.edu
Subject: It's okay

Funny job to have if you're shy. I thought all Smile Awhile
volunteers were super friendly. I also thought they were
mostly retired nurses. Or at least old.

From: turnerj@northwoods.edu
To: sheinmand@northwoods.edu
Subject: RE: It's okay

You're right, I'm an exception, but how do you know so
much about Smile Awhilers?

From: sheinmand@northwoods.edu
To: turnerj@northwoods.edu
Subject: RE: It's okay

Alas, this isn't my first time at the rodeo. So why are you
a Smile Awhiler if you're so shy?

From: turnerj@northwoods.edu

To: sheinmand@northwoods.edu

Subject: RE: It's okay

My mom works at the hospital. She pulled strings to
get me the job. She thought it would be good for me to
practice talking to strangers.

From: sheinmand@northwoods.edu

To: turnerj@northwoods.edu

Subject: Not okay

Covered in vomit.

From: turnerj@northwoods.edu

To: sheinmand@northwoods.edu

Subject: RE: Not okay

I guess that makes me feel less shy, surprisingly.

The longer this conversation goes on, the more
shocked I am. Partly that I'm being funny with a boy, and
partly that I'm being funny with *this* boy: David Sheinman,
senior class *president*, who makes microphone announcements in the cafeteria every week. I consider him a school
celebrity, though it's possible not everyone thinks of him
in that way. This year, I've been eating lunch alone all fall,
so I have no distractions and nowhere else to look. He isn't

good-looking in the standard, high-school-athlete way (he's very thin for one thing, and he also wears glasses, which I think are cute but would probably knock him down a point on Missy's one-to-ten scale). Still, I could tell you the color of his eyes—hazel, with surprising yellow flecks—and a few other bits of trivia. Like this: he carries a cloth handkerchief that he sometimes coughs into before he starts his announcements. Then he folds it up and slides it into his pocket, like somebody's grandfather would do. I'm not sure if noticing these things means I have a crush on him or if it means I'm a strange person who notices weird things. I don't have much experience in this area.

When I first walked into his hospital room, I knew who he was right away. Even though his back was to the door and he was lying on the bed, clutching his stomach, I could tell by his thin arms and his hair, which is brown and curly and long enough that he sometimes tucks it behind his ears. He was obviously in pain, like maybe he'd been admitted for appendicitis and they hadn't given him any pain medication yet.

In that moment, I surprised myself. It was like I forgot who I was—my shyness; my disastrously bad handling of friendships; my nonexistent experience with boys—and became my mom for a few minutes. Or at least a nurse-like person assessing a situation. His breathing sounded rattly, like maybe in addition to whatever was going on with his stomach, he was also having an asthma attack. I know those can be more dangerous than people think. When I said hello and he made a noise like he was starting to choke, I got really worried.

I put my hand on his back, something my mother would have done to check his breathing. I left it there long enough to make sure I was right: he was definitely having trouble breathing and he had a fever.

"Hang in there," I whispered. "I'm going to get you help. I'll be right back."

It *was* well handled on my part.

Uncharacteristically so, I have to add. I only wish now that I'd left it at that and hadn't gone back to check on him a few hours later after he'd been taken care of—cleaned up, wearing a new hospital gown, with an IV drip that must have included pain meds because his eyes were half-closed and he was smiling.

"Hi," I said, surprised that he was still alone. Where were his countless friends from school? Or his family, who should obviously be there? "I'm just stopping by to see how you're doing."

"Are you my angel of salvation? I don't know how I can ever thank you."

He held out his hand like he wanted me to cross the room and hold it, which was crazy and not something I could possibly do. We weren't friends. We didn't even know each other. We happen to go to the same school, but so do fifteen hundred other kids, and that doesn't mean you hold someone's hand while they're lying in bed with hardly anything on.

"Actually, I have to go," I said awkwardly. "I just wanted to make sure you were okay."

"I'm okay. I'm also David."

I knew that of course. I also knew that his last name was Sheinman because every week when he stepped up to the cafeteria microphone, a few people yelled, "Shine on, man!" which I thought was some kind of rude slang until I heard his last name. I'm always guessing at these things because, for most of my life, I was homeschooled by my artist dad, who prioritized visiting museums and painting together in his basement studio over any activities involving other kids.

I stopped homeschooling two years ago, which means I should be savvier about things like hecklers and their slang by now, but I'm not.

Eventually, I figured out that people weren't making fun of David; they liked him. Maybe he isn't as popular as the football players and the cheerleaders, but that group always listens to his announcements and claps afterward. If he mentions someone by name because their club is having a meeting or a bake sale, that person usually stands up and waves. After they sit down, their friends all say, "You just got Shined on," but not in a mean way. He is like a mascot to the pretty-girl/jock crowd, except he dates Sharon Dinow, one of the pretty girls, with blond hair that she styles every morning or else wears in a neat, bouncy ponytail. Dating her means he's not a mascot really, but more like a part of that crowd.

"Do you want to tell me your name?" he said. He was still smiling, but his eyes were almost closed. He must have been on a lot of pain meds.

"Jamie Turner," I said, and then, in a fit of nervous confusion, I kept going. "We go to the same school. You don't know me because I'm in tenth grade and I don't belong to any clubs or anything. I don't even have any friends really. I'm not that type."

Instead of being horrified by all this, his smile spread. "What type are you?"

"I don't know. Never mind. I hope you feel better," I said, and left.

My face stayed red for about an hour afterward.

Of course I didn't expect him to get in touch.

I prayed he was so doped-up he'd forget the whole thing.

Then I couldn't believe it. I got home and opened my computer to an email that sounded so casual I assumed he'd mistaken me for one of his friends: *Hey. How's it going?*

I thought about it for a while and finally wrote back: *This is Jamie Turner. From the hospital.*

He wrote: *I know. I thought maybe we could be pen pals.*

I didn't understand. Hadn't I already proved how bad at socializing I was? I might listen to his announcements every week at lunch, but that didn't mean I went to any of the activities he suggested. I don't like crowds or marching bands or girls getting drunk and falling down bleacher stairs, which happened at the only football game I'd ever been to.

For a whole day, I didn't respond.

Maybe he was still giddy on pain medicine, or maybe he was playing a trick—popular older boy pretends to be nice to younger geeky girl. In the end, my response was an overworked attempt to not sound too paranoid. It was meant to say, essentially, *Hi back, now let's not worry about pretending we're friends just because you're in the hospital and we go to the same school.*

I never expected the rest. That he'd respond every time within two minutes. That he'd be a good writer and funny, too. That even when I was honest and told him *I'm shy*, he didn't seem to mind.

All of it was a surprise, but none more so than his final note at the end of this flurry of exchanges.

From: sheinmand@northwoods.edu
To: turnerj@northwoods.edu
Subject: Gotta go

I've got visitors right now, so I have to go, but it looks like I'll be here for another week at least. When do you work again?

Most kids on the pediatric floor stay in the hospital for a night or maybe two at the most. Even kids with cancer don't stay for a *week* unless they're getting a bone marrow transplant, and then they stay on the isolation unit of the oncology floor. This whole time I'd assumed he had appendicitis or a kidney stone because he was in so much pain and was holding his stomach. But those things don't put you in the hospital for a *week*.

I remember him coughing when I walked into his

room and flash on the memory of his cloth handkerchief at school.

I spin around to see my mom, who's only pretending to read on the sofa behind me. I know she's been watching me.

"How long would someone with bad pneumonia stay in the hospital?" I ask her.

"Depends on how they respond to treatment."

She hasn't worked as a nurse on the pediatric floor in more than a year, but even if she did, I know she'd never tell me someone's diagnosis.

Instead of leaving the computer, I tell her I have a little more research I need to do for homework and poke around online. I google symptoms and clues, including the fact that he knew I was a Smile Awhiler, which means he's spent at least a little time in the hospital before. I type in *labored breathing, fever, chest pain, gut pain*, and then add *recurring hospitalizations*. A few possibilities come up, but nothing seems quite right until I remember him saying he knew about nebulizers (all too well), which means his lungs must be part of the problem, and I add *chronic cough* to my search.

A few minutes later, I've read enough to guess what he might have.

And now I wish I didn't know.

DAVID

I don't know why I'm writing this girl.

Actually, that's a lie—I do know why. I'm writing her because it's easier than writing my real friends, who I've been lying to for months, pretending I'm busy when really, I've been too sick to do anything or go anywhere. It's a complicated business, having something like cystic fibrosis, which is a big deal, except you spend most of your life pretending it isn't. You say, "It's like asthma, only I cough a lot. I'm not contagious; my body just makes extra mucus," which is gross but acceptable if you smile sheepishly. Or else you shrug and say, "It's like diabetes. Incurable but manageable. You get used to it."

Which you do. Sort of.

But how do I tell people, after years of pretending this is only *like* diabetes: *Hey, with my pancreas crapping out, the doctor thinks I might have that, too?*

Two weeks ago, I was okay. Or at least I could pretend. I was standing in the cafeteria, doing my lunch announcements, planning for homecoming. Then, one afternoon in AP Bio, I felt a new pain in my chest, like a tiny man with an ice pick was moving around my lungs, stabbing wildly. It was so bad I broke out in a sweat. I thought I might pass out in the middle of class. I held on to my desk and concentrated on not throwing up. And then . . . it passed.

By the end of class, I could stand up. In the hallway, Sharon asked why my shirt was wet and I laughed.

"Just running some wind sprints," I said.

She raised her eyebrows in surprise. Sharon is the hardest part of all this. We've been together for two years, and she knows how bad this might get, but neither one of us wants to be the first to say it.

That day, Sharon didn't ask again about the shirt I'd

sweated through even when we were alone in the car, driving home. I didn't mention it, either, or the tiny new hissing sound in my chest, like one of my lungs had popped a hole. For the next two days, I didn't say anything to anyone. The pain had shifted to a dull ache—new but not alarming. On Wednesday night, I went to sleep thinking, *Maybe this is nothing. Maybe I'm okay.* Then, in the morning, I woke up so sick I coughed blood into the sink and crawled back to bed, where I vomited on myself and thought, *I can't pretend anymore.*

The first time Sharon visited, she came with our best friends, Ashwin and Hannah, which meant that—for another day, anyway—we weren't going to talk about how sick I truly am. We kept it light, like this was one of my usual hospitalizations. A round of antibiotics. A "tune-up," as we call them. I saw her eyes slide away from the drainage tube in my chest and the new machines I'm attached to. By the end, it was hard for her to figure out where to look.

We talked mostly about school issues and how I shouldn't worry about anything while I'm in here. Ashwin will cover student council meetings and lunch announcements; Sharon will run the senior-class-committee activities.

"You just have to get well, that's all," Sharon said.

There was a surprising firmness in her voice, though. I *have* to get well. She believes she can *will* these things to happen.

And maybe she can. Telling her it will be harder for me to get well this time isn't something I can do in front of other people. It will throw us both off. It might even make her angry. It's hard to predict and better to avoid.

All of which means, I'm writing this girl Jamie because it's nice to talk to someone who isn't horrified by the shape I'm in. I've never told her any lies or pretended to be fine around her. These machines I'm attached to and the tube snaking out of my chest aren't scary to her. She's seen puke in a nebulizer mask, which is at least slightly more unsettling than anything going on with my body right now, though not by much.

CHAPTER TWO

JAMIE

"WHAT HAPPENS TO KIDS with cystic fibrosis?" I ask my mom, trying to sound casual. We've been living in this apartment for only six months, but its tiny size means we've developed new habits, like eating break-fast together, which we do every morning now.

"Why? Have you got one on the peds floor?"

"I don't know. Maybe. I'm just curious."

"It's a tricky one. There's a wide variation."

"But in your experience—"

"In my experience it's pretty bad."

"How bad?"

"It gets worse as they get older. Their mucus gets very thick, and their bodies can't clear it, so they get chronic infections in their lungs. Usually, they're okay when they're young, and then, when they hit adolescence, the infections get worse and put them in the hospital more. They keep getting weaker until eventually their lungs wear out."

"But the average life expectancy is older now, right? Because of new treatments?"

"Yes, some people live into their thirties, but we don't see them as much. The ones I knew got sick in high school and were trying to make it to college."

"Did they?"

"One did! Her name was Fiona—I remember her. She was lovely. Very smart."

"And the others?"

She hesitates. "The ones I knew didn't make it, no."

I know my mom will probably ask around and find out who I'm talking about. She won't tell me his story, but she'll know it.

Rita, the psychiatrist I haven't seen in almost a month, said the secret to going back to my old life was to start living it and, sooner or later, I'd feel like my old self. It was probably good advice, but the problem is: I don't have my old life. Or I do, but it doesn't look anything like the one we're living now. We used to have a small but nice three-bedroom ranch house. We owned two cars, and no one had to share a computer.

Since my dad died a year and a half ago, we have none of these things, but we do have bills we'll be paying off for years from credit cards he never told my mom about. When the bills first came, she asked me if I recognized the charges. It looked like art supplies and groceries, the usual things. It took me a while to understand he'd been buying more of *everything*. Spreading it out over different cards.

It didn't make sense, but a lot of things didn't make sense after he died.

My mom stopped talking about money (with me at least) and tried to focus on the positive. "It's good to get a fresh start," she said when we moved into this apartment complex next to the hospital, where the dumpster doesn't get emptied until the trash spills over and takes up three parking spots. She works so hard to stay upbeat that I try to as well. I don't talk about the other factors in my life that have also changed this year: the friends I no longer have, or the lunches I eat perched alone at the end of a table full of people I don't know.

I don't tell her that I sit in some classes with an open notebook in front of me and afterward I have a blank sheet and no memory of anything that was said.

I don't say that it's hard to remember my old straight As or why they once felt like little prizes when I mostly got them for neat homework and lab reports three pages longer than they needed to be. I don't tell her the homework I turn in these days is scribbled illegibly ten minutes before class. It would break my mom's heart more than it's already broken, and I can't do that to her. Which means I should concentrate and do a better job, but I can't do that, either, so I'm not sure how all of this is going to end.

The odds are: not well.

For now, though, we've got a rhythm. Neither one of us spends too much time alone (unless you count school for me, where I'm alone for most of the day). After school, I come to the hospital most days, where I tell my mom some version of the same thing: my classes are going better than I expected, and yes, we were right to sign me up for a non-honors, lower-stress course load.

"I'm fine, Mom. I promise," I say, because I am. Or at least fine enough that I don't spend an hour (each way) traveling on a city bus to see Rita these days. Instead, I try to be like my mom and stay busy and cheerful. Saying that makes my mom sound superficial, which I used to think she was, but I don't anymore. Now I understand it's a survival strategy and she's trying to survive. We both are.

Another thing Rita said before I left the hospital this summer was that I should trust my instincts. "You might not have a great deal of experience with friendships, but you're smarter than you realize about other people."

I'm not sure where she got this idea, because she couldn't be more wrong. If I've learned one thing this year, it's that my instincts about other people are horrible. Worse than horrible—they're catastrophically bad. That's why I spent my first month of school avoiding the girls who used to be my best friends and doing nothing with anyone after school. Usually, I do my homework at the hospital because, even if you don't have a problem with depression, you might start to develop it if you spent too much time alone in our apartment. Two days a week, I volunteer. The other days, I meet my mom for dinner and make up stories about school so she won't worry too much. If she asks how I'm doing "making new friends," I tell her it's slow but I know it'll happen.

"Don't worry about me," I say. "Seriously. I'm really

okay, and plus, worrying doesn't help."

Am I okay? It's hard for me to judge. At lunch I watch my old friends sitting at a table by themselves in the corner. I think about the only conversation I've had with any of them this year, when Bethany found me at my locker the first day of school and seemed so friendly at first that I thought we were going to pretend we'd forgotten what happened at Missy's sleepover last spring. She asked me how my summer was and what classes I was taking. I studied her face for clues. Did she *really* not know how my summer was? I couldn't tell.

Then Bethany said, "I just wanted to tell you, Missy thinks it's a bad idea for you to eat lunch with us. She's still pretty mad, so I said I'd talk to you. Is that okay?"

Is what okay? I thought. I didn't understand what she was trying to say.

Later I figured it out. She meant, *Is it okay if you don't eat lunch with us?* Apparently, she also meant, *Is it okay if we all ignore you and don't say hi even though we were best friends last year?* Because that's what they did.

Rita was wrong about me having good instincts for people. I've got a long history of having no instincts about people. Every Tuesday and Thursday afternoon, I roll a cart full of games, books, and DVDs into rooms with sick kids. Usually, they ask why my movies are so old and my games are so bad. No one even looks at the books. Most kids aren't here long enough for me to learn their names or get to know the parent sitting next to their beds. Bad DVDs can do only so much, I've learned. I might wear an apron with a happy face on it, but I'm not sure if I've ever cheered anyone up.

Until now.

I can't stop thinking about this simple fact: helping David shifted something inside me. It made me feel stronger. For a few days now, I haven't thought about myself or my own problems, which is such a relief it's hard to describe.

I can't tell my mother about this, though, because I'm sure it won't last. I won't really become friends with David or anything like that. He's senior class president, with a lunch group of friends that sometimes spreads out over two or three tables. He's popular in a way that I couldn't even, in my wildest dreams, imagine being. I know how imbalanced this is. If I say anything to my mom, she'll tell me to be careful and remind me that I'm fragile, which I already know. I also know that, for some reason, I don't feel fragile when I'm emailing with David. I feel like a different person. Like some version of myself I imagined becoming when I first told my dad I wanted to go to real school with regular kids and stop spending all my days making art with him.

DAVID

I was right. The tests are back, and the news is bad. Dr. Chortkoff doesn't look up as he recites the list from his tablet: I have a collapsed lung on one side and an infection on the other. My pulmonary-function tests are lower than they've ever been. I also have a blockage in my intestine that's keeping my pancreas from doing its job and is the reason I've lost so much weight recently.

It's a lot to take in. I feel my throat tighten.

"Is *anything* working?" I say to fill in the silence.

"Your teeth look good," he says. "But of course I'm not a dentist."

I like jokes like this, but my parents don't. They're furious. They want to know what he's going to do about all this. It's my senior year, they remind him.

"He can't spend the next six months *sick*," my dad says.

My dad has a hard time sitting down in the hospital. He spends most of his visits pacing around rooms, which he's doing now.

Dr. Chortkoff keeps going. "In my experience, there's never really a good time to get sick. It happens when it happens. There's not much we can do to control it." He looks at my mother as if he's trying to measure her state of mind. "There's one option I'd like to broach with you all. Given these numbers I'm looking at and the overall decline in David's health since last spring, I think it's time to talk about getting him on the organ donor list for a lung transplant."

My mom gasps and puts her hand over her mouth. I'm shocked, too, and I'm the one who's been sleeping twelve hours a day and feeling terrible. Does he really think I'm *that* sick?

He stares at his tablet screen, as if he can't bear to see

my mom's eyes fill with tears. Even I have to look away.

My mom believes that having a positive attitude is 90 percent of staying healthy. When I was younger, she used to tell me I had a different kind of cystic fibrosis than the other, sicker kids I saw in the clinic, some of whom were already wheeling oxygen tanks beside them as they played with the toys in the waiting room.

"We're lucky. Your CF is milder," my mom would whisper when we got to the elevator.

For a long time, I believed her because mostly I *was* healthy. I was thirteen the first time I was hospitalized, which is later than most CF kids. After that, it was once or twice a year for a course of IV antibiotics when an infection hung around too long, but it never felt scary or even like a big deal. Dr. Chortkoff called them tune-ups, so we did, too.

"Four days of this, and you'll be raring to go," he'd say.

Usually, I was.

But last spring, I spent a week in the hospital and came out with just as little energy as I crawled in with. "It's your PFTs," Dr. C said, meaning my pulmonary-function tests. "They're not bouncing back yet, but they will. Give it time."

They haven't bounced back. This lung-transplant idea shouldn't be such a shock, but it is.

I press the cannula against my lip, hard. I don't want to cry in front of Dr. C.

"He's too *young* for that," my mom snaps. "He's been healthy for seventeen years. He does his lung treatments religiously. He shouldn't be a transplant candidate for another ten years!" Her eyes have a wild fire behind them, as if she'll do anything to make her nonsensical point: *I'd rather have him die than admit he's sick enough to need this.*

My dad, pacing back from the window, tries to sound more reasonable. "What Linda's trying to say is that this is David's senior year in high school. He's the *president* of his class, and he's got so much on his plate—not just school-work but also college applications, and homecoming is right around the corner. That might sound silly to you, but—" He stops for a second, as if he's trying to decide what *won't* sound silly. "This is his last year to have *fun* with his friends. Can't we see how this collapsed lung heals and then wait until the end of the year before we make any big decisions?"

Dr. Chortkoff looks at me. "David, what do you think?"

The room starts to darken. I'm getting extra oxygen, but it's never enough. My throat tightens more. I have to concentrate on breathing to get any air at all.

I know about lung transplants from CF chat rooms. I know it's a big deal to go on the list. You have to wait a long time—sometimes a year—to find a match. After the surgery, recovery takes months and requires an arsenal of medications, including steroids that make you moody and fat and that covered one of my online friends in back acne that I wish I'd never seen a picture of.

I also know that for the last four months I haven't felt right. At the beginning of the summer, I got a job at a grocery store, thinking it might boost my energy to stay busy, but standing up for so long made me dizzy. I'd scan a bag of lettuce and see spots in front of my eyes. I told everyone I was quitting to concentrate on a college-level online course I was taking, which I never signed up for and no one ever asked about.

For a while, I don't say anything. And then I take the deepest breath I can.

"I don't know if I really have a choice. I think Dr. C is right—I have to do it," I say.

My mother gasps again.

My dad shakes his head and says, "You realize what you're saying, don't you? This will affect your whole year. Your work on student council, your college applications, everything. If lungs turn up in December, that's it, you've got to take them. Forget the winter formal. If it happens in May, never mind prom."

My parents spent my childhood shuffling me to activities so I wouldn't feel like a sick kid and no one would treat me like one. I understand why he's saying this, but I also see from Dr. C's expression: he sounds a little crazy. I've heard about people who get on the organ transplant list too late and die waiting for lungs. I know if you're serious, you don't schedule your transplant around parties you don't want to miss. You get on the list, and you wait for the call.

"I don't want to die," I say softly. "That's all."

Dr. C explains the process. His main point seems to be that it isn't easy getting on the transplant list. You have to be sick enough to really need the lungs but healthy enough to survive the surgery. I suspect he's building up to something else and I'm right: he's concerned about my weight loss. If I'm serious about a lung transplant, I can't be underweight.

"I know you've resisted this in the past, but I'd like to recommend that we put in a G-tube. We can't really move forward until you've regained the weight that you lost this year."

He's right; I *have* resisted this one. Vain as it sounds, the idea of pouring cans of Ensure into a tube attached to a hole in my stomach has always sounded horrifying to me, like one step away from being on a ventilator. Maybe I get this prejudice from my parents, who've always hated the idea of medical devices attached to my body and have said no to Port-a-Caths every time I was offered one. But what if Dr. C is right? If I'm losing weight no matter how much I eat, what other options do I have?

Before I can say anything, my dad holds up a hand. "Look, this is a lot to take in, Doctor. Can we have some time to talk all this over?"

"Of course," Dr. C says, but after he leaves, we don't say very much.

In my family, we're good at not talking about our problems. We soldier on and work hard and think about other things. We rise above like a phoenix, never once mentioning the pile of ashes we live in. We talk about talking, but we never actually do.

Eventually, they have to leave—my younger sister, Eileen, is home alone, and she's got her own problems we're not talking about, either.

After they go, I text Sharon. Earlier, I asked her to come by alone today, without Hannah and Ashwin.

Okay. Why? she had texted.

Just not up for crowds, I wrote back.

Hannah and Ashwin aren't a crowd, David. They love you.

Now I write her again. *Just got some bad news. I'll wait till you get here.*

I'm so sorry! I'm in an emergency meeting for homecoming. I'll call you once it's over.

Okay, I write back, but I know if she's in the meeting, she might not be here for an hour, if she comes at all. Homecoming is a week and a half away. They're probably freaking out.

I don't know what to do.

Sharon and I had a hard summer. We met in sixth grade taking ballroom dance lessons, which might sound absurd, but in our area, where lots of kids have Russian grandparents, it isn't so crazy. In Russia, ballroom dance is considered an art form that every child should learn the basics of.

I used it as my alternative PE credit to escape the embarrassment of having coughing fits in front of my friends while we ran around the gym. For years, I pretended that was the only reason I kept taking classes, but the real reason was, I liked it.

I liked the formality of bowing to a girl when you asked her to dance. I liked escorting her onto the floor with her hand tucked inside my elbow. Most of all, I liked the breath-catching novelty of having a girl in my arms and being told what to do with her.

Sharon was one of the best dancers in our group. She'd moved here from Texas, where she'd already been taking lessons. It took me a few years to catch up with her, but when I finally did at the start of ninth grade and we'd danced enough waltzes without any gaffes on my part for her to ask me to enter a competition with her, I fell in love. With dancing. With Sharon's ambition and her sparkly dresses. With doing anything she asked me to do.

She got me to join student council at school.

She talked me into running for president.

She believes we can do anything we set our minds to.

This year, she wants to raise enough money to bring prom prices down so all seniors can attend. The first week of school she launched her campaign with a T-shirt and bake sale that got her an article in our local paper with the quote: "I know every senior class says they're the best, but I believe we really are."

She does, too.

Sharon is like my mom this way: She believes staying positive will make good things happen.

It's after seven when she finally calls back, too late to stop by. She has to get home and babysit her younger brothers while her mom does a house showing.

"What was your news?"

"Never mind. We can talk about it tomorrow."

"It's okay. Tell me."

I don't want to now. She sounds tired. She's worried about the things anyone our age *should* be worried about. Homecoming decorations. A test in calculus tomorrow. How can I tell her the scary-depressing thoughts that have filled my mind this whole afternoon? *If this collapsed lung doesn't heal, I might not be back to school for a very long time. It might get so bad, I can't come back at all.*

For now, I can't. It's not in our vocabulary. I was a different person before I met Sharon: anxious and shy and scared of anyone finding out why my cough never went away. Sharon changed all that. I told her the truth one night at Starlight, and she helped me tell others in a way that made it seem like nothing. She was the first one to tell other kids it was like asthma, only rarer. She made it sound mysterious yet strangely appealing.

"He goes into the hospital occasionally, but mostly so the doctors can study his lungs."

I don't know where she got that idea, but I never contradicted her.

Now I'm not sure how to tell her the truth. Needing new lungs is the scariest news, but all of it is bad. If the tube draining yellow bile from my chest is hard for her to look at, it's pretty hard to imagine what she'd say about a permanent hole in my stomach with a plastic screw-on cap. In the CF world, they're pretty common. In the real world, they're hard for anyone to hear about and not want to vomit.

I don't want to drive her away, so I don't say anything. I tell Jamie instead.

From: sheinmand@northwoods.edu

To: turnerj@northwoods.edu

Subject: Question for you

What do you think when you see kids with G-tubes? Be
honest: they're pretty disgusting, right?

From: turnerj@northwoods.edu

To: sheinmand@northwoods.edu

Subject: RE: Question for you

Not at all. You can't see them under a shirt. And if you're
wearing a bathing suit, well—some people look at it as a
novelty piece of body jewelry.

From: sheinmand@northwoods.edu

To: turnerj@northwoods.edu

Subject: RE: Question for you

If you're in a coma.

From: turnerj@northwoods.edu

To: sheinmand@northwoods.edu

Subject: RE: Question for you

Definitely if you're in a coma, but even if you're not.
You can think of it as an atypical piercing. It's not your
earlobe, it's your stomach, and the hole's a little bigger,
but still. You'd have to pick the right color, though. I

wonder about the ones that are bright pink but are called "flesh-toned." Like they'd be "flesh-toned" for a salmon but not really for a person.

From: sheinmand@northwoods.edu
To: turnerj@northwoods.edu
Subject: RE: Question for you

Does that mean you're recommending sky blue?

From: turnerj@northwoods.edu
To: sheinmand@northwoods.edu
Subject: RE: Question for you

It's your call. You'd have to look at your wardrobe, see what you've got that matches.

It's amazing how good Jamie is at her job. I didn't tell her I needed one, but she figured it out and doesn't seem particularly thrown off by the prospect.

For a while, neither one of us types anything. Then I refresh and see this:

From: turnerj@northwoods.edu
To: sheinmand@northwoods.edu
Subject: RE: Question for you

Seriously, though, the important thing is they work. I've seen kids come into the hospital looking like skeletons.

They get a G-tube put in, and a few weeks later they look like regular kids again.

I don't want to ask her if I look like a skeleton. I don't want her to think I'm stupid and vain, which I obviously am.

From: sheinmand@northwoods.edu
To: turnerj@northwoods.edu
Subject: RE: Question for you

It's nice you're saying this, because the doctor thinks I need one.

From: turnerj@northwoods.edu
To: sheinmand@northwoods.edu
Subject: RE: Question for you

Great! Take a before and after picture with a week in between. You'll see what I mean. You'll be transformed.

It's strange. Now that she's said this, I want to do it. I want to take a picture and see if I look different a week from now.

JAMIE

Is this flirting?

I assume it isn't, but I have zero experience so I've got no idea. I don't think it's possible for someone who has a girlfriend and is semifamous in a school-wide context to flirt with someone who is mostly invisible like me.

As strange as it might sound, I think it's the social-status imbalance between us that makes me surprisingly not nervous talking to him. I'm not fantasizing about impossible things happening, like him breaking up with Sharon. I'm not even fantasizing about being friends when he comes back to school. I know that won't happen. I've looked through old yearbooks in my library study hall, and I've learned more about him.

As class president, he runs student council, which includes every popular person who doesn't play football or isn't a cheerleader. He's also president of Leaders for Tomorrow, a club where everyone wears business suits for the yearbook photo, including the girls, who look especially uncomfortable in tight skirts and jackets. I've found him in two other club photos and in a bunch of candids. He's a pillar of this school in a way that I never will be, which means in any other setting, we wouldn't have much in common. Or anything, really. But in this one, we do.

Once, I almost stopped by his room. I was at the hospital anyway, waiting to have dinner with my mom, and I walked up to the floor, just as I saw his girlfriend, Sharon, go inside. I couldn't see David, but I heard his voice.

"There you are!" He sounded happy and relieved.

I know he's been dating Sharon for a long time because there's a picture of them holding hands in a yearbook from their sophomore year. Sharon is pretty in a way that's hard for me to even wrap my mind around. She wears makeup so well that I can't even imagine her leaning into mirrors and putting it on. It's like her pretty blue eyes have eyeliner and shadow *tattooed on*, so it never smudges the way it does for me after ten minutes.

So, no, I don't imagine taking Sharon's place. Which means we're not flirting. We're situational friends. Like bunkmates at a camp where the activities are bad and the food is even worse. I know (sort of) what he's going through. I know what it's like to be in the hospital and feel alone.

Of course I'm not going to tell him that, though, because we're not *that* good of friends.

From: turnerj@northwoods.edu
To: sheinmand@northwoods.edu
Subject: RE: Question for you

When are they putting it in?

From: sheinmand@northwoods.edu
To: turnerj@northwoods.edu
Subject: RE: Question for you

If I say yes, they'll do it tomorrow.

From: turnerj@northwoods.edu
To: sheinmand@northwoods.edu
Subject: RE: Question for you

You should definitely say yes. Seriously. I could stop by
tomorrow afternoon and take your picture. You'll see
what I mean. You'll start gaining weight pretty quickly
afterward.

I shouldn't be saying any of this. We're never supposed
to talk with patients about anything medical. We're not
even supposed to ask how they're feeling in case they tell
us something important—a new symptom maybe—and
we don't realize what it is. I'm definitely not meant to say
a G-tube sounds great. But I've been thinking about his
weight and reading all the reasons CF patients have trouble
absorbing food. Their mucus gets too thick for their pancreas to work. They need enzymes with every meal, and
even then, they only absorb about half the calories they eat.

From: sheinmand@northwoods.edu
To: turnerj@northwoods.edu
Subject: RE: Question for you

Are you working tomorrow?

From: turnerj@northwoods.edu
To: sheinmand@northwoods.edu
Subject: RE: Question for you

No, but I live nearby, and I usually come over to eat
dinner with my mom.

From: sheinmand@northwoods.edu

To: turnerj@northwoods.edu

Subject: RE: Question for you

Where do you live?

This is the sort of question I lied about last year until I learned that lying only compounds whatever problems you're hiding in the first place and eventually becomes your biggest problem, until you're so stressed out from lying, you explode one night at a sleepover like a volcano vomiting truth all over a bunch of girls in sleeping bags.

This year, I've vowed not to do it again.

From: turnerj@northwoods.edu

To: sheinmand@northwoods.edu

Subject: RE: Question for you

The Desert Paradise apartments.

He doesn't answer for a while. Maybe he's trying to think of a response that doesn't mention the moldy broken sofa that's been sitting in our parking lot all summer. Maybe he's so shocked, he doesn't know what to say.

From: sheinmand@northwoods.edu

To: turnerj@northwoods.edu

Subject: RE: Question for you

How's that?

From: turnerj@northwoods.edu
To: sheinmand@northwoods.edu
Subject: RE: Question for you

Not as bad as you might think from the outside. You don't need a hazmat suit or anything. We were a little worried before we moved in, but it turns out it's okay. It's what we can afford, and it's close to the hospital.

I feel proud of myself typing all this. Everything I'm saying is true, and he's not signing off or making excuses to end this chat. Of course, I also remind myself: he's trapped in a hospital room, and I'm not telling him the whole story, which I never will, because no pledge to be honest would get all that out of me.

When I was in the hospital, no one was allowed internet access. No social media. No email. Those things weren't helping us, the counselors said. We had to learn who we were, apart from social media, before we could start building healthy relationships with it. Apparently social media is a big reason why a lot of teenagers end up in psychiatric hospitals. The way Rita explained it, we Snapchat and Instagram so much of our lives that we can't identify the difference between a post and a fact. For me, this wasn't the problem, but it was interesting to hear other people talk about their internet addictions. I was surprised by how many kids raised their hands to the question "Have you ever trolled chat rooms posing as someone other than yourself?"

Out of twelve, four kids had.

Three kept their hands up when asked the question "Have you perpetuated the charade longer than you were comfortable with?"

"Have you put yourself in a dangerous situation because of your internet habits?"

Two hands for that one.

I wonder if what I'm doing now with David would qualify as a dangerous situation. I may not be using a fake name, but the person I am with him is different from any version I've ever known of myself in real life. I'm pretending to be things I can tell he likes—upbeat, down-to-earth, easygoing. Even if I like the person I'm pretending to be, it still feels dangerous. I'm not sure why exactly, but it does.

CHAPTER THREE

DAVID

THIS MORNING, DR. C is going over everything I'll need to do to get on the transplant list: Gain weight. Get my blood sugar under control. Have no sign of infection.

My mother interrupts him. "I should probably tell you we've been talking to other doctors. We want to get a second opinion before we rush into anything."

Dr. C is the leading CF specialist in a two-hundred-mile radius. We all know this. Still, he nods. "That's fine, Linda, but I've consulted with some others myself. I'm afraid they've all said the same thing. Without a transplant, David will probably have two years at best."

We all look away. He's never been this precise before. Never put a timeline on my life. Two years means I won't make it to twenty. Two years means I'll never drink legally. Two years means I won't finish college even if I go.

No one says anything.

We stare at our hands or out the window. My dad picks up a Kleenex box and studies it. We wait for Dr. C to leave, and when he finally does, we keep saying nothing all over again.

In the bathroom, I study myself in the mirror and decide it's official: I've never looked worse. Whatever new medications I'm on have hollowed out my eye sockets and bloated the rest of my face. I look like a skull with three chins. Beyond the horror of my misshapen face is the color of my skin—simultaneously yellow and gray, like a thin covering of moss is growing over the doughy plain where my cheeks used to be.

I can't stop staring. I think: *If I'm going to look like this, maybe dying is okay.*

I have no idea how long I stand there, but when I come out, my parents are gone and my sister, Eileen, is there instead, flipping through a magazine.

"You don't have to say it. I know I look shitty."

Eileen narrows her eyes and shrugs. "You want some blush?" She digs through her purse. "Never mind, I don't have any. How about some lipstick instead?"

She pulls it out and uncaps it. I'm scared she's serious. "I'm not putting on lipstick. Sharon might stop by later."

Waiting for Sharon is a force of habit. All summer, I lay around in bed at home, waiting for her to text about when she'd stop by. Readying myself, then pretending to be casual. But after everything we've learned today and seeing how I look, I'm not even sure I want to see her.

"Yeah." Eileen recaps her lipstick and shrugs again. "You're right. She's probably not worth wasting my lipstick on."

Eileen used to like Sharon when we first started dating, but now she makes comments like this. I'm not sure why.

I sit down on the bed. My G-tube surgery is scheduled for tomorrow morning, which means in twenty-four hours, in addition to looking horrible, I'll also have a hole in my stomach. I feel like crying. I wish I could ask Eileen for a hug. She used to be the huggiest little girl I've ever known, sitting in my lap during my doctor's appointments so I wouldn't get scared, but that was all a long time ago.

"Thanks for sticking around, Lee-lee." I've been coughing most of the day. My voice sounds like I could audition for an anti-smoking ad.

"Mom and Dad will be right back. They went downstairs to get something to eat."

"That's okay. This gives us a chance to talk. You and me."

She gives me a funny look. "About what?"

She sounds nervous. This whole fall, we never talked. I gave her rides to school in the morning, but never after school. Usually I had club meetings or else I was driving Sharon home, which meant I couldn't take her because no one has to give their little sister a ride when they've got their girlfriend who they don't see enough of as it is. Those were my rules. No wonder she doesn't mind telling me the truth about how I look.

I try to think of a topic. "How about G-tubes. Do you think they're gross?"

Eileen widens her eyes and smiles. "Not at *all*. I told Dad we should pour a beer in there and see what happens."

Eileen likes to say shocking things to get our parents' attention. Unfortunately, it works, so this year she's started *doing* shocking things to up the ante.

"Did he laugh?" I feel a coughing fit coming on. I hold my breath so it'll pass.

"Of course not. He gave me the David's-very-sick-we-can't-make-jokes speech."

Holding my breath doesn't work. Laughing turns into a coughing fit instead. She watches me carefully. Unlike Sharon, Eileen doesn't look away. "You're not *that* sick, right? This is just one of your tune-ups, I assume."

I shouldn't be surprised, but I am. I'm not doing a great job of talking about what's happening with my friends, but apparently our parents are doing an even worse job. I go for some water to calm my heaving chest. "It's a little more than that this time," I say through my heaving coughs.

She narrows her eyes. "Is that why Mom and Dad are being so weird?"

"Why—what are they doing?"

"Mom keeps calling doctors, saying she wants a second opinion, and Dad keeps going to Whole Foods and buying food for you."

This sounds about right. He's been annoying the nurses for days, filling their refrigerators with containers of food he's hoping I'll eat. What I don't understand is why they haven't told her the truth. "I'm sorry Lee-lee. Seriously. They're screwed-up, and I know my being sick doesn't help." I don't have the breath right now to tell her anything else. I need to, though. We need to start telling each other the truth.

She closes her eyes, and for a second, I think she might start to cry, but no. Eileen is fourteen now and doesn't cry anymore.

Our parents' mistakes with Eileen started so long ago, it's hard to know exactly where they began. Seven-year-old Eileen would test a limit, get punished, and then, riding on a wave of parental guilt, get whisked out for Froyo, where she'd wordlessly ask, *Can I fill a cup with all candy toppings and no Froyo?*, to discover the answer: yes, apparently, but with an eye roll.

It's like we've had two sets of parents. Mine have their eyes trained on me all the time, attuned to every numerical fluctuation in my life: PFTs, GPAs. A dip in one and we spend a whole dinner discussing next steps. For Eileen, who established herself as a solid-C-student-reaching-for-Bs years ago, they'd just as soon not look too closely at anything, so they don't. "Oh, *Eileen*," they say, and then feel guilty at what their tone implies: exasperating Eileen. Overindulged Eileen. It must be hard for parents to resent a child for seeming spoiled and not recognize their own hand in the problem.

I suspect that's why they've adopted the myopic, hands-off approach they maintained all last year, until the end of August, when the police brought Eileen home at three o'clock in the morning wearing only a bathing suit bottom and two tank tops.

"Found her at a party with all older kids," the police said. "You should probably keep an eye on this one."

Of all our parents' ineffectual responses to Eileen's transgressions, my dad whispering to me, "Should we ask her where her pants are?" might take the prize.

You'd think such a warning would have produced a bigger response than it did. Instead of being angry, they took Eileen out for a "special lunch" to talk. Later, Eileen did a hilarious imitation of Mom avoiding the subject of the party the whole meal. Though we laughed about it, we still haven't talked about what she *was* doing at a party with older kids in the first place. I've tried to fill in the gaps that our parents miss, but there are some even I can't bear to look at. Some weekends neither parent can remember which friend Eileen is supposedly spending the night with. This fall, Dad read an item from the police blotter in the paper about a party by the railroad tracks. I watched Eileen's face ready itself for the confrontation: *Yeah, I was there. I wasn't doing anything wrong.* And then it never came.

To me it's so obvious that I've tried to find a way to say to our parents: *Parties are pretty appealing to Eileen, have you noticed?* Alcohol, bands, boys—they're all like a cup full of candy toppings these days. Hard to resist and definitely more interesting than getting good grades. Thinking about this worries me. If I'm in the hospital for a long time, I'm scared that Eileen will go down a self-destructive path, because in our family, dying or coming close gets you the most attention.

As screwed-up as all this is, Eileen has never resented me, which still surprises me. When she was younger, she used to sit with me through my treatments, thirty minutes a day, morning and night. I couldn't talk because I was breathing medications from a nebulizing machine, but she didn't care. She'd sing or tell her own stories or lean with her forehead against my buzzing machines.

I want to talk about all this now, but I'm not sure how to start.

"This isn't one of my regular tune-ups. My lungs are getting worse, and I'm going to be in here for a while. There's nothing I can do. You have to stay out of trouble."

"What do you mean?"

"You know. Maybe find some new friends who aren't into breaking the law."

"Are you saying I should join some *clubs*?" Maybe one of the reasons Eileen stopped liking Sharon is because she was always suggesting that Eileen should join more clubs and "get more involved."

"It's not a terrible idea."

She makes a face to say: *Yes, it is.* Eileen once told Sharon that clubs are for people who are too anxious to have real friends.

"I'm saying maybe you should find things to do that aren't dangerous."

"Like what?" She smiles, even though I haven't said anything funny.

I'm stuck. It's impossible to imagine her volunteering in the Smile Awhile office without thinking it would be funny to sneak her own DVDs onto the cart and offer five-year-olds *Reservoir Dogs* or *Kill Bill*.

"I don't know. I don't understand your friends. I don't know what you guys were doing at that party in August."

"Aysa made me go. There was a guy she wanted to see, and then she left with him after ten minutes, so I had no way to get home."

She doesn't say the rest. *Except with the police.*

She looks sad. Aysa used to be her best friend. Why would her best friend think it's okay to leave her alone at a party where everyone is older and she knows no one? I still remember Eileen as the little girl who worried so much about her stuffed animals' feelings she rotated who got to sleep on her pillow every night. I also remember the ways she used to help take care of me. How she'd line up my pills in the morning and put a gummy worm at the end. Even if our parents haven't told her what's going on, she understands more than they think. She knows what I'm up against. That's why she's here.

We don't have parents who know how to talk about the messy truths in our lives: that one of us is dying, and one of us sometimes acts like she wants to. We have to talk about it with each other.

"You're a good person, Lee-lee. You deserve to have real friends who won't do crappy things like that." I can't tell if she's listening. She seems to be studying the ends of her hair.

"Yeah, maybe. I kind of hate my friends these days." She looks around the room like there's something else she wants to say but she's not sure what it is. "I don't know. Sometimes it's like I've spent all this time with them and we don't really know each other. I'll say something, and everyone will just stare at me."

It's strange that she's saying this. This is exactly how I've felt every time my school friends come to visit. I spend all day waiting for them, and then when they get here, I can't understand what they're talking about. When I tell them something funny that a doctor said, they don't get the joke. I wonder if what's happening to me feels like it's happening to Eileen, too—where everything ordinary seems wrong all of a sudden.

"What do you talk about with your friends?"

"Nothing really."

She shrugs and flips through a few pages of her magazine. I don't know how much longer we'll be alone, but suddenly I want to say something important in case I die in the next six hours, which isn't likely but seems possible, as sick as I feel. The problem is I'm not sure what I want to say exactly: *We didn't get super lucky in the parent department. You have to look out for yourself. Don't give up on school just because it's hard.*

What I really want to say is: *Don't let me (and my illness) define you. Find what you're good at and throw yourself into that.*

Or maybe this: *Mom and Dad don't see the truth like you and I do.*

I open my mouth, but instead of words coming out, I have a coughing fit that goes on and on. For a second, I'm afraid my nose will start bleeding or I'll throw up in bed, both distinct possibilities in this new fragile body of mine.

When it subsides, Eileen's eyes are wide. "I'll kill you if you die" is all she says.

Our parents aren't the only ones bad at talking about what matters.

JAMIE

This is the first time I've seen David since we started emailing. It's my regular Smile Awhile shift, so I don't have to worry that walking into his room might be weird.

"Knock knock," I call. "Smile Awhile is here."

This is what we're supposed to say in every room we walk into so no one mistakes us for a nurse or a doctor. As if anyone might.

He looks thinner than he did last week, and paler. His face is gaunt, like he's losing weight in places he shouldn't lose weight—his shoulders, his eye sockets. At the same time, his cheeks look puffy. It makes me realize that I never took his picture last week. When I stopped by, Sharon was here, so I wrote him later to apologize, and he said it was fine—his sister was happy to take as many bad, unflattering pictures of him as he wanted. Now it's pretty clear, whatever miracle I promised a G-tube would produce hasn't happened yet.

A few days ago, my mom told me she'd talked to her old friends on the floor and, yes, I was right, David has CF.

"It's okay to tell you because it makes him an 'extra precautions' patient. Masks and gloves are recommended when you visit. They're not required, but you should definitely wear them for his sake."

He's sitting in the dark, which I assume means he must have been sleeping when I walked in. "I'm sorry," I whisper through my mask. "I can come back."

"No," he says softly. "It's okay. Don't go."

I leave my cart full of DVDs by the door and step closer to his bed. "Are you okay?"

I haven't heard from him for two days. Yesterday, I wrote him but tried to keep it casual. *Just checking in to see how you are.* He never answered. I assumed he remembered what grade I'm in (tenth) or who I really am (nobody) and realized we shouldn't pretend to be friends, online or otherwise. Now I wonder if it's something else completely: He's sicker than I realized.

He's attached to more machines than he was last week. His breathing is shallow, like lying here in bed is making him pant. "I don't want to be alone. I thought I did, and I told people not to come . . ."

His voice is thin, like he's not getting enough oxygen. He should be wearing a mask, not the cannula. I almost suggest it, but he obviously wants to talk, and he wouldn't be able to wearing a mask.

"I don't know what to do. I can't stand having visitors, and I can't stand being alone."

I know this feeling. I pull a chair over and sit down next to his bed. I may not have many (or any) social skills, but I know how to sit quietly with someone who is sad.

For a while, we don't say anything. His eyes are shiny but he's not crying. He wouldn't do that in front of me, of course. He might be sad, but he hasn't lost his mind.

Or maybe he has.

"I think I'm losing my mind," he finally says.

I also know this feeling. I know it doesn't help when someone else says, *You're not.*

Instead, I say, "Okay." I see a pile of textbooks in the corner that looks as if it hasn't been touched. Calculus on top; physics underneath. I'm not going to tell him his schoolwork matters now, because it doesn't.

"You've got a lot of time on your hands. Maybe you need a project. Something that requires using your brain but doesn't tax it too much. If your brain is busy, it's harder to ruminate. Ruminating too much isn't great for anyone." I know a lot about this, obviously. I look back at my cart. "I have something we could try if you'd like." I pull out a box of origami paper and put it on the rolling table in front of him.

His mouth flickers, like he wants to smile at the idea of origami, then he changes his mind. "No thanks."

"Maybe you're a little intimidated by origami. That's okay. I was intimidated at first, too. It requires some dexterity. I don't know how good your fine-motor skills are."

He narrows his eyes. "My fine-motor skills are fine. They're the only thing that is."

"Well, good. Then you should try it."

He looks at me for a long time. I feel my armpits tingle. I've never sat so close to a boy and had him really look at me.

"Is this what they teach you in Smile Awhile school?"

"No. There isn't any Smile Awhile school. There's six hours of training that feels like sixty, but, no, there's no school."

I wait for a bit. I know that when someone is in this state of mind, "suggestions" can feel like water filling up your brain and drowning out any other thoughts. They can make you angry and sad at the same time. Still, I have a hunch about this. I move his table closer and slide a piece of origami paper toward him. I take my own paper and demonstrate a few basics: a mountain fold, a valley fold, a few reverse folds.

After a minute of watching, he starts to fold, too.

"What are we making?" he finally asks.

"I'm not saying. One of the first lessons origami teaches is the pleasure of delayed gratification. Sometimes you make a hundred folds before you see anything take shape."

We keep folding for a while until, without looking at me, he says, "Do you know what I have? Did anyone tell you?"

"My mom did, yes. But only because you're on precautions. Ordinarily she wouldn't."

"Is that why you're sort of wearing the mask?" He almost smiles because I'm not wearing it anymore. It kept falling off, so finally I've let it stay bunched under my chin.

"Should I put it back on?"

"No. You won't make me any sicker than I am, I promise."

I keep folding, staying a few steps ahead of him so he can get the idea of where we're headed: with two reverse folds, what looks like a broken kite becomes a perfect, long-necked bird. I hold it out for him to admire.

He smiles—a real smile, for the first time since I walked into the room. "Wait, are you pretty good at this?"

I smile back. "I don't want to brag, but yeah."

"Like are you one of the best teen origamists in the country or something?"

"*The* best, actually." I laugh. Behind his nose tube, he laughs, too. It's a nice feeling, cheering someone up. I don't know if I've ever done it before. "No, I just started this summer. But I like that it takes a little concentration, and you definitely get better with practice."

He nods and looks down at his own. He's made a mistake somewhere; it doesn't look right. "Is there such a thing as abstract origami? Where it doesn't technically look like a bird but it captures the essence of bird?"

"No. There's really nothing like that. If that happens, you pretty much throw it away and start over."

"Wow. This isn't stressful at all then."

DAVID

To make the bird Jamie's just finished out of the mess of folds I have, she has to take me back, step-by-step. "Are

53

you keeping up with your homework?" she says as she unfolds my mistakes.

"I don't have much. I took light classes this semester because of college apps."

"And how are those going?"

I point to the bag draining bile from my chest. "Not great. It's hard to get excited about applying to college when you may not have lungs to breathe with when you get there."

I never talk like this. I never do things like point to a bag of disgusting bodily fluids and make someone look.

Jamie looks down and shrugs. "Right. But working on the assumption you'll get better, what colleges are you interested in?"

"I'm pretending Brandeis is my number one choice."

She raises her eyebrows. "It's not?"

"I don't know. My college search is a little different from other people's, but no one wants to talk about it."

"I don't mind. Talking about it."

She's bizarrely unflappable. I don't know why I'm telling her all this, but now that I've started, I keep going. I tell her everything I haven't told any of my friends yet, including Sharon. I tell her the doctors say I'll probably live for two years at most if I don't get new lungs and getting new lungs will require six months, at least, of full-time recovery. Add to that the reality check on lung transplants that no one likes to mention: chronic rejection is a huge issue. Five years after a transplant, only 50 percent of recipients are still alive. "It's all a little bleak, right? It's like what's the fucking point of applying to college with odds like that?"

I have to admit, just saying all this makes me feel better. Now my chest isn't so tight. I can breathe a little deeper. I tell myself it's okay because I don't really know this girl and she's not going to talk to any of my friends.

Then it occurs to me: I've just told a stranger who goes to my school that I might be dying. "Please don't tell anyone I said this. I have this whole thing at school—where everyone thinks I'm fine. They know my diagnosis, but we pretend it's a mild case and not really a big issue. I know that sounds crazy, but I really don't want people to know."

She puts the finishing fold on my bird, turns it upside down, and blows into a tiny hole in the bottom. Amazingly, it puffs out and becomes a swan.

"It's not crazy at all. I think a lot of people have stuff they don't talk about with their friends. The good news is, I'm not allowed to say anything. When you start this job, you have to sign all these papers. I'm not allowed to tell people that I've even met you."

JAMIE

I'm not the best teen origamist in the country, of course.

I'd never tried origami until this summer in the hospital. Doctors who'd read my file kept telling me I should give art therapy a try, and I refused because I didn't want to smell paint or turpentine. I didn't want to watch watercolors bleed across a page. I was nervous that being near those things would remind me of my dad and make me sadder than I already was.

Then my roommate, Joan, said they didn't do much painting in the art therapy room. "Mostly it's origami. Everyone starts out by making a house. Then you add decorations. It sounds stupid, but it's kind of cool."

I liked Joan, who was an old hand at being in the hospital. It was her third stay, and she had the best advice for getting through the days. Mostly it boiled down to: keep busy.

Origami is cool? I thought. *Has she lost her mind?*

In a way, she had, of course. We all had.

So I went. And it *was* cool. I made the house to start out with and came back for another session so I could try something else. The next design was multifunctional. With the same twenty folds, you could make something that was either a boat, a hat, or an animal puppet depending on how you opened it up and held it. "You decide," Ms. Yu, the thin Japanese woman leading the class, told us. "Origami is the art of transformation. It's a small piece of paper that becomes many things. You're in control."

The next day, a new group came in and we made houses again. This time, Ms. Yu brought out a box of artist markers after we were finished folding. Nice markers—the expensive kind that make thin or thick lines of bright, saturated color. I was surprised. I didn't mind the smell; in fact, I kind of liked it.

"Now you can decorate your home," Ms. Yu said.

When everyone's house was done, we put them all together on one small table.

"We made a community!" the teacher said, clapping. "Many people living in peace together. Different colors, different shapes, all living in harmony together."

"Maybe in Japan that works," Brian said. He was both funny and probably the most depressed one among us. "Here, not so much."

"Yes here," she said. *"Right here!"* She pointed to the ground emphatically. It was hard to tell if she meant here in America or here in the art therapy room of Cactus Grove hospital. "Many differences make you stronger together!"

I don't know why I thought origami might cheer David up, but it worked. On Thursday, I get another idea.

"I have a new project for you," I tell him.

He's sitting up in a chair today, which is nice to see, but he's also wearing an oxygen mask around his neck. Maybe he needed it to make the trip from the bed to the chair.

"This would be in addition to origami, though. You've gotten off to such a strong start on that one, I'd hate to see you stop now." I didn't think I could be funny with him in person the way I am online. But apparently I can, because here I am, making a joke. He laughs. I notice he's saved both of the birds we made on his bedside table.

I pull out a stack of DVDs I've brought from home. "Old movies! You can watch these while you fold."

He squints. "Seriously?" His voice sounds strained, like talking is hard for him today.

"You'd be surprised how compelling they are. And educational in their own way. I spent most of my homeschooling years studying these, which might sound strange, but I had kind of an unconventional teacher. My dad thought schools put too much emphasis on reading and math and ignored important subjects like filmmaking and art."

I spread out my assortment. "Some people are scared of falling asleep if a movie is in black and white, so it's fine to start with something in color. *The African Queen* maybe. Or *Oklahoma!* perhaps?"

I've brought six movies from the hundred or so we have at home. I watch as his fingers trace the titles on the spines. He pulls one out of the stack, and I'm surprised—it's probably the least well-known but one of my favorites: *Top Hat* starring Fred Astaire and Ginger Rogers.

"Great choice!" I say. "Though I have to warn you it's a terrible movie, plotwise. You'll spend most of the time scratching your head over the implausible story line. You might even think, 'Did someone get *paid* to write this?' But then Fred and Ginger dance 'Cheek to Cheek' and you forget all that. It's pretty magical."

"Sounds good," he rasps, pulling his mask up to his face.

I'm right—talking is hard for him today. I'm glad I have the movies. "Fred and Ginger it is!" I stick the DVD in the dusty player stored below all the TVs on the pediatric floor.

"We should probably keep going with some origami while we watch—this isn't a movie you want to pay super close attention to."

He smiles and nods, like he's grateful for the excuse not to have to talk.

I start him on a new origami project, but I don't stay for very long—I still have to make my rounds, which ends up taking a while. There are a lot of new patients who spend forever looking at my cart before realizing I don't have anything they want. I never do.

When I come back to David's room, two hours have passed and he's back in bed. The movie is over, and a finished crane is sitting in the middle of his table.

He's also fast asleep.

It's scary how easily he tires out. One movie and one origami bird and he's done.

CHAPTER FOUR

DAVID

BEFORE JAMIE GOT HERE on Thursday, I'd had a session with a pulmonary therapist and coughed up about two cups of mucus. I could barely breathe, much less tell her why I had picked that movie. It's Monday now, and since then I've watched *Top Hat* twice and it's brought back a million memories of Starlight and dancing with Sharon. I text Sharon and ask if she's ever seen the movie.

Fred Astaire and Ginger Rogers, I write. They're amazing.

??? She writes back.

They dance. Ballroom. The more I have to explain, the less magical it seems.

Oh, right! Should I watch it? Sharon writes. I'm trying to finish an AP English paper this weekend.

I can't write, *Yes, you should definitely download it and watch it this weekend.* Jamie's right. On many levels, it's a dumb movie. But Fred Astaire's dancing is like nothing I've ever seen before. It's like his body doesn't obey the law of gravity. He floats. Even though he's thin, prematurely bald, and a little sickly looking, he's this superathlete, capable of anything. The whole time I watched, I didn't cough or think about my lungs at all.

You don't have to watch it this weekend, I write, but at some point you should. It'll make you nostalgic for our Starlight days.

We stopped taking lessons a year ago, in the fall of our junior year. We told our teachers (and ourselves) that with student council and our AP-heavy schedules, we had no time left for anything else. Neither one of us mentioned the trouble I was having keeping up with everyone else. I'd make it through two dances and I'd have to sit down for ten minutes and catch my breath. At our last class, I tried a merengue that left my chest screaming and my face red. I spent the rest of the night on the sideline, watching Sharon dance with other people. A few days later, she told me that she felt too overworked and stressed to keep doing dance class. She never once mentioned my episode at the last class. She blamed her labs and her committee obligations; she never blamed me.

Now I write, Do you ever miss it?

Not at all, David. I don't know why you're even thinking about this.

I don't know why, either, but I am.

The next day, Eileen texts me at two in the afternoon.

Eileen: Can I stop by after school before Mom and Dad get there? I have a little problem.

Me: Sure.

The problem isn't so little, as it turns out. She's been suspended from school for getting in a fight, which I don't understand. I picture her friends screaming at each other the way they sometimes do. Why would she get suspended for that?

"It got physical," she explains. "There was some shoving and some hair pulling. Aysa claims I broke a wire on one of her braces."

The fight was with her best friend, *Aysa?*

"I couldn't help it. She was being really mean to other girls we're friends with. I don't know what her problem is."

She hugs her backpack in her lap. In her own way, Eileen has a high moral bar. She stands by her friends, even though none of them stand by her or seem worth the effort.

"It's only a one-day suspension. It's supposed to be a warning to me."

I notice that her backpack looks empty. If this had happened to me (which it never would, unless you look at being hospitalized as a kind of suspension), I would have filled my backpack with books to catch up on homework. Eileen doesn't bother.

"I was thinking that maybe instead of staying home, I'd come here tomorrow, and Mom and Dad wouldn't have to find out."

Is she serious?

"I'm sure the school has already called them."

"They did. That's why I put my phone number on the school forms, not Mom's."

"Wait—they called and you *pretended to be Mom?*" It's

hard to imagine. Even harder to picture is the fact that back in September, she *planned* this in case she got into trouble.

"You just have to act shocked and mad at your kid. I'm not the first person to do it."

I have to draw a line. I need to take charge in a way that our parents can't or won't. But I also don't want to get Eileen in more trouble. "Okay, you can come here tomorrow, and I won't tell Mom and Dad, but I'm going to ask you to do something, and you have to say yes."

"What is it?"

"Do you promise to say yes?"

"Fine."

"Okay. I want you to sign up for dance lessons at Starlight."

She rolls her eyes. Our grandmother, who died two years ago, tried to get her to sign up, too, and she always refused.

"Yeah, no, thanks."

"I'm serious, Lee-lee."

She stares at me. I stare back so she knows: I really am serious.

"Take it or leave it. Sign up for dance class at Starlight or I'm calling Mom right now."

"Why do you want me to take ballroom lessons that are stupid and pointless and I'll never use?"

"Because I'm starting to think they were the best thing I ever did for myself. They opened my eyes and made me realize the world is a bigger place than I thought."

True, I was only eleven when I started, so my world was

pretty small to begin with, but I met a dance coach who was only fifteen when he emigrated from Russia without his family to find a better life. It put my own problems in perspective. I also met kids from other schools who didn't know the unathletic loser I really was. Every Wednesday night felt like a fresh start. That's what Eileen needs, I keep thinking. A fresh start.

"They also taught me a lot about kindness and decency and being thoughtful to other people. Lessons you don't get in school."

I know watching *Top Hat* has made me overromanticize my Starlight days, but I can't help it. I feel like this is *exactly* what Eileen needs.

"Plus you got a girlfriend."

"Plus that."

"You think I'll go there and meet some great guy?"

"No, I think the kids there are nice and polite and you need people like that in your life right now."

"How do you know what I need?"

"It's a hunch. And you'll love the dancing part, I swear." Suddenly, I get another idea, even better than the first. "What if I suggest someone you could do this with? A girl I met here. She's your age, and I think you'd really like her."

"No one my age will voluntarily take ballroom dance classes, I can promise you that."

"She will. Trust me. You'll like this girl. She volunteers here, but she also goes to Northwoods. Don't ask too many questions. You're doing this. Think about Baba. She'll be watching you from heaven, and it'll make her very happy."

"And if I do this, you won't tell Mom and Dad?"

"I promise."

"Fine."

Later that afternoon, I tell Jamie my idea the minute she walks in, and I'm surprised: she seems more dubious about this idea than Eileen.

"Just because I like Fred Astaire and Ginger Rogers movies doesn't mean I can dance. You know that, right?"

"Right, except you'll love it! I know you will!" I tell her about my grandmother and taking lessons for six years. "It's also a good sport for someone who doesn't reliably breathe well. Once you do it for a while, though, you get to love it, I swear. And the more you learn, the more you appreciate the people who do it well. Like Fred and Ginger."

I'm putting on a full-court press here, invoking their names.

"It's not that I don't want to—" she starts to say, and stops. I fear what's coming: *It's just that I don't want to.*

I thought she would jump at this: nerdy kids, an old-fashioned activity. It seems like it would be right up the alley of a girl who loves black-and-white movies from the 1930s.

"Okay, the truth is, I want my sister to do it, but she'll be more responsible if someone signs up with her. She needs to make some new friends. The kids at the dance studio are different from the ones at our school."

Jamie looks worried, and it occurs to me: maybe she already knows Eileen and the trouble she's been in.

"You can take one class for free. If you don't like it, you don't have to keep going." Do I sound desperate? I can't tell.

"I'm sorry. You're right. I'm shy, and I get nervous about going into new situations, but you're right. I should try it."

Her neck is flushed, like she really is shy and what I'm asking is hard.

"How about this? If you sign up for a dance class with Eileen, I'll watch one movie every day for the next week. You pick which ones. Except not too scary. I scare pretty easily."

"You'll let me choose?"

"Absolutely."

She laughs. "Hitchcock it is then. You should start with *Rear Window.*"

"Did you hear that part I said about 'not too scary'?"

"I did. But you also said I get to pick."

This has obviously cheered her up. She smiles as she opens the origami book.

"I also want you to try folding a frog today. That's an advanced-beginner animal, but I think you're ready for it."

She sets up the movie and says she'll come back after she finishes her rounds. At the door, she turns. "Did you say your sister's name is Eileen?"

"Yeah. Do you know her?" I hope my fake-casual tone isn't obvious.

"I do. She's in my life science class. I can't believe she's your sister. She seems so—"

I get ready to hear the worst: Scary? Dangerous?

"I don't know—more artsy than you."

I laugh. "I guess that's one way to describe her."

JAMIE

I don't know how to break this to him, but I've watched Eileen in class and there's no way she'll want to sign up for dance lessons with me. She might not have the high-achieving crowd that David has, but she's just as popular as he is.

"The thing is, she has a lot of friends, David."

"Right, it might seem like that, but they're not great people. All they do is get her in trouble. She needs better influences in her life."

"And you think I'd be a good influence?"

"No offense, Jamie. But yes."

His smile makes my breath catch. I can't say no. Even if I wanted to, which I don't. He looks more like his old self these days. His eyes have a sparkle again; his smile is so big his glasses ride up.

In life science, I watch Eileen from my seat three rows behind her. She looks nothing like David. His hair is light brown and curly; hers is much darker, maybe even dyed, to go along with her general alternative look, which includes heavy black boots, torn stockings, and a confusing mix of accessories: a scarf tied around her wrist, her hair pulled into a messy bun with Mardi Gras beads. I've noticed her before, mostly because of things like the beads. She dresses with an artist's eye for color. One day she'll wear layered T-shirts in Gauguin reds and oranges, the next she'll be all Van Gogh yellows and blues. It's interesting. She looks nothing like my old group of friends, who always shopped together and dress alike in a standard uniform of T-shirts and jeans.

Life science is part of the non-honors course load I signed up for this year to lower my stress level and avoid my old friends. After everything that happened last spring, I was happy to get away from that crowd, but it's hard to tell if this current schedule is the answer. In this class, I sit behind a boy who spends the bulk of every class period covering the inside of his textbook with elaborate and surprisingly well-drawn dragons, like he's hoping to be a tattoo artist one day. I've never talked to him, but every time he opens his book, I wonder how many other people have secret stashes of artwork they keep hidden away like I do.

My dad would have been fine with my schedule this year ("You'll be surrounded by artsy types!") but my mom worries ("You know you're smart enough to do the work—maybe you shouldn't limit your options."). More and more I'm realizing my mother's instincts are probably right, but for now we decided this was all I could manage, so I sit in classes where teachers hand out "cheat sheets" with the notes we should have been taking all along. This month our unit is the "Criteria for Life," and posted on a bulletin board behind the teacher's desk is:

Living things are made of one or more cells.
Living things use energy.
Living things reproduce.
Living things maintain homeostasis.
Living things respond to and interact with their surroundings.

We're supposed to use these criteria to debate whether a substance is alive. Water? Fire? Virus? As Ms. Fisher, our teacher, has said, the "thinking process" will be on the test, not the list, so it's interesting that from where I sit, I can see Eileen has copied them all down in her notebook in fancy handwriting with a curlicue border of climbing roses and little animals. Maybe she's a bored doodler, but she also seems like she might be a decent artist. As if she's studied some manga and knows how to pencil shade. *But why the little animals and flowers?* I wonder, and then it occurs to me: *Living things.*

After class, I wish I could say something to her, but I can't mention her brother without saying how I met him. Which means I can't really say anything. I have to wait for her to ask me about this dance class idea. *Which means it'll probably never happen*, I tell myself.

In the hall as I walk away, I hear a voice behind me. "Jamie, can I talk to you for a second?"

I spin around. It's not Eileen. It's Bethany, who hasn't talked to me since the first day of school, when she looked at my schedule and asked me not to sit with our old friend group at lunch. I've passed her maybe twenty times since then, and she has never said hello.

"Missy wants to talk to you. She thinks we should clear the air so she doesn't have to worry about seeing you in the hall and feeling awkward."

"It's not that awkward, Bethany. We're just not friends, that's all."

She rolls her eyes like I'm missing something obvious. "But you're not friends with *anyone else*. You just sit by yourself watching people all the time. You shouldn't *do* that. It scares them."

Does it? I wonder. *What are they scared of?*

"She just wants to talk. She thinks maybe we should all give each other another chance."

Bethany was the first friend I made when I started school in eighth grade. Up until then, I'd been homeschooled by my dad, who had no friends himself and never saw any reason to help me make any. The first time Bethany had invited me to her house I'd clapped my hands in gratitude.

"Yes!" I'd said. "Sure!" I'd hoped making friends might be as easy as getting over that initial awkward hump.

For six months, we were each other's only friends, which made Bethany nervous.

"If we don't have a bigger group before we get to high school, we might get left behind," she'd worried.

Toward the end of the year, she'd set her sights on Missy.

"I think she's looking to expand her group. I heard her complaining about her lunch friends in English today."

I wish one of us had recognized a red flag when we saw

one. Missy is a girl who is always looking for better friends than the ones she has. She sits on the fringe of the cafeteria, keeping tabs on the popular people who hardly know who she is. She tracks their love lives and their friend fights in a way that even I understand disqualifies her from joining their ranks. When you care that much about people who don't know your name, it's creepy.

I wonder if they've learned this lesson by now. I have to admit, though, Bethany standing here like this softens me a little.

"She says it's fine if you want to eat lunch with us today. I think you should."

"Okay," I say.

I spend the rest of the morning second-guessing this idea. It might be sincere, but it also might be Missy, restless and bored, wanting a chance to take another swipe at me in front of other people.

I show up to their table ten minutes after lunch has started because I don't want Missy to think I'm too eager. I'm not the same person I was last spring. Unfortunately, I'm still not completely sure who I am, which makes my voice sound a little shaky. "Hi, Missy. Bethany said you wanted to talk to me."

Missy looks up and doesn't say anything for a while. She isn't the prettiest or smartest in this group, and I've never understood why everyone gives her so much power, unless the explanation is simple: when you're unpredictable and capable of saying incredibly mean things, everyone is scared of you.

Apparently two new girls have joined their group. I don't know their names, but they both look nervous, like they've never seen someone stand up to Missy before. Come to think of it, neither had I before I did it last spring. I feel like telling them not to worry, I'm not about to do it again.

"That's right," Missy finally says. "I don't like worrying all the time about running into you. I just want to clear the air."

"Okay."

Long silence.

"I'm pretty sure you should start by apologizing to all of us. Me especially, but to Nicki and Bethany, too."

I look at both of them. I try to say with my eyes, *Is she really going to do this in front of other people? Do you see how she makes everything worse than it needs to be?*

Their expressions say they don't.

"I'm sorry, you guys. I was going through a lot of stuff last spring, and I wasn't really myself for a while. I took it out on you all, and I shouldn't have." My heart is pounding, but it's not because my mouth is saying the wrong things like last time. To me this sounds like a good apology: reasonably heartfelt and fairly mature.

Except Missy doesn't think so. "Yeah, I don't know. What you said at my sleepover was pretty unforgivable."

I don't want to have this argument. In fact, I don't want to be friends with them, so why am I even standing here?

I look up and see Eileen sitting with her own group of

friends, two tables away. From the outside, they look like they're better friends to each other than my group ever was. They're more touchy-feely, straightening each other's bra straps and reaching into each other's pockets. But watching Eileen, I can tell she isn't really part of their conversation. She plays with her food and stares at her phone, like their talk is noise she has to filter out to keep her thoughts straight. I remember this feeling so well that for a second, I want to go over to her and ask if she's okay.

She doesn't look like she is. Mostly, she looks lost—like she has no idea what she's doing here. Maybe she's worried about her brother and she can't talk about it, or maybe it's something else. Maybe she's keeping a secret the way I did, but she's not even sure exactly what it is. It catches my breath for a second—how much she reminds me of myself last spring.

Like maybe we actually *could* be friends.

I don't know why seeing Eileen makes me feel empowered, but it does. I turn to Missy and say, "Sorry about this, but I can't eat lunch with you guys. Today or ever, probably."

That night, I get a message from David.

I loved Rear Window. I want more Hitchcock.

Even though I don't have a shift, I stop by the next day and bring him *North by Northwest* and *Vertigo*. He messages me the next day to say he loved the first one but *Vertigo* freaked him out a little.

David: That is the psychologically creepiest movie I've ever seen. Jimmy Stewart is evil. He's trying to change her the whole movie.
Me: Exactly. You think he's the hero, and he's really not. It's twisted.

After that, I bring him *Laura*, which freaks him out even more. "Oh my God, she's been alive this whole time?" he gasps at the big reveal. He's the perfect audience for these movies. Everything shocks him.

"As alive as you and me," I say.

On the other hand, *Who's Afraid of Virginia Woolf?* is kind of a downer.

"This might be reminding me of my parents a little too much," he says. "Except for drinking too much and fighting all the time. Mine don't do that because they've got—you know—yoga at night and work in the morning. But looking at each other with bitter disappointment and making up stories about their children. They definitely do that."

"What stories do they make up?"

I've met his parents only once, a few days ago. Even though David looked happy to see me, they seemed confused. They knew I wasn't a friend from school. It was awkward, and I left pretty quickly.

I haven't mentioned Eileen or the dance class idea since then. I still haven't said anything to her in class, and she hasn't, either.

"They like to pretend that I'm not really that sick and I'm definitely not going to die anytime soon."

It's the first time he's ever said anything like this. We both get quiet. I want to say a bunch of things:

You're not dying right now.

Maybe it's okay to be in denial about some things.

They love you, and that's what people do when they love someone.

I don't say any of it, though. Instead, we sit quietly for a while.

Finally, he asks, "Did you really watch these movies in elementary school?"

"Yes. I'll admit I didn't always understand the plots, but my dad would talk about visuals and how a director had set up a shot, and I'd watch for things like that."

"Weren't some of them—a little disturbing for a young kid?"

It's hard to explain what those years of being home alone with my dad were like. "Maybe a little, but it was part of our homeschooling curriculum. He was an artist, so we did a lot of art together. And we watched movies."

"And that was it?"

"We had to cover some things for school, but mostly he let me choose what subjects I wanted to learn. We went to museums and worked in his basement studio a lot. It was great for a long time. I loved it. Then I got a little older and realized I was the only sixth grader in the world who'd never read Harry Potter. I wanted to learn other things."

Does that sound normal? I can't tell.

★ ★ ★

David keeps asking to do more origami even though he's not very good at it. His fingers are shorter and wider than most people's. I didn't notice it until he held up a hand and pointed it out. "It's a weird CF thing. We're stubby-digited. Go ahead. Laugh."

I don't laugh. Instead, I bring in an abalone paper folder the next day, shaped like a letter opener. "The pros use this to make their folds crisper. You can, too."

He smiles. "Should I wonder about the fact that you own something like this?"

"Does it make me a nerd? Possibly. It also means your origami will get much better."

I'm right. With the next bird he tries, his folds are a hundred times better. He laughs as he holds it up. "I did it! I made a decent crane even with my club fingers!"

After a while, we've got a pattern. He watches the movies I bring after I leave, and we spend my visits folding origami. Today, when I walk in, the origami book is open to a new page.

"Have you ever done a tessellation?" he asks. "They look so cool, don't they?"

"They're pretty advanced, actually. They might look simple, but they're not." I look down at his paper, an accordion of folds. Tessellations are folded patterns on flat paper that have to fit perfectly. "You've got a decent start, though."

"Should I admit that I've been working on this for two

hours, or should I lie and pretend it's taken me much less?"

I smile. "Maybe you should take a break."

Recently, we've been telling each other stories from our childhood. Not the hard ones that I avoid, but funny ones. He tells me he's trying these tessellations because they remind him of the armor he used to wear when he was obsessed with anything medieval.

"Armor, castles, anything like that. I had a pretty extensive collection of swords at one time. Don't laugh."

"I'm not laughing." I smile. "And capes? Did you have any hooded capes?"

"As a matter of fact, yes. Some really nice ones. There was a store downtown that sold old costumes, and I used to beg my mother to take me. I'm only just realizing now that makes me sound like a geek."

"Not at all. It just sounds like you were probably shopping with some geeks. Did you do *Lord of the Rings* every Halloween?"

"I was Frodo one year. And Robin Hood another."

"With tights or without?"

"I'm not going to answer that."

"You don't have to. I can guess."

"Fine, yes, I wore tights, and, yes, everyone thought I was Peter Pan. Even though obviously Peter Pan doesn't carry a quiver of arrows."

"That doesn't sound embarrassing at all."

"Didn't you have some Halloween costumes that were a misfire?"

I don't have to think about that one for too long. "I'm not sure Marie Antoinette quite worked out the way I was hoping."

He laughs, which turns into a cough.

"Everyone thought I was Cinderella even though I was carrying a piece of cake on a plate."

"Overinvesting in props was always a big mistake for me."

"That, or choosing random historical figures most kids haven't heard of. That's a mistake, too."

"I bet you looked great."

"I did actually. My dad spent a long time making the dress. He was kind of a Marie Antoinette buff. It was his idea . . ." My voice wavers. I hope he doesn't ask any more.

He doesn't because we're interrupted by a nurse, rolling her cart into the room to take David's vitals. Whenever I'm here for this, I try to remember the numbers they're recording. I want to keep track and see if there's any good signs in there but it's hard for me to tell. It's also hard for me to know exactly what I'm hoping for. Of course, I want him to get better as quickly as possible, but I also know that when he does, he'll leave the hospital. He'll still be sick and waiting for a transplant, but if he does it at home, everything will change. He'll go back to his old life of being senior class president with a million friends and Sharon for a girlfriend, and I'll go back to my old life of being nobody to anyone.

★ ★ ★

When I leave his room, my mother is waiting for me at the end of the hallway. I'm surprised; usually she meets me down in the cafeteria.

"All set?" She smiles, trying to look cheerful.

"Yeah," I say. We haven't talked much about David since she told me his diagnosis. She's busy at work and tired when she gets home. I haven't told her that I've been stopping by more often, on days I'm not working. Now, I say, "David seems better. He's more energetic."

"Good," she says, and starts walking.

The whole way down to the cafeteria, we don't say anything. Finally, we get to our table with our food and she says, "I have to tell you, I don't think it's a good idea for you to spend so much time with him."

"I'm careful, Mom. I always wear a mask," I say, even though I don't. I wear one into the room, but I don't always keep it on.

"I'm not talking about germs. He's facing something that you shouldn't have to deal with, Jamie. You're not ready. You want to think about him, but I have to think about *you*."

"What do you think he's facing? What are you even talking about?"

"He has a terminal genetic disorder. You know what that means."

"You think he's going to *die*?"

"Yes. Sooner or later, he will."

I remember her saying this the first time I asked about

CF, but this is different. David was incredibly healthy up until a month ago. "One of his lungs collapsed and it takes time to heal, that's all! Plus, things are changing a lot. There're new treatments for CF every day. People don't die in their teens anymore."

"Yes, they do, sweetheart. Some people live into their thirties, but some aren't so lucky. I've seen this before. And I know that the sicker these kids get, the more they need to save whatever strength they have to be with their family and their friends."

"I'm his friend, too!" I say, much louder than I expected to.

"Even if he likes you, Jamie, it makes his life harder—can you see that? It adds one more person he has to deal with. You might not realize how little energy he has right now."

I think about the way he fell asleep last week from the strain of sitting up in the chair. I think about how often he's wearing an oxygen mask when I walk in. Though I haven't wanted to dwell on it, I know the G-tube hasn't worked the miracle I promised. He's gained a little weight but not a lot. I know he's not getting better. He won't—not really—until he gets new lungs. "Has he complained? Or his parents?"

"No, of course not. They're too busy processing this all themselves."

I can't stop visiting him just because he might be sicker than I realize. I won't do it. I look my mother in the eyes. "Then how do you know what's best for him?"

CHAPTER FIVE

DAVID

"**J**AMIE KNOWS YOU," I tell Eileen the next day. "You have life science together. She sits three rows behind you, and she likes the way you dress. She says you have an artistic eye. Some of your outfits remind her of Van Gogh."

Eileen looks wary. "She didn't say that."

"She did. I swear."

"Is she a freak?"

I smile. "Maybe. But in a good way. It's good for us to get to know someone different. She makes me think about things." I don't bother trying to explain. I'm hoping she'll understand when she gets to know Jamie.

Eileen looks at the shelf beside my bed, where I'm displaying my small paper menagerie. "What? Like origami?"

"Yeah. Plus, other things. I like her. You will, too."

"Okay."

She shrugs as if this doesn't matter much to her one

81

way or another. I'm not sure why I care so much. "You have to be nice to her, though. She doesn't have a lot of friends."

"I know. I can be nice."

"I know you *can*, but sometimes you aren't."

"But I know *how*. Why are you being so weird about this?"

"I'm not being weird. Or if I am, so what? She's a tenth grader who watches Fred Astaire and Ginger Rogers movies. If you mention a TV show from the last five years, she'll have no idea what you're talking about. How often do you find someone like that?"

"Never."

"Exactly."

Suddenly, I'm nervous. Maybe this isn't such a great idea. Spending as much time with Jamie as I have over the past week is confusing. Visiting with my friends is hard; visiting with Jamie isn't. Some afternoons with her, I'll look up and realize two hours have passed and I didn't even realize it. Even Sharon doesn't stay that long. She hates the disinfectant smell and is scared of the tubes I'm still attached to. She doesn't want to pull anything out or knock anything over. Back in school, Sharon and I have almost everything in common (three classes, two clubs, plus student council). In here, not so much.

It's not like that with Jamie, but maybe that's because nothing in a hospital room resembles real life. To me, Jamie seems like a perfect friend for Eileen—smart and funny, with a good head on her shoulders. But maybe that's because she's been a great friend *for me*. Suddenly I wonder if I want to share Jamie, even with Eileen, who I love and want to help. "You're right. I'm being weird. Never mind. Skip it. Do dance classes by yourself and see how you like it."

"No way. I'm curious now. I want to meet this weird girl."

After Eileen leaves, I think about how hard it's been lately, seeing my school friends. Every visit, they spend the first minute pretending they're not shocked at the sight of me. I'm getting used to it now: the inhaled breath, the widened eyes. Everyone starts with the obligatory lie "You look *good*, David," then we quickly move on to school topics. Yesterday, Ashwin spent an hour talking about a new crisis on the fund-raising committee. Toward the end, I dozed off, which made me feel bad. I think of Ashwin as my best guy friend, even though we've never done any of the things boys usually do—sleep over at each other's houses or waste whole weekends playing stupid video games. How can I when my breathing treatments mean nebulizing medicines for a half hour every morning and evening? Sharon is the only one in our friend group who knows that my bedroom is lined with breathing equipment and my bathroom shelf is lined with medications. It's weird to realize this now: No one else has been in my bedroom.

Maybe it's not so strange. The only time I've been to Ashwin's house was in ninth grade when he invited me over to "make pies." It didn't make sense until I got there, and then I understood: the idea was his mother's. Nervous that Ashwin wasn't making friends, she suggested this party and bought six pie crusts and the ingredients to fill them.

"I invited two other guys, but they thought it sounded weird," he said sheepishly. I saw it all then—his mother in the background wearing a sari, religious talismans on the wall. He had his own secrets tucked away at home, just like I did.

We had a great time that day. We ate ourselves sick, and for years afterward, we've made jokes about bringing pies to school events. I've always meant to become better friends with Ashwin, but I never have. I don't know why. I was busy with Sharon, or it seemed risky. Like spending more time with him would mean letting him see the truth about my CF, that it was a bigger deal than I let on, and more work to take care of.

Now it feels like it's too late. He can see the truth, but thinks it's better to talk about our old subjects. To pretend I'm the same person I was last month even if I'm not.

Jamie was right about origami. To me, it's more relaxing to sit here, working on something that's hard and also doesn't really matter, than it is to see my old friends. I've been doing it for two weeks now, and each animal I make is a little better than the last. It's comforting to line them up. A row of legless creatures, wounded and waiting. Like me.

I also like the conversations Jamie and I have while we fold. They have nothing to do with school or which colleges everyone is applying to. They're random and weird and make me think. Last time she was here, Jamie explained, "In Japanese, the words for 'frog' and 'return' are pronounced the same way, so a geisha would fold a frog and give it to a favorite patron to let him know that she would welcome his return."

I laughed, even though I don't think she was trying to be funny. "That's an amazingly strange detail to know."

"I agree. The origami book I read was from the 1970s. I don't think the women's movement had made it to Japan at that point."

Hanging out with Jamie is easier than seeing my friends. It just is. She doesn't walk in the door and gasp at the sight of me still attached to these machines after almost three weeks. She doesn't look at me and see everything I'm currently not—healthy, stable, on top of my game. I know I'm a mess right now. Seeing me sick doesn't make her sad. Maybe it's a low bar to build a friendship on, but there you have it. There's a tube in my chest and a hole in my stomach. All the bars are pretty low right now.

JAMIE

Every time we have a nice conversation, I almost tell David the truth. It's happened a few times. The words float up, right there, on the tip of my tongue: *Something happened last spring after my dad died. At first it was like I was numb and sleepwalking. I couldn't taste food or understand what anyone was saying around me. I couldn't read more than a sentence at a sitting. I couldn't do homework or anything else except compile examples in my mind of how phony my supposed friends were. Finally, during a sleepover, I told them they were shallow and manipulative and I hated them all. I left in the middle of the night, and when I got home, I realized the person I hated most of all was me.*

I want to tell him, *I volunteer in the hospital because I have no choice. I have to stay busy to keep the darkness away.*

I haven't because I don't want to scare him.

He might know about brushes with depression because of his illness, but I don't think he knows the terrifying depths of it. If I tell him I was in the hospital this summer for three weeks, it won't feel like we have more in common. It won't mean laughing about hospital food and orange-juice cups with peel-off foil lids. It'll mean we won't laugh about anything again because nobody thinks depression is funny except for other kids on a psych ward who laugh more than you might expect, but of course I don't see or talk to any of them anymore.

I almost tell him the truth.

But I don't.

CHAPTER SIX

DAVID

APPARENTLY, MY MOTHER IS softening. She's talked to enough outside specialists to agree with Dr. C's assessment, and now my parents are doing what's required to get me on the transplant list. They're submitting their own health histories and talking to a psychologist about their ability to support me in the year I'll spend recovering from the operation.

"A year?" I gasp when I hear this. "Is that what they're saying?"

"Yes," my mom says. "That's what they're saying."

This news sends me back to the message boards on my CF websites. My mother doesn't think I should spend too much time on these boards. "It's not good for you to read depressing stories. CF is the only thing you have in common, and you aren't defined by your disease." I don't tell her, *I've been lying in bed for three weeks, draining bile from my chest and breathing with one lung. At this point, I'm pretty defined by my disease.*

Breathing Together is my favorite CF site. As a general rule, the sicker someone is, the more time they have to write posts, so it's not hard to find other people my age on the transplant list. I weigh where each person seems to be, healthwise—who sleeps with oxygen, who needs it all day, who's using a bi-pap 24/7. I'm not approved for the list yet, but I'm curious where I'll end up once I make it on. My number will be determined by how sick I am, which makes it one of those competitions you don't want to win, but also do. It's confusing.

Everyone who goes on the list says some version of the same thing: *I don't want to die without trying my hardest to live.* They also concede that there are some problematic statistics to consider: a third of transplanted patients reject their new organs right away. Another third develop chronic rejection after a year or so. Only about half of transplanted lungs last more than five years. Meaning a lot of people go through all of this and don't live that much longer. Even so, everyone on this board still wants to try. *I hope to be part of the lucky 50 percent and still be alive in five years*, they say.

Five years is the goal everyone is shooting for.

Some people on Breathing Together are already old by CF standards. One woman is thirty-one and married with an adopted child. To me, she sounds greedy, wanting five more years than she's already gotten. "My goal is being alive until my child turns ten," she writes. "Is that too much to ask?"

It kind of is, I think. Especially if my goal is being alive next year.

I think about Lester Freeman, the only person I've known personally who's had a lung transplant. I was thirteen when we met; he was the same age I am now, a senior in high school. We were hospital roommates because back then they didn't keep CF patients apart the way they do now, for fear of spreading our bad bacteria to each other. At the time, he seemed sicker than I am even now, but going on the list energized him. He told me if he got a transplant, he was going to make some changes in his life, which he did. After the surgery, instead of going to college, he moved to San Diego to spend all his time surfing. Three months after the move, he wrote me a note saying he was happier than he'd ever been. "I spend every day on the beach and every night with my girlfriend." I pull up his old messages now and reread them, which I shouldn't do, because I know how the story ends: after six months, he contracted an infection in his new lungs that raced through his body and shut down his organs in the course of a single weekend. On a Friday he posted pictures of himself smiling on the beach. On Monday he was dead.

Now that my parents have adjusted to the transplant idea, Sharon is the hardest person to talk to about it. I put off telling her as long as possible. She's accepted the tube snaking out of my chest, the hole in my stomach, the cannula under my nose. She can look at these things without stopping midsentence and losing her train of thought. But a surgery that will involve cranking up my rib cage like a car hood, cutting out organs, and replacing them with ones from a dead stranger will be harder for her to handle, I fear. She likes to be in control, or at least feel like she is. Getting on the transplant list means you control almost nothing about your life. You wait. You don't make any big plans. Even little plans are hard, because you don't know how you'll feel or how much energy you'll have.

On the website, people write about this all the time. *Thought I could manage seeing a movie today. I was wrong.*

I finally break the news to her the day after she gets the fundraising totals from homecoming. Apparently, it went really well—plus they've raised more money for senior events than any planning committee in the past—so she's been in a good mood this whole visit.

"I have a little good news, too," I say.

She looks up, surprised. "You're being released?"

"No, not that good. The doctor thinks I'm ready to get on the transplant list. I'm going to try for some new lungs."

Her hand goes to her mouth. Tears rim her eyes. "Oh my God. Oh, David—"

"It'll be okay, Share! It means I'll be able to do things again. I can climb a flight of stairs! I can sit near a candle at a party and not have a coughing fit! I'll be almost normal!"

She nods with her hand still over her mouth. She doesn't say anything.

"I might not get approved for the list yet. And if I do, it might take a long time for lungs to show up. It doesn't change anything right away."

I don't want to tell her too much at once. Like how

long recovery will take if I get the surgery this year. Or how, after a transplant, you shift from managing one condition (cystic fibrosis) to managing another (transplant rejection), which requires taking more pills (if that's even possible), and more vigilance. I won't have CF in my lungs anymore, but I'll still have it in other places like my pancreas and my liver, which are, at best, only limping along in the jobs they're meant to do.

Finally, Sharon takes her hand away from her mouth. "It's great. I'm so happy for you," she says, even though she's crying.

I laugh.

"I *am*," she snaps, wiping the tears away. "It just changes our plans for this year, that's all. I'm not crying about you, I'm crying about stupid things, like the winter dance. This means you probably won't make it back to school in time for that, I guess, right?"

"Probably not."

"I know that doesn't matter. I'm being so stupid." She turns away to blow her nose and wipe her face. When she turns back, she takes a deep breath. "What matters is you getting *well*. That's all. Don't even worry about me."

I hold out my hand. She comes over and sits down on the side of the bed. This whole time, she's hardly done this. She's scared of pulling out a tube or unplugging a machine, I think. I'm so grateful, I almost start crying, too.

"With new lungs, I'll be able to dance again. Maybe we could go back to Starlight."

"Why do you keep bringing that up?"

"Wouldn't it be nice to go back there and dance again? Especially if I'm not breathing like an eighty-year-old with COPD?"

"You never did that."

"Yes, I did, Share. That's why we quit." Isn't it better to be honest about all this, I think, but looking at her face, I'm not so sure.

"I don't know if I want to go back. Aren't we kind of done with that?"

Are we?

She doesn't look at me, so I'm not sure what she's thinking. Now that she's seen how fragile I am, maybe the idea of doing anything like that scares her.

After she leaves, I log back on to Breathing Together, where I find a message board for older teens with a thread titled, The 50K Question—Is College Worth It for Us? The posts seem equally divided on both sides of the question. One person argues that dying in our twenties and leaving our families with a big student loan debt is kind of like "screwing them over twice." Others point out that college is full of health-compromising issues for us—sleep deprivation, alcohol consumption, lots of young people who don't wash their hands. "It's like paying a lot of money to increase all your risk factors."

A few people maintain that whatever the risk, it's worth it. "College is the place where most people discover who they really are. You can't learn about independence living in your parents' basement."

For my friends, college—where they're applying, what their chances are—has been an obsession since last spring, when everyone started their school visits. Ashwin fell in love with Brown; Hannah with Bates; Sharon called me from Tufts.

"This is it, David. I can *really picture* myself here." I was too sick to go on a college tour, though I told my friends that my parents couldn't get away from work. Still, I pretended to fall in love from afar with schools in the same area. "They all look great," I said. I told people Brandeis was my first choice because it was thirty minutes from Tufts, Sharon's first choice. I couldn't picture what I'd do in college, so I imagined it being like an extension of high school, where all of us would meet up, wearing down jackets and hats. On my college questionnaires and "interest inventories," I checked "engineering" and "math" as possible majors, but it's hard for me to imagine pursuing either one. Those majors sound like a mind-numbing grind of hard work and stress with no real point beyond the lucrative job you'd get if you survive four years of that drudgery. When my posttransplant odds are five years, at best, I have to ask myself: Do I really want to spend four years working toward getting a job I'll never be well enough to do?

The more I read on Breathing Together, the more I think the pro-college people sound a little deluded. If I only have a few years left, why spend them fulfilling other people's expectations? Especially when I've spent most of my life doing just that. Starting clubs, running for office, piling up AP credits. It all made sense while I was pretending my health wasn't an issue. Now it doesn't.

Of course my parents don't see it this way. A few days ago, my mom asked how the essays were going for my applications. Today she's at it again.

"Maybe it would help if someone read what you've written so far."

I tell her, as gently as possible, that it might be better to wait.

"Wait for *what*, sweetheart?"

"Just wait. I want to see how I feel in a month."

"I don't understand why you're lying in bed with all this free time and not using it productively—"

She sounds like Sharon, who likes running on a treadmill and doing her AP English reading at the same time. Time is the main thing they both hate wasting.

"Maybe I *am* being productive, but I'm doing different things than you want. Maybe I'm starting to see a different future. Even if I get a new pair of lungs and feel great, I'm not sure I'd want to rush off to college next year. It might be better for me to slow down a little."

It feels strange to say this out loud. It's the first time I've told anyone what I'm thinking (besides Jamie, who doesn't really count because she doesn't know the old me).

The whole time Mom's been here, she's been straightening the room. Now she sinks down in the chair beside my bed. "This is *exactly* what we're worried about. You have one little health setback and you're ready to give up. We're not going to let you do that."

"I'm not giving up. I want to consider all my options and think about taking a gap year at least." Now that I've started this conversation, I don't want to back down. I haven't been to school in three weeks. To me, this seems like a reasonable thing to say.

She looks down at her phone, which has pinged with a message. "All right, I wasn't sure whether to tell you this or not, but I've talked to Dr. Chortkoff about putting you on Prozac. I think it's a good idea right now."

"You think I'm saying this because I'm *depressed*?"

"I think you're seeing things in a very negative light these days. It's not helping you make good decisions. Dad and I agree on this."

"I *am* looking at reality, Mom. The truth is a little depressing right now."

"That's what I'm saying. That's why you need medication."

"But maybe I also need to *talk* about all this. And think about what I really want to do with the rest of my life."

"You've spent your whole life taking AP classes and doing extracurriculars. You have an exceptional transcript. The school counselor said your college list might not have been shooting *high enough*. She thinks you should include some Ivy Leagues—maybe Cornell or Princeton. This is *Ms. Lowenstein*, who never tells anyone this. Usually she reminds everyone that community colleges are excellent backups."

It's true. She's the world's least optimistic college counselor, but I can't help wondering how my mother heard this. Did she call her up, looking for a message like this?

"You were all set to apply to eight schools—now you've been sick for three weeks and suddenly you're thinking that's not a good idea? What if you get better and don't need the transplant? What if you get it and feel great five months from now? Why would you want to eliminate your options for next year?"

Later, when I tell Sharon about all this, she agrees with my mom. "I don't understand what you'd do instead of college. It's not like any of us will still be around, and you don't exactly love spending time with your family. I don't know, David. It seems like you're seeing things through a pretty dark lens right now."

Am I? I honestly don't think I feel depressed. I feel like I'm seeing some truths for the first time, but when my dad visits he goes into a whole speech about the importance of staying positive.

"They say it's the best medicine there is! You visualize your future as a healthy, well person, away at college, having fun like everyone else, and your body *responds*."

"Come on, Dad, is it really being so negative to say I might die in the next few years if that's what the doctors are saying? I'm looking at the whole picture. I feel different than my friends, and I feel like even if I make it to college, I'm not sure I'd have anything in common with eighteen-year-olds who've always been healthy and don't know what this is like."

I thought my dad would understand, but he keeps shaking his head like he's not sure what to say.

"That's most of the world, David. I'm sorry but it is."

"I know. It's not only that, though. It's about taking control of the time I have left. I want to figure out my priorities and set my own agenda. Is that so crazy?"

"Of course not. Except you don't have any alternative plans."

"But I do! Okay, look—here's an example. There's this girl who volunteers here. She's Eileen's age, but she was homeschooled most of her life. Up until eighth grade she spent all her time going to art museums and watching old movies with her father, and she's *interesting*. She's more interesting than me because she's *thought* about what she wants to learn. That's what I want to do."

"You want to go to art museums and watch old movies?"

"No. I want to take control of the time I have left. I want to decide what's interesting to me and learn more about that."

Even after all this, I've apparently convinced no one, because the next morning, Dr. C says my parents have asked him to put me on a generic antidepressant. "Is that something you're interested in?"

"No. They think I'm depressed, but I'm not. I'm just rethinking my life a little right now. If it's going to be shorter than I expected, I want to make sure what I'm doing means something. Is that so crazy?"

He gives me a look. "Not crazy, no. Just hard."

He says he'll check back in with me in a week to see if I've changed my mind.

JAMIE

When Eileen finally approaches me about signing up for Starlight, it's pretty much as awkward as I imagined it might be. Her mouth doesn't move from the thin, angry line it was in when she walked up.

"My brother says I have to sign up for this weird dance class and you're doing it, too."

"Well, I haven't signed up or anything. I don't know too much about it."

"Basically, you learn to waltz and cha-cha in case you want to try out for *Dancing with the Stars* someday."

I laugh. "It seems pretty random that teenagers actually do it, right?"

"Only weird teenagers. Like my brother and his girl-friend."

Even though it's obvious Eileen wants no part of this activity—or me, for that matter—I have to admit, I don't mind the prospect of spending time with her. I like the furious way she rolls her eyes about her brother and makes fun of Sharon. In my old friend group, Missy was sarcastic without ever being funny. Eileen seems funny. Though I'm not completely sure, of course, so I don't laugh.

"The new session starts Wednesday. If you want to go, we can give you a ride."

"That sounds great. I like ballroom dancing. And weird teenagers."

She rolls her eyes again, but there's the start of a smile in the corners of her mouth, like maybe she doesn't mind this idea as much as she's pretending to.

That afternoon, I tell David that I finally talked to Eileen.

"Did she tell you she hates me for making her do this?"

"No. She made fun of it a little, but I think it might be okay."

"You're a hero. Seriously. Eileen might have a bad attitude, but I think you'll love it."

He's already told me that he had to drop out because of his health, though he told other people it was about being overscheduled and making time for college applications. I can tell it makes him sad to think about the way he's sacrificed things he loved for a future he's not sure he wants anymore. Recently, David's been talking more about his friends and their college applications. Usually, I don't say much, because what do I know about applying to prestigious East Coast schools? My mom got her nursing degree at a community college, and my dad finished two years of art school before dropping out. When I told David this, his eyes lit up. "Art school? *Really?*"

Maybe I keep bringing my father up because he always gets this reaction. David has romantic ideas of being an artist, even though I tell him he shouldn't. "My dad went to Trinity Arts, which is really hard to get into, but he never liked it that much. He thought the teachers tried to impose their own aesthetics on the students. He'd already sold a few paintings, so it didn't hurt him too much to leave. Or that's what he said, anyway."

"But he made money at it? People bought his paintings?"

"For a while, yeah. He was profiled in *Art World* magazine once. It was before I was born, but I've seen the copy. He was kind of a big deal when he was younger."

"So he was famous?"

"Well, no. Famous is different."

I think about the corner of my mother's bedroom where the paintings he made the last ten years of his life are stored now. For months after he died, she visited his old galleries to see if they'd be willing to try to sell them. She heard the same thing every time: they loved his early work; his recent stuff, not so much. She pressed them on it—suggested old clients, people whose houses they'd visited and gone to parties at. They wanted to help, but there wasn't much they could do.

"You can be successful for a while, but it's hard to keep making money, I guess. Art buyers are fickle. They want whoever's young and hot."

"Still, that's pretty cool," David says. "He made his living as an artist."

I don't say anything more.

I wish I could tell my mom how often David writes me now. Every afternoon, I get home to two or three emails.

He writes about different things—his thoughts about college (he doesn't want to go), his thoughts about his friends (and the hard time he's having relating to them), even his thoughts about his health. Yesterday, he told me he'd started reading a book that someone online recommended called *Meditations* by Marcus Aurelius. He was the emperor of Rome a zillion years ago, which apparently meant he was always going into battle, and every time he did, he expected to die, so he wrote a lot about living life to the fullest while one can. In David's latest email he sent this quote: "Why do you hunger for length of days? Death is only a thing of terror for those unable to live in the present."

If I show my mother these, she'll see only more reason to worry.

I know she doesn't want me to get in over my head, which I understand. I also know that David will probably get better soon, and when he does, he'll return to his old life and the world we don't really share. When he talks about living life to the fullest after he gets out of the hospital, I have something like the opposite thought: *I have to make the most of this friendship while he's still stuck in here.*

On Wednesday, I get home to a frantic IM:

DAVID: Jamie, where are you? Weren't you going to stop by this afternoon? Shouldn't you already be here?

For a second, I wonder if I could just show my mother this. Would it be enough for her to believe that we're friends and he wants me to visit him? I don't because then she'd read the rest of our messages and put a stop to all of them. *It's too much*, she'd say. *You're not ready for this.* Instead, I write him back quickly, before she gets home.

> **ME:** Maybe you forgot—our dance class starts tonight.
> **DAVID:** That's right! So I guess I won't see you today, unless you want to stop by and show me what you're wearing.
> **ME:** Absolutely not. I didn't have a skirt or the right shoes, so I had to borrow an outfit from my mom, which means I'm going to look like a middle-aged nurse, off-duty.
> **DAVID:** They talk a lot about dress codes, but they don't really mean it. You'll look great, I'm sure.
> **ME:** I really won't, trust me.
> **DAVID:** Have a great time. Tell me how it goes afterward!

"I know I look ridiculous," Eileen announces when I get in the back seat. She sits up front next to her dad, who nods hello but doesn't say anything.

She doesn't look ridiculous; she looks *great*. Her hair is down, which I've never seen before—styled and curled around her face in a pretty way. She's also wearing about half the makeup she usually wears in school. No black eyeliner, no dark lipstick, just a little mascara.

"You look great, Eileen. Seriously."

The ride is quiet and a little awkward until Eileen surprises me by asking whatever happened to the girls I used to be friends with in middle school.

"Do you *know* them?" I ask. What I mean is, *Do you know me?*

"Missy and Nicki? Yeah, I never liked them. No offense, but you can do better."

I can? I thought. *With who?*

This whole time I've assumed that Eileen lives in a different league than me, friendwise. She talks to other kids in our class and moves down school hallways saying hello. She seems buffered from the abyss of friendlessness that I live in. Now I wonder if she plays the same games I do. Does she sit mutely in a group she's no longer part of? Does she perch on the periphery of conversations she never joins?

The first hour of our lesson is in a small group with two other beginners and will be followed by a larger group lesson in the big studio. Tonya, our teacher, is a middle-aged woman with bright red hair and strappy black sandals. She introduces us to two dance coaches who will partner with Eileen and me as we learn our first moves. They look at least five years older than us and are both ridiculously handsome. One is dark-haired, with a beard; the other is blond with blue eyes.

"Girls, please meet Stenyak. And Antonin."

They bow in front of us, which makes me blush and Eileen laugh.

"Seriously?" she says, looking around behind her.

Tonya runs us through the basics: dance position, box step, and the one-two-three, cha-cha-cha. After about twenty minutes, she dismisses our partners with an apology.

"We're busy tonight! We must spread our extra gentlemen around, you don't mind, ladies?"

Eileen offers to be the leader and dance with me after they go, but Tonya shakes her head. "That won't be necessary. You dance alone for now and follow my steps."

Dancing alone makes me realize how thrilling it was to dance with a partner who knew what he was doing. The fox-trot—slow, slow, quick, quick—with our empty arms in the air, isn't the same as having a tall boy with his hand on your back, standing close enough for all your clothing to touch.

For the second hour, we move into the larger studio with the big group. David is right—there are a lot of kids our age here, but I don't recognize any of them from school. Though no music is playing, most of them are dancing anyway, working on steps they've just learned in their smaller sessions. Of course beginners aren't doing this, so we sit for a while and watch really good dancers strut their stuff. I've been at this for an hour and I don't even recognize a correlation between the moves we've just learned and what these people are doing.

"Where are the bad dancers?" Eileen whispers.

If I were here with any of my old friends, we wouldn't be having fun like this. We'd be silent and self-conscious and terrified of being found out as beginners. Eileen doesn't think this way. When two boys sit down next to us, she leans across me and introduces us both. "This is our first night, and we have no idea what we're doing. She might be okay"—she hooks her thumb at me—"but I'm terrible.

What do you guys think—do you want to dance with us?"

They smile and reassure us. It looks hard at first, but we'll catch on quickly, they say. Of course, they'll dance with us. They'd love to.

Eileen is impossible to resist. I don't understand why David said she needed better friends and "influences" in her life when she seems so confident to me, hardly like someone who is easily influenced. With our new partners, we start with a basic box step on the edge of the floor, so we don't crash into the better dancers who can move in circles without bumping into each other. About halfway through the song, my partner pulls me closer.

"Shall we try a turn?" he whispers.

"Okay," I say, sounding a little breathless.

A moment later, he's turned me into the river of couples swirling clockwise around the room. After two spins, I realize: it's possible to be led around the dance floor by someone experienced enough to make you look like you know what you're doing. With every mistake I make, he adjusts his own feet for a swift recovery. Once, when it seems like my confusion might actually knock us over, he grabs my lower back and brings me in tighter to steady me again.

"There you go," he whispers. "You're fine now."

From the corner of my eye, I see a flash of Eileen and her partner spinning around, too. At the end of the song, we return to our chairs, breathless. "That was awesome," she says, smiling. She's worked up a sweat. I have, too.

None of this is like what we imagined.

As the night wears on, though, I notice something.

Watching Eileen in action is like watching a how-to demonstration on flirting with older boys. She sidles up to our first partners and asks where exactly in Russia they're from.

"Do you know Russia?" Stenyak asks.

"Not at all," Eileen says, not breaking eye contact. "I'm just making conversation."

For a while, her approach seems generalized to include every older boy in the room. She finger-waves, and smiles, and walks with a twist in her step so the formfitting dress with the flared skirt she's wearing almost touches the knees of the boys she walks past. She's a beacon that draws every eye to her and then insists, too loud, that no one should watch her dance, she's terrible at this.

Toward the end of class, Tonya announces that a special guest has come tonight to help her demonstrate the last dance, a merengue. "Everyone please welcome Nicolai, Arizona's newly crowned Latin-Salsa Swing King!"

The door opens, and a handsome young man wearing all black glides into the room to take his place beside the teacher up front.

A few people clap; others look confused.

A moment later, Nicolai and Tonya are moving through a merengue so graceful it catches my breath. It's impossible to look away and impossible to fathom how they stay so connected to one another as their hips swivel and their feet take them in one direction and then another.

Eileen leans into my shoulder. "Okay. So how do we get a chance to dance with him?"

For the next five minutes, we form separate lines. Leaders (boys) on one side; followers (girls) on the other. We practice the moves until Tonya claps her hands and says, "All right then. Let's partner up and try this."

Eileen, who was standing beside me, disappears. A moment later, I see her across the room, in dance position with Nicolai. I have no idea how she's managed it, but maybe this is what David warned me about: *She likes to take risks.*

Even though there isn't much time left, Eileen manages to dance once more with Nicolai. She doesn't sit next to me for the end-of-class wrap-up where the teacher goes over dates and reminds us of the social next month. We aren't supposed to have our phones in class, but from across the room, I watch Eileen pull hers out to show Nicolai something. He nods at her screen, and she bumps his shoulder with hers. I try to imagine touching David like this—easily, jokingly. I wish I could, but I can't.

The next day, I don't tell David any of this. I tell him we had a great time. "Eileen is different than the girls I was friends with last year. In a good way."

"Did she do anything weird?"

"What do you mean?"

"Just weird. She can be weird."

Where on his weird scale would flirting with Nicolai rank? It made me nervous, but maybe it was nothing. She didn't mention him after class or on the ride home. Maybe dancing with him was a small thing in her world.

"Do you know any kids who still go to Starlight?" I ask him.

"Not too many. There was one guy I started with. We used to be pretty good friends and then he got more serious about entering competitions, and we drifted apart. He's probably still there. He was a little strange, though. Even though we used to hang out all the time, someone told him why I coughed so much, and he never talked to me again. Couldn't handle it, I guess."

"That's *terrible*."

"Some people get freaked out, that's all."

I think about how our dance coaches bowed when they met us. How often Tonya talked about the importance of manners. It made me think: *David is right, forcing people to be polite makes them all seem nicer.*

Now I wonder if that's true. "Was he really a good friend?"

"I thought so. For a little while, at least. Maybe he was mad I never told him myself. I don't know. He'd gotten caught up in competing by then. Some girls had started paying him to enter competitions with them, so he was under a lot of pressure."

"Paying him? Are you kidding?"

"Maybe you noticed there's a slight shortage of guys. That's how the dance coaches make their money. They're here getting certified to become dance teachers. A few of them are from Russia and they're younger than you think. They're on their own, and they don't have any other source of income. But Nick just wanted to cash in on it so he makes people think he's from Russia and sells his services."

I swallow hard. "Nick? Is his real name Nicolai?"

"Yeah, but we always called him Nick."

"Tall, with brown hair and a beard? Really good at salsa?"

"Yep, that's him. Did he talk to you in his fake accent?"

"No," I say. I don't add: *But Eileen has her eye on him.*

"Well, now you know. You should probably avoid him."

CHAPTER SEVEN

DAVID

AFTER I GET THE news, Jamie is the first friend I tell. I know she'll be happy for me and everyone else will have hesitant, hard-to-read responses.

> **ME:** So now it's official. I've been approved for the organ transplant list.
> **JAMIE:** Congratulations! That's great!
> **ME:** It is great, but also strange. When the doctor told us, I kept worrying that my mother would start crying and I'd get mad at her and we'd get in one of our ugly new fights. And then it was weird. She was fine, and I was the one crying. I don't even know why. I know I shouldn't admit this. Please don't tell anyone at school.
> **JAMIE:** Who am I going to tell? And of course you should admit it! It's pretty overwhelming. And scary.
> **ME:** Yeah.

JAMIE: And potentially great.

ME: Potentially.

There's no way to talk about how truly terrifying this is when I've been waiting almost a month to get approved for this list. Maybe I should have talked about this first with Sharon, but she's at a Youth Leadership Retreat this weekend, where they couldn't bring their cell phones. We haven't communicated in three days, which I thought would be hard, but instead I've been chatting with Jamie a *lot*.

I don't know if she's thinks it seems strange. She doesn't say anything if she does.

JAMIE: So what happens now?

ME: When I leave the hospital, I'll carry a pager everywhere I go, and they'll page me when they get a pair of lungs.

JAMIE: Are they saying you might get out soon?

ME: Not likely, since I had a temperature this morning. But let's talk about something else. Tell me about your day. How did the life science test go?

JAMIE

I keep being surprised at how interested David is in the details of my life. I don't even remember mentioning the life science test. Maybe Eileen did, and maybe he thinks of me as an extension of her. Maybe he's the kind of big brother who wants to know what his tenth-grade sister's life is like, so he asks me.

ME: I did okay, but that's because she gave us most of the questions ahead of time.
DAVID: Is it possible you're taking a slightly too easy schedule?
ME: It's possible. In three out of four of my academic classes they don't assign homework. We just do it in class, where the teacher can help us.
DAVID: How about reading?
ME: In English we've only done one play and a poetry packet, and we read all those aloud. She did say something about reading a whole book before the end of the year.
DAVID: I think you should definitely consider some honors classes next semester.

I remind myself, *He doesn't know me or what I'm capable of.* He's saying this to be nice. Or maybe he's practicing the pep talk he wants to give Eileen. It's all pretty confusing— feeling like he knows me and then reminding myself that he doesn't really.

Today I'm bringing him *Splendor in the Grass*, starring Natalie Wood and Warren Beatty, as part of my plan to tell him the truth about what happened this summer. I thought of it two days ago, but we didn't own a copy, so I had to go to the library and check it out. Plus, I had to work up my courage. Natalie Wood and Warren Beatty (in his first movie!) play a glamorous high school couple. He's rich; she's poor. He's under family pressure to succeed; she's under family pressure not to be one of "those" girls (meaning slutty). But the crazy intensity of her sexual feelings tips her over the edge, and she makes a scene at a school dance, wading into the local reservoir still wearing her party dress. ("Water is always a metaphor for sex," my dad explained to me when I was twelve.) That night she's put in a mental institution, where she stays for two years.

Because Natalie Wood is believable and also beautiful throughout—even in the hospital—I'm hoping this is the perfect way to tell David the truth. The more he talks about his own future and how he's rethinking everything—not following the same path his friends are on—the more I want to tell him my own story. *I never had real friends or a path to follow.* I want to watch this movie with him and say, *Something like this happened to me.*

Minus Warren Beatty. And I didn't stay for two years.

But as he knows, three weeks can feel like a pretty long time when you're in a hospital.

Once we start this conversation, I know I'll have a lot to say, and old movies will help me. I can tell him there are more suicidal characters in Frank Capra's movies than any other director's, but everyone still thinks of him as an upbeat, life-affirming storyteller because look how *It's a Wonderful Life* turns out. Maybe I'll tell him there was a time, before I was in the hospital, that I was obsessed with movies about people in psychiatric hospitals. I loved the way those characters seemed fragile but strengthened by their experience. And wiser somehow. Like they were the only ones who saw the truth about the world they had to step away from.

It's certainly true in *Splendor in the Grass*. By the time Natalie Wood gets out of the hospital after two years, the stock market has crashed and Warren Beatty has lost all his money. He's a farmer with a wife and baby and a yard full of chickens. Next to him, Natalie looks like the one with the promise of a better future. I want David to watch the movie before I tell him. That way he'll see for himself: people do get better.

After four weeks of being friends, I want David to know the truth: I had a terrible time last spring. I didn't understand the way depression worked—that it feels physical for a long time, like something else is wrong. Your bones ache. Food tastes different. You're always tired because you never sleep. You can't think clearly, and you're too exhausted to do anything. He's complained about the ways his body has taken over his decision-making—that he's too tired to do homework, too unfocused to read much.

"You're sick," I tell him. "Your body is working on other things. You have to give yourself a break."

Now I want to explain how I know this: Depression is a sickness, and the worst part is that your mind can't remember what better feels like. You get well by doing a whole bunch of little things that sound like they won't help but eventually they do. You have to eat right and get exercise and take your medication, but mostly you have to be patient, the way he has to be now. Maybe I'm ready to tell him this because I'm scared he'll leave soon and I want him to know why his friendship matters so much to me. I want to tell him, *Helping you has made me better.*

I run through the other rooms I have to visit first. Most of the kids have seen me before, and most of the parents are too tired to talk much. "Can I bring you anything else?" I always ask. They always smile and shake their heads.

I've saved David's room for last so I can stay longer. But as I get nearer, I see a red sign posted on his door. I push my cart closer to read it, though I've seen these signs before and I know what they say. LIMITED STAFF. NO VISITORS. FULL PROTECTIVE MEASURES REQUIRED.

To the side of his door is another cart with masks and gloves, sterile jumpsuits and booties. Beyond that is a bin for used items. I know what all this means: he's tested positive for pseudomonas or another bad bacterium.

Though it takes me another minute, I also know what this really means: he's much sicker now. If lungs become available, he might not get them.

CHAPTER EIGHT

DAVID

OPEN MY EYES, SEE where I am, and shut them again. Moving hurts. Even the nurses lifting my arm to check my IV hurts. My chest aches every time I breathe.

I lose track of days.

My whole family comes in, wearing masks and sterilized coveralls. The only thing I can see is my mother's eyes filled with tears.

I assume I'm dying.

"Are you in pain?" my dad asks.

I can't answer with my oxygen mask on so I nod. When I open my eyes again, my parents are gone.

Someone puts on music that hurts to listen to. I recognize the song; I remember once liking it. Now it hurts to hear it, and I ask the person moving around my room to turn it off. I don't open my eyes, so I don't know who it is.

★ ★ ★

This morning, I wake up and keep my eyes open. There's a packet of saltines on my bedside table. I can't move, but I can stare at it without feeling nauseous.

After some experimentation, I realize I can pull my computer onto my bed.

I must be slightly better. I still can't sit up, but I can read lying down. There are four messages from Jamie. There are other messages, too, but I read hers first.

JAMIE: I don't know if you're reading these, but in case you are, I want you to know, you're on quarantine now, so I can't come visit you. They're really strict about that. Family only. I would be there if I could.

JAMIE: Write when you can. I'm thinking about you.

JAMIE: I hope you're okay.

JAMIE: I broke down and asked Eileen today how you're doing, and she said you're okay. They've got the bacteria under control. Yes, it's pseudomonas, and I've read enough about that one to know this must feel like a setback, but I promise you it's not. You're going to get your lungs and you're going to get better. I know you will.

She doesn't know that pseudomonas are the one bacterium you can never get rid of once you get them. Even if I get new lungs, they'll still be in my body. It's not easy to type, but I want her to know the truth.

ME: I won't get better. Not now.

JAMIE: You're writing again! I'm so relieved!

ME: I'm not better. I'm just typing.

JAMIE: That means you ARE better. You might feel worse right now because you've had a temperature, but you're okay. You're going to get well. It'll just take some time, though.

ME: I'm not going to get well.

JAMIE: What do you mean?

I can't read the words anymore. The room is starting to spin.

I type *Bye* and shut my computer.

It's impossible to distinguish night from day. I have no idea how much time has passed. I ask every nurse what day it is, and then I can't remember what they tell me.

I have crazy dreams. Where I'm angry and screaming at everyone in my family. In one, I'm standing alone on a beach, yelling "LET ME GO!" to my parents and Eileen.

When I wake up, I'm sweating.

"I'm dying, right?" I say to the nurse. "You can tell me. It's okay. It's better to know."

"You're not dying, David. The infection is going down."

I don't understand why no one will tell me the truth.

I write Jamie again.

ME: I know I'm dying. Why won't anyone just say it?

JAMIE: Because you're not. You're just sick.

ME: I'm never going to get out of here.

JAMIE: Yes, you are.

ME: This is too hard. I don't even remember what being well feels like. I don't think I'll ever get back there, and I don't want to spend another day like this.

JAMIE: Your mind is playing tricks on you. That's what happens.

ME: I don't want to be in this room anymore.

JAMIE: Would you like me to call you? Would it help to talk?

In all this time, we've never talked on the phone. I don't know why not. Suddenly, I think, with perfect clarity: *Yes. The sound of Jamie's voice will help.*

ME: Yes. Call me, please.

She calls, and we talk for almost an hour. She tells me she knows the way I'm feeling. That I'm not alone and I have to trust her. I listen to what she says, even though I'm drifting in and out of sleep.

"Your brain is telling you lies right now. It's saying you won't get better, but you will. It's hard to believe that, because brains are stubborn. They think they're right when they're not."

I ask if she minds if I sleep a little while she talks.

"Not at all. That's probably the best way to get through this. Just sleep, and I'll stay right here telling you you're going to be okay."

She does.

And it's strange. The next morning when I wake up, I am.

JAMIE

I'm nervous about seeing him again. It's only been a week since I spent all that time on the phone, telling him he would get better and now here he is—sitting up in bed, smiling and looking better than he has in weeks.

"Jamie! I've been waiting for you to come! Guess what—I'm better!"

"Wow. That's great!"

"I mean they're not about to let me out, but the antibiotics are working finally, and I feel my body moving in the right direction. I'm putting on some weight again. I'm not falling asleep an hour after I wake up."

"That's really great."

His eyes have a sparkle that they haven't had in weeks. His voice isn't so breathy. I'm happy, but I'm also confused. Does he not remember our last conversation and how low he was?

"So a lot has happened, and I've been wanting to talk to you. Sit, sit."

He waves at the chair I usually sit in. His energy is making me nervous. I don't understand where it's coming from. How could he be so much better already?

"I've made a few big decisions. The first one is, I'm

not going to apply to any colleges. I told my parents that instead of wasting money on college, I'm going to pick my own books, watch classic movies, and learn what I want to learn! Just like you! It's going to be great!"

"Wow," I say, because I can't think of anything else. I wonder if I should remind him: *I left that life behind to go to real school.* "What do your parents say?"

"They hate the idea, of course. But I told them, they either let me make this choice or I'll figure out a way to kill myself."

Now I'm really uncomfortable. I stand up. "David—"

"Sit, sit. I'm just kidding. They'll come around. They don't love the idea, but I showed them all the books I ordered, so they can see that I'm serious."

He opens the drawer beside his bed that's full of books. Apparently, I wasn't the only one he reached out to online while he was sick. Amazon must have been another.

"What did you get?"

"I'm starting with a few philosophers and psychologists." He reaches into his bedside drawer and pulls out a stack of books. *Meditations*, by Marcus Aurelius, which he's already told me about. I don't recognize the others: *The Power of Positivity. Looking Up in a World of Down.*

"I don't get it," I say.

"I started feeling better the day after I talked to you. Thank you, by the way. I have no idea how long you stayed on the phone, but whatever you said, I woke up the next morning feeling much better. Like a hundred percent. I had energy again and focus, and now I've been reading nonstop for the last three days. These books are amazing. Did you know that the most popular class at Harvard is called Positive Psychology? It's about finding happiness. Sixteen hundred overachieving kids take it every year, and do you want to hear the basic message of the class?"

He's talking too fast. His enthusiasm becomes a coughing spell that lasts almost a minute. Not the worst I've seen, but it takes the wind out of his sails.

"Stop overachieving?"

"How did you know?" He smiles and spits what he's just coughed up into a washcloth beside his bed. "It's crazy, Jamie, but they've got all this research to back it up. They've done a bunch of studies, and they all say some version of the same thing: after your basic needs are met, having money doesn't make anyone happier. In fact, your happiness level goes down slightly after you make a million dollars. Success doesn't affect the level, either. You want to know the only thing that really works?"

I don't answer. He's on such a roll, I don't need to.

"Making a habit of optimistic, positive thinking. You have to train your brain not to see things negatively by replacing those thoughts with positive ones. I know it sounds a little simplistic. I was skeptical when I first started reading all this, but the more I research, the more sense it makes to me, and I really think this is what I'm meant to be doing. I've finally found it! This is my project."

I look down at the books. "Thinking positively is your project?"

"Yes, but it's harder than you think. There's a book based on the class, and it lets you pick different exercises. This is mine." He opens the drawer again and pulls out a green plastic box with index cards inside. "I'm writing down quotes. Five a day. Enough that I can forget them, and my second exercise will be pulling them out and re-reading them. Here's one: 'To be interested in the changing seasons is a happier state of mind than to be hopelessly in love with spring.'"

He lays a stack of maybe fifty cards on his rolling table. I reach over and pick one up: "'The golden moments in the stream of life rush past us and we see nothing but sand; the angels come to visit us, and we only know them when they're gone.'"

"See, I love that one."

I put it back on his table. "Okay."

"Why? You don't?"

"No—it's just—it's nothing. I'm not much of an aphorism person."

"These aren't aphorisms. Do they seem like aphorisms to you?"

I pick up another one and read it: "'Most people are as happy as they make up their mind to be.' Yeah, that sounds like an aphorism to me."

"These are quotations from famous writers on the greatest question every human being faces: How can I be happier? Aphorisms are stupid posters like 'Hang in there, Baby' and 'A smile is a frown turned upside down.'"

"The guidance counselor at my middle school actually had that on the wall."

"I know. I had the same guidance counselor. She was an idiot."

DAVID

I don't understand. I expected my friends to roll their eyes and make fun of this, but I thought Jamie would love it. This is my own project. My own special study, like the ones she got to do with her dad. Only this isn't about art, it's the question I've been asking myself for the last month: If I have just a few years left—too long for a bucket list, but not long enough for a family or career like everyone else— what will make me happiest?

To me, reading these books makes a ton of sense.

To her, it doesn't.

"These aren't idiotic, David. They're just—I don't know. Never mind. It's a good project. It is."

"But you think it's stupid."

"No, I don't think it's stupid. Yes, I think it's a little simplistic, that's all. I'm not sure positive thinking works the way people want it to."

"This is the crazy part, though—it *does* work. The research *shows* it. If you do the exercises and put the effort in, it really does work. You should try it. I could lend you some of my cards."

I don't know why I'm pushing it. I've been working on this project and for a week I've wanted to tell her, *I thought I was dying, and then I remembered what you said. Find a project for yourself.* It's worked. The more I read and write down quotes, the more I want to learn about all this. I'm not thinking about my lungs or my infection or the sorry state of my body. *I'm lying here in bed, just as sick as I was last week, and I'm genuinely happier.*

I haven't told anyone else because this feeling is fragile and one eye roll might kill it. I'm telling Jamie because I assumed she'd understand.

But no. She stares at the chunk of cards I'm holding out. She doesn't want to take them, I can tell.

JAMIE

I understand why he thinks I'd like this. Last week, I told him he needed to think more positively, to picture a future where he isn't so sick.

Now I don't want to touch his stupid cards.

"No, thanks, David," I say softly. "I'll stick with origami for now."

I try to keep my voice light, but I feel my face get red and my hands get clammy. I'm not going to turn this into an argument where I have to explain, *I was talking about something different. "Get happy" talk and positive thinking feels like bullshit to someone who's been depressed. It says it's your fault for not being able to think cheerful thoughts. It makes everything worse.*

He takes his cards back. "Okay, never mind."

He looks hurt.

"David, I'm sorry."

"No, no. It's not for everybody. I understand."

He can't look at me, which makes it even worse.

"I should probably get going. My mom is waiting for me." I've never used this excuse before because I've never wanted to leave his room before.

"Sure, yeah, okay. Will I see you tomorrow?"

He's never asked this question because I always come.

"Why?"

"It's your regular shift, right?"

"Oh, right. Yeah. I'll see you tomorrow."

In the year and a half since my father died, I've tried to make sense of his sadness.

"Making art was the only thing he ever wanted to do," my mom has told me. "He wasn't depressed because you left him to go to school. He was depressed because he never became the artist he wanted to be."

What neither one of us ever says is: *I'm not becoming the one I wanted to be, either.*

I loved all those years of painting with my dad, and I loved the year I got to take art class in middle school. I loved being chosen for a citywide art show downtown, where representatives from every grade got to display work around city hall. The assignment had been to choose a favorite children's story from childhood and reimagine new illustrations for it. I'd picked *The Runaway Bunny* because the story always fascinated me and the illustrations always confused me. In my version, I played with perspective, putting the baby bunny on adventures in the foreground and the mama bunny in the distance, keeping an eye on him. My teacher loved it; my dad, not so much.

"I thought they didn't start telling you to be a children's book illustrator until you got into art school, but I was wrong, I guess. Nowadays they start in middle school."

Something happened after that show. It wasn't just what he said about the assignment. It was his silence when I brought home all my other work from that semester. Work that had gotten lavish praise from the teacher, who told me I should explore all the mediums before choosing one to pursue.

"You're a bit of a Michelangelo," she said, smiling. "You could probably do any of them."

I knew she didn't mean I had his talent; she meant I was good at drawing and painting and maybe sculpture. For weeks, her words floated around in my mind. I'd done work at school that year that I really liked. Pieces that were different from anything I'd done at home with my dad. I was excited for him to see them. I even worried that he might go overboard and get sentimental.

You did all this without me? I imagined him saying, and I would rush in to reassure him.

You're still part of this. Your voice is always in the back of my head. Which was true. I thought we might cry and hug and reassure each other while he looked over everything.

But no. He flipped through the portfolio quickly and for a long time didn't say anything at all. Finally, he closed it up and said, "Looks like you're moving on."

The next semester, I didn't sign up for art. I wanted my

dad to know that I wasn't moving on—he was my first and most important teacher. I'd go to school for academics, and I'd learn art from him.

Except he hardly worked anymore. On weekends, he'd go downstairs to his studio in the basement for only an hour or two. Over the summer, it got worse. He hardly went down at all. We took none of our old field trips to museums and art shows. Instead, we both went quiet. Some mornings, my mother left for work and we retreated to separate corners of the house, not saying a word until she came home.

At the time, I was confused.

Now I understand: This is what depression looks and feels like. Silence. Stillness. Torpor. David's talk about foregoing college to pursue his "happiness research" feels like he's taken the idea of being homeschooled and gleaned the wrong lesson from it. He thinks learning and doing what he wants will mean being happy. I haven't told him about the last year of my dad's life. How I still believe he would have been better off if he'd taken the job teaching art at our community college when it was offered instead of refusing it because he "didn't want any distractions." Having no responsibilities meant he accomplished nothing.

In this past year, I've done no art at all, and instead I've embraced my mother's philosophy: work hard, do your job, think about other people. So far my mom has been right. Even friendless and overwhelmed at school, I've been happier this year than I was last year. But how do I tell David that without telling him everything else?

★ ★ ★

The next day I stand at the foot of David's bed with my cart at my side. I've been awake half the night trying to figure out what I want to say.

"I'm sorry I was weird yesterday about your happiness project. I have a problem with depression, and the idea that you can control your mood with upbeat sayings—I don't know. It pissed me off."

"Why?"

"Because you can't. If you don't know depression, I can't explain it, but it's bigger than that. Deciding to be cheerful or think positively doesn't help. It makes it worse actually."

It's strange—I'm not as nervous as I expected to be. My heart isn't hammering; I don't feel dizzy the way I did yesterday when he talked about this.

"I'm doing better now, because I'm on medication, but it's not like that's a miracle cure. I still have to think about it. I'm always worried that it'll come back."

He nods but doesn't say anything. I can tell he's listening.

Tell the truth, I think. "Sometimes I feel okay, and sometimes I'm not sure. I still do weird things that I can't always explain. Like eating lunch by myself in the cafeteria and storming out of here yesterday. I don't always have reasons why I do certain things."

"When you have a genetic disorder where the odds are pretty good that you'll die at some point before you hit thirty, you have some idea of what depression probably feels like. It's not the same, I know, but things can feel pretty bleak sometimes."

I think about our phone call when he was feverish and sick.

David keeps going: "Would it make you want to storm out of here if I told you about one more thing I read in my happiness research?"

I smile. "It depends, I guess."

"It turns out the country with the highest happiness index is Denmark, of all places, where it's winter eight months a year. The reason is this concept they have called hue-guh." He opens his laptop so I can see how it's spelled: *hygge*. "It's crazy. The spelling, not the idea. The idea is that real happiness is about simplifying your life so you can see what's right in front of you and find happiness there." He points to his lap and then widens his hands so it's clear, he doesn't mean his lap, he means here, in this room. What's right in front of us.

"Here? In the hospital?" I say.

"Well, no, actually not right here. The lighting is too fluorescent to be *hygge* in here, but the point is that you look at your life *as it is.* You learn to savor what you already have. You don't need to apply to colleges and go someplace where you won't recognize anyone or know yourself. Happiness is where you feel at home. Most people already have the components for happiness. They just have to realize it."

"Like stop and smell the roses?"

"Yeah, sort of. *Hygge* is usually described as the feeling you get when you're curled up in front of a fireplace with a cup of hot cocoa and there's a snowstorm raging outside. It's about atmosphere, and coziness, but it's also about the storm, too. I think it's really about finding pockets of comfort in the face of hard times. Where you defy the shitty elements in your life and be happy in spite of them."

He looks at me like there's something more he wants to say but isn't sure he should. He coughs. Then he must decide to go ahead, because he closes his laptop. "I'm telling you all this because I wanted to say that your visits and folding origami and watching movies and everything we've done—they've given me some *hygge* here in the hospital. Thank you for that."

I feel my throat tighten. I want to tell him the truth—that if I didn't have these visits to look forward to, I don't know how I'd make it through the loneliness of school right now. I wouldn't. It's what I couldn't tell my mother when she told me I shouldn't visit him so much, because I can't say this to anyone. If I didn't have David, I wonder how bleak and friendless this fall would have felt.

"You don't have to thank me," I say. "You really don't."

"Okay, then. Now that we've gotten that out of the way, I want to ask you a favor. A big favor. Promise you won't say no right away."

"Okay."

He claps his hands and rubs them together. "I've been in this hospital for over a month now, my longest stay ever, and you can certainly testify to the fact that I probably started losing my mind about four weeks ago, am I right?"

I can't tell where this is headed or if I'm meant to agree with him or not.

He keeps going. "If you're talking about someone's psychological health, I'm guessing that pretty much the worst thing you can do is confine them to a hospital bed in a room by themselves and then wake them up every three hours to find out how they're doing. It's not waterboarding, but it's close."

I nod. Even my mom would admit this is true.

"So here's my idea"—he leans forward to whisper—"I need to get out of here. Not a full-on escape. Just a mini escape. For an hour or two. You bring clothes for me to wear. I change downstairs in a bathroom. I put them on, and you and I go outside. We breathe real air again. Maybe we even get real food. I'm talking about two hours tops. No one will even know I'm gone."

"I can't, David. I can't violate hospital rules like that."

"Jamie, listen to me. We're sitting here talking about depression, and I'm lying here every day trying to keep it away. I need to breathe fresh air and taste real food and eat with a utensil that isn't plastic. I need to feel like a person again, not a patient. I'll never get better if I can't remember what better feels like. I've been here more than *four weeks*. I know it sounds melodramatic, but I feel like I'll die if I don't get out of here. I can't say this to anyone else, Jamie, but I can tell you."

Now I'm not looking away, and he isn't, either.

"I have a four-hour window. My IV antibiotics happen twice a day, morning and late afternoon. Each one takes about three hours. What I do in between is up to me. Last week, the doctors gave me permission to leave the peds wing during the day to go somewhere quieter and do my homework, as long as I stay in certain areas of the hospital. They'll assume I'm downstairs in a conference room working."

We look at each other long enough for me to read his face. I don't know what to do. I love that he seems so energetic and upbeat about this idea. He's right—it makes him seem healthier. I *want* to believe he is, but I know it's not true. No doctor would say he's well enough to leave the hospital. But they have said he's well enough to leave his room. To leave the wing.

I take a deep breath. "Okay. I'll help you, but only with some conditions. We're not going more than a block away from the hospital. We need to be able to get back here quickly if anything happens. That gives us one restaurant to choose from."

"That's okay."

"It's Denny's," I say. "You won't have to eat with plastic forks. Take it or leave it."

"It sounds great." He grins. The biggest smile I've seen in a long time.

"It won't be great, but it's not far from the side exit where we can leave without attracting attention. You'll also need clothes obviously. Do you have any here?"

"Just T-shirts and pajama pants."

"Can you ask Eileen to bring you something?"

"She wouldn't mind breaking rules, but she'd probably

tell our parents as part of making her point that I'm not perfect."

I'm not sure what other choice we have. "I guess I could bring you some of my dad's clothes. Even though we moved, my mom saved most of them. I'm not sure why. She just couldn't bear to give them away."

"Is that okay?"

"Not really, but we'll be careful, and I'll bring them back. She doesn't need to know."

"Thank you, Jamie." He holds out his hand the way he did the first day he was in the hospital, when I came back to check on him.

He wants me to come over and take it. He can do things like this—hold hands with someone who isn't his girlfriend—because he's older and confident and doesn't think holding hands is a big deal. But if you're me, and you've never held anyone's hand—if you've spent too much of your life being homeschooled or depressed—it's a big deal. It is.

For a long time, I stare at his hand. I wish I were a better actress. I wish my heart wasn't beating so hard that I'm afraid he might hear it. I wish my hands weren't sweaty.

"It's okay, David. I'm happy to help you."

I give him my hand. He squeezes it with both of his and closes his eyes as if this—holding my hand—helps him relax. He takes a deeper breath than he usually can. "Thank you, thank you," he mouths.

I want to relax, but I can't. My heart is beating too much. My throat tightens. It's hard to breathe. I wonder if this is what he feels like most of the time: dizzy and light-headed because he has to pant.

Over dinner in the cafeteria that night, it's hard to make eye contact with my mom, knowing what I've just agreed to do. I wish I could tell her everything and explain the real reason I said yes and how it has to do with Dad. More and more I've been thinking the worst part of his depression was how he never talked about it or asked for help. If I learned anything while I was in the hospital, it's the importance of this part—you have to ask for help, and you have to accept it when it's offered. I know David isn't depressed, but he's giving me something my father never did: a chance to help him.

"Is everything okay with those girls at school?" my mom asks. "You look a little preoccupied."

"It's fine, yeah."

"Do you feel like you're starting to make better friends?"

It's a loaded question, she knows. I think about David, first and foremost, Eileen second. "Yeah," I say. "I do."

Eileen and I have now been to two more classes, and I've told my mom a little bit, but not everything. I haven't told her that I'm supposed to be keeping my eye on Eileen and lately, she's been making me nervous. Last week, Nicolai showed up halfway through class.

"Oh my God, there he is," Eileen whispered to me.

"Isn't he kind of a phony?" I said, trying to sound casual. "I don't think he's even from Russia."

She shrugged. "He never said he was."

"He didn't?"

"No. He's a senior and he's a great dancer. What's the big deal?"

I wanted to tell her what David had said, but he'd asked me not to repeat our conversations. "I've heard he's not a great guy."

"Oh, please." Eileen smiled. "I'll be okay."

Twenty minutes later, she was dancing with Nicolai, smiling and laughing as they spun circles around the other couples on the floor. Toward the end of class, though, he left early, walking right past Eileen and me without saying anything. She held up her hand and called, "Nicolai! Wait!" loud enough for everyone to hear and stop talking.

He didn't turn around.

The next week, he was there early and they were all flirtation again—smiling and signaling to each other in what looked like some coded language I didn't understand.

"Is something going on with you and Nicolai?" I asked.

"No," she said. "Why would you think that?"

How could I say anything or stop what she wouldn't even admit? We weren't really friends. We'd been thrown together, and one of us had been charged with keeping an eye on the other. I hadn't even done a good job with that.

CHAPTER NINE

DAVID

REAL AIR IS AMAZING. Even though I'm wheeling an oxygen tank beside me, so I'm not breathing 100 percent real air, it still feels different. It's colder than I expected, which is thrilling and—actually a problem. With all my circulation problems, I get embarrassingly cold easily.

"Oh God, I didn't bring you a sweater," Jamie says, seeing me shudder. "Should I run back and grab something out of lost and found?"

"Isn't that full of clothes from people who've died?"

"I don't know, maybe. But if you're freezing, who cares?"

I let her run back because it gives me an excuse to sit down and rest on a corner bench. Walking this far—half a block, maybe two hundred steps—has left me breathless. I need to collect myself so I can take it all in.

Nothing about this street is pretty. It's four lanes of

traffic and a block full of strip malls on the other side—a nail salon, a drugstore, and a "Checks Cashed Here" place. A month away from all this, and I feel like I'm seeing it with a fresh pair of eyes. Or maybe I never really *looked* before. I'm feeling so light-headed. I don't even realize I'm sitting at a bus stop until a bus pulls up and the door opens.

"You getting on?" the driver says after looking at me for about ten seconds.

"Oh, I'm sorry!" I laugh. "No, I'm just resting!"

I'm still smiling as the bus pulls away. It's like everything has changed! The world has filled with buses that stop if you sit down on a random bench to catch your breath!

"What's so funny?" Jamie says when she reappears, holding a bright red cardigan sweater.

"Nothing," I say, hoisting myself up to put on the sweater.

"My only fear now is that the ninety-year-old woman who lost this sweater will be in Denny's and ask for it back."

"That would be awkward."

For the rest of the walk, I smile. Everything seems funny suddenly. The image of an old woman wanting this sweater back. The bus driver thinking I was waiting for a ride. I lied a little bit when I told Jamie no one would notice or care if I left the hospital. If I asked, I'm sure they would have said no. Now I'm just happy I never asked.

"So the good thing about Denny's is that you can order breakfast all day long," I say when we get there and sit down. It's probably been ten years since I've been to a Denny's, but nothing seems to have changed, including the menu. "I don't know about you, but I'm thinking about biscuits and gravy."

"Why? Has it been too long since you've eaten something that looks like throw-up?"

"I'm just curious, that's all. But now that you say that, I'm reconsidering."

"And well you might be."

I laugh. One of my favorite things about hanging out with Jamie are these funny little sayings she has. "Where does a fifteen-year-old get a phrase like 'Well you might be'?"

She smiles and lifts her menu so I can't see her face. "Just decide," she says. "We only have an hour left to eat this crap and get back."

JAMIE

It came from my dad, of course. Even as I remember the hard times with my dad, I also keep thinking about the funny things he used to say. Some of them still make me laugh out loud, which makes no sense. After everything that's happened, how can he still be funny in my mind? But he is.

Once, at the National Gallery of Art in Washington, we walked into a room we thought was empty and then we noticed a guard in the corner, fast asleep in a chair. I was always nervous around museum guards because I was a child and inevitably one followed us from room to room.

My dad went over and stood near him, squinting as if he were examining a piece of art. Finally, he turned around and said, "It just doesn't feel alive to me, you know?"

My dad also said things like "And well you might be," when I was young and told him I was bored at the museums he dragged me to. It's unnerving how often I channel my dad's joking style when I'm talking to David. Whenever he mentions it, some part of me forgets for a second and wants to say, "If you think I'm funny, you should meet my dad." Then I go quiet.

Recently a new worry has cropped up in my mind: *David likes the Dad-like qualities in me most of all.* Even as I find comfort in being like my mom—working hard, thinking about others, learning practical skills—my dad is in me, too, popping out daily to make this boy laugh. It feels like a high-wire act, too risky to get away with for long. I can't imitate parts of my charming, suicidal father and be sure that only the charming part comes out.

I change the subject after we've ordered, a turkey club for me and something called a breakfast skillet for him. "Apparently it comes in the skillet, which sounds like it might be a little dangerous, but it's the kind of risk I need to start taking, don't you think?"

He can't stop smiling, which makes me smile. Extended sensory deprivation has left him giddy at the sight and smell of what most people would call pretty greasy food.

"What does Sharon think about you being in the hospital for another two weeks?"

This is a new development, designed around an aggressive plan to treat the pseudomonas bacteria he's tested positive for. To stay on the organ transplant list, he needs to get this bacteria under control, which means two IVs a day of powerful new antibiotics. The bacteria will never leave his system completely, but it is possible to manage it. He's even found some people who blog about living with pseudomonas. Some people are doing okay five or eight years after contracting it. The big thing they can't do is come into contact with other CF patients. What your body learns to live with could easily kill another person quickly.

Of course I don't tell him I know all this. But knowing it makes it easier to feel okay about being here. The two-week extension is mandated not by his numbers but by the companies who manufacture the antibiotic he's on.

Now that I've asked, I don't know why I've mentioned Sharon at all. If my dad is a risky topic in one way, Sharon is equally risky in others. It might turn this whole meal into one of David's monologues about how "generous" Sharon is, putting up with his illness. I hardly need David to remind me that "a lot of girls would just run away."

"Sharon is . . ." He waggles his fork by pushing down on the tines. "Sharon. I don't know. Yes, she's sad that I'm still sick, and I guess maybe I don't want to talk about Sharon."

"Okay."

"I also don't want to talk about my health. I'm sick of talking about my stupid body."

"Gosh, what's left?" I say. "Origami, I guess."

He laughs, and I think: *Would Dad have made that joke?* It's hard for me to know what he would have thought of origami, because he wasn't around when I discovered it.

DAVID

Being out with Jamie is different from being out with Sharon. Usually, when Sharon and I are out by ourselves, we spend most of the time talking about our friends, which has always seemed fine because they offer an almost unlimited buffet of problems-that-aren't-our-own to go over. Like Hannah, who is so anxious about college admissions that apparently she no longer sleeps.

"She keeps saying Adderall isn't as bad for you as everyone says," Sharon told me last week.

"Except for the addiction part," I pointed out.

"Right. Except for that."

It's always felt fine to focus on our friends because we have about the same number of equally screwed-up ones. Recently I've started to wonder if we dwell on other people's problems to avoid looking at the possibility that we might have some problems of our own. Lately, she's been visiting less and calling in the evening instead. She doesn't want to bring in any germs, she says, or run the risk of making me sicker than I am. To me, it's pretty obvious that the hospital scares her so much she makes excuses not to come, but neither one of us wants to have that conversation.

"How come you don't talk about your friends from school?" I ask Jamie. "Isn't that—I don't know—a big topic for tenth-grade girls?"

She smiles, but I can see a wince behind the smile. "For some tenth-grade girls, it's a bad topic. It turns out we're not all alike. I know that might come as a shock."

"I guess not, considering you seem about five years older than you are."

"Yeah right," she snorts. "That's the reason I never get invited to anyone's house anymore. My maturity."

"Did you used to get invited?"

"I used to have a few girls I thought of as friends. But it turned out I was wrong."

"What kind of girls were they? Not that I'm an expert, mind you."

"The kind of girls who are competitive about everything, but then they never really win at anything, so they take out their frustration by being mean."

"On *you*?"

"Yes. Don't sound so shocked, David. That's why we're not friends anymore. Because they were nice to me for a while and then they decided to be mean to me instead."

I laugh, which I probably shouldn't. "I'm sorry, I just have a hard time picturing that. Why would anyone be mean to *you* when you're like the nicest person in the world?"

"I guess Missy didn't get the memo about me winning that award. She thinks I'm cruel in ways that I need to atone for."

"Come on. *You?* Really?"

"I don't remember exactly what I said but supposedly the b-word was involved."

Now I laugh so hard, I have to readjust my cannula. I can't help it. I'm so happy to be outside the hospital, everything seems funny. "I can't picture that at all, but I love it."

"It's nice that you find it funny, but it's kind of ruining my life. I have to plan my whole day at school so I can walk down hallways and not run into her."

"What would happen if you ran into her?"

JAMIE

We've been here for forty-five minutes, and this whole time, he's been smiling. I've already told him this story isn't funny, and his expression keeps saying, *Yes, it is.*

And it occurs to me: maybe this *is* funny. If Dad were alive, he'd have made jokes about Missy the day after it happened. By now he'd have turned it into an elaborate story that had very little to do with what actually happened. I tell David the first part. How Missy got the idea that she wanted us to be friends with cooler guys, not the ones in our classes but the soccer players who none of us knew.

"She invited them to her house and told them she was having a big party, like fifty people. When they showed up, it was just four of us and four of them. You could tell they thought it was weird, but she acted like nothing was wrong and teamed us up into boy-girl pairs and forced us to play get-to-know-you games where you ask each other embarrassing questions and tell the group afterward whether you thought your partner lied or not. Does that sound like a strange game to you?"

"Very."

"To me it was. The guy I was paired with got mad and

left after about a half hour. Then the other guys all said they had to go, too. Afterward, I told Missy we shouldn't trick people into being friends with us, and she said it was my fault. That my guy would have stayed longer if I'd been friendlier to him."

"She sounds awful, Jamie."

"Sometimes she's not. I don't know. She said the popular kids played games like that all the time."

"No. Popular people would never do something overtly mean like that. They'd be much more subtle. Of course, they'd still be mean."

"Really?"

"Unfortunately, yes."

I give him the edited version of what happened the next weekend—how Missy invited us all for a sleepover to talk about planning a "real party" with the fifty people she was pretending to be friends with last time. After listening to her talk for what felt like forever, I blew up and started screaming uncontrollably. I tore up the list she was making. I said she was full of bullshit. That none of these people were our friends. That she had no idea what it meant to really be a friend. "For this split second I thought they would all agree with me. Like it would be a relief that someone had finally said the truth out loud. But it turned out—no."

"Marcus Aurelius would say the best revenge is to be unlike him who performed the injury. Or obviously *her* in this case."

"Since Missy only cares about being popular, and I

have no friends, I guess I've accomplished that."

"You can't say that anymore. You have friends."

"Who?"

"Me and Eileen."

He says that as if it's simple, but it's not. I'm not really friends with Eileen, even though I like her. And once David comes back to school, we probably won't be friends there, either.

On the walk back to the hospital, he seems to have *more* energy, not less. Maybe he was right when he said his health would get better outside the hospital. He's definitely walking faster now. Almost like he's forgotten where we're going.

"Here's the thing about girls like Missy," he says. "You got under her skin by speaking the truth."

We're almost back at the hospital. I stop walking so he can catch his breath.

"It was stupid of me. I created a lot of problems, and I shouldn't have. That's all."

"Still, it's good to speak the truth. We should all do it more."

We're standing about ten feet from the side door of the hospital.

"Look," I say. "We're back!"

His whole expression changes. The smile fades. "Oh my God, you're right."

"Are you okay?"

"Yeah. It's weird—I just . . . forgot for a second."

My heart breaks a little. "I think it's okay if you want to do this again. I mean—you're right. You're stronger than they think. You should be able to get outside once in a while."

He looks up at me, with an expression that I haven't seen on him in ages—happy and hopeful. "You'd do this again?"

I don't promise anything. I can't; it's too risky.

The whole elevator ride up, we don't speak. When we're back in his room, he surprises me. "My friends can be the same way. So phony that being around them sometimes feels lonelier than being by myself."

I'm shocked to hear him say this. I know his friends don't come around as much as they used to, but I assume they all keep up with him online. He's never complained about them before, but now that I think about it, he doesn't say much of anything about them.

The next day at school, I sit a few tables away from David's friends. From a distance they look like they're having a great time—laughing at each other's jokes, leaning in to hear what someone else is saying. They're not all beautiful like the table full of football players and cheerleaders, but they exude a certain confidence, like they know they're going to take over the world someday.

I can't help watching Sharon. She wears more makeup than most, which might be her Texas roots showing, because most girls—even popular, pretty ones—don't bother. They just walk around school, gorgeous in outfits they look like they slept in—yoga pants, tiny flannel shirts, shearling-lined slipper boots. Sharon tries to look casual, but can't help color-coordinating her outfits and using a curling iron on the hair that she sweeps back into a pony-tail.

I'm close enough to hear some of their conversation. No one talks about David. Maybe they're all used to his being in the hospital, but still, it seems strange. Even after Ashwin, David's vice president, gets up and does a horrible job with lunch announcements—reading from his phone, squinting at dates and mispronouncing names—no one says, "Where's 'Shine on, man'?" or "When's David coming back?"

In life science, we're learning that one criterion for life is the capacity to return to homeostasis, meaning that all living things work to heal injuries and eradicate illness. I wonder if this makes a student body a living organism, already working to eradicate illness? I also notice this: Eileen walks by Sharon and doesn't say anything. Sharon even looks up and sees her. I would have thought they'd say hi to each other, but apparently I'm wrong.

Even though we've been to three dance classes, Eileen and I don't talk at school beyond saying hi. I don't want her to worry about some awkward moment at lunch where I try to sit near her table and hope for an invitation. Which is why I'm surprised when I get a text from her. I'm sitting all the way across the cafeteria, and somehow she knows that I've been watching David's friends.

Eileen: Those people are all ridiculous.

I laugh and look around. When I see her, she doesn't look up.

Me: Why?

Eileen: They're just fake. All of them. They pretend to be big do-gooders, but they're not really.

Me: What about Sharon? She's okay, right?

I've been dying to ask her this question but haven't because I don't want Eileen to know how much I think about David. Part of me wants Eileen to say, *Sharon's the worst of them all*, and part of me doesn't want to hear that, because David is so obviously loyal to her. I don't want to hear that she doesn't deserve it. It'll make me sad and furious at the same time.

At breakfast this morning my mom asked me, straight out, if I had a crush on David. Apparently, she's not worried about David being too sick anymore, she's worried about him being too appealing.

"No. God, Mom, why would you even say that?"

"Because I have to ask, and I also have to say that's not a good idea."

"Well, I don't, okay? He's a senior, and he's got a girlfriend."

"I'm just saying it would be natural on your part. He's a very nice guy and good-looking, too. A girlfriend rules out dating him, but it doesn't rule out you having a crush on him."

Her words have been playing in the back of my mind

all day. My mother is right. I can't let myself have a crush on him. It's too dangerous. I have no group to fall back on, no safety net to catch me when he gets well enough to come back to school, sit with his old friends, and barely acknowledge me.

> Eileen: She used to be. Now, not so much.
>
> Me: Why not?
>
> Eileen: She's changed. David doesn't see it, but I do. He thinks they're this important couple that everyone looks up to. I keep telling him, Hello? No one cares about you two.

I'm dying to ask more, but when lunch period is over, she disappears up the hall in a crowd of her friends. It's strange—even though Eileen doesn't talk to me at school, I get the feeling she kind of likes me. In dance class last week, while we were waiting for the lesson to start, she asked (out of nowhere) how far I'd ever gone with a guy. I gave her a one-eyebrow-raised look like maybe she'd forgotten who she was talking to.

"I've never gone anywhere with a guy. Remember—I was homeschooled and then I spent most of middle school being stupid and shy."

"Oh, that's right." She smiled. "But what does that mean? Like—nothing? Ever?"

It's fun to shock Eileen this way.

"Nothing. Ever. No dates. No spin the bottle." I'm a novelty to her—like someone from *Little House on the Prairie*.

"So what do you do when you go to parties?"

"I've never been to one." I shrugged. Too late, I

remembered Missy's party and realized this wasn't technically true.

"Are you serious? *Never?*"

"Maybe one, but it had eight people total. I don't think it counts."

When I asked Eileen how many boyfriends she'd had, she had to use her fingers to count. "Four since sixth grade. I don't count the ones before. That was all kid stuff."

"*Four?* Really?" I didn't add: *And we're only in tenth grade.*

She rolled her eyes. "Some of them were stupid. My friends dared me, so I did."

"How many did you really like?"

"I don't know. One. Sometimes I think the chase is more fun than dating." As she said this, her eyes drifted over to Nicolai, who looked up just as she was looking over. I watched both of them carefully. Neither one smiled or waved the way they did earlier. They just exchanged a knowing look that scared me.

Instead of saying anything about Nicolai, Eileen said, "It's weird you've never gone out with anyone, because you're pretty hot."

I laughed. "No, I'm not."

"Do you seriously not know that?"

"I'm *not.*"

"So why do all these boys line up to ask you to dance?"

The answer was easy: They didn't. Or they were being nice. Or they wanted to ask Eileen, and she'd already been asked. It had nothing to do with me being hot, which I'm obviously not.

Four days later, on Monday, after our lunch texts, Eileen surprises me by waiting for me after life science. At first I worry that she knows I left the hospital with David and she's going to tell me not to do it again. But no.

"I've got a surprise for you," she says. "But you have to meet me at my locker after school."

"What kind of surprise?"

She smiles. "You'll see."

If this were Missy, the surprise would be something mean, like a complimentary makeover or a coupon for Weight Watchers. She'd give it to me with a hug and say, "I was talking with the others, and we decided you should get this."

"Okay," I say.

Eileen's locker is on the art corridor, a hallway I haven't walked down this whole year, right next to Mr. Standish's room. Mr. Standish teaches painting and 3D sculpture. I know this from the tour I took at the end of eighth grade, not because I've ever taken these classes. On the tour, I memorized where these rooms were—four altogether, three more than we had in middle school, where we also had strict limits on supplies, including all paints except watercolor. Here, the closets bulged with expensive paints and supplies. I eyed the tubes of oils and raised my hand.

"What's the limit on supplies?" I asked, and Mr. Standish looked surprised.

"None," he said. "This is a painting class. We give you all the supplies you need."

Since I've gotten to high school, I've been scared to

come down here. I still don't know if I can be around the smell of art supplies.

"It's good to avoid triggers," Rita once said. "But don't be afraid to go back to things you loved. Even if they remind you of your dad."

I have been afraid. Terrified, really.

When Eileen walks up, she seems a little nervous. "You don't have to do anything with this," she says, spinning the dial on her locker. "But you keep saying you have to borrow your mom's clothes for class, so I thought, here, maybe you'd want to borrow mine."

She pulls a white plastic bag out of her locker and hands it to me. I peek inside. It's the dress she wore on the first day—formfitting, low-cut, and sexy. I blush a little at the idea of wearing it myself.

"I know it would look great on you, so I just thought why not?"

"Won't everyone remember that it's your dress?"

She narrows her eyes like she can't tell if I'm kidding. "I don't think they have any rule against borrowing your friend's clothes."

Missy never let anyone borrow her clothes. "Then they get stretched in all the wrong places," she once said. Realizing how mean this might sound, she added, "Because some people's boobs are so big, Bethany."

"Is this really okay?" I say. "What if I stretch it?"

She laughs like I'm joking. "It's spandex. You're supposed to stretch it, then it goes back."

"Okay." I smile. I can't get over it. Eileen doesn't care

about the things other girls care about. A minute later, she's gone and I'm alone in the hallway. All the doors are open. By school policy, teachers must stay for an hour after school to help any student who needs it. The old me would have seen this as an extra hour every day with the bounty of art supplies no one was counting. I would have been in one corner every day after school, which is why I'm surprised when I lean in and no one is there. "Can I help you?" Mr. Standish says from his desk.

I recognize him from the tour, but he doesn't recognize me. "I'm not in your class."

"That's okay."

"Are people who aren't in your class allowed to come after school?" I have no idea why I'm asking this. I certainly don't intend to do it.

"Well, it's better if you're enrolled in a class. Current students have priority. But as you can see, I'm not swamped at this point. Usually I get old students asking if they can come back and finish up projects. I always say yes to them, so maybe, yeah, it's something I'd consider."

"I'm asking for someone else," I say quickly.

"Okay. Well, tell your friend to come talk to me."

On Wednesday I have to stand on the side of the bathtub to see what I look like in Eileen's dress because this apartment didn't come with a full-length mirror and it's never occurred to us to buy one. It's hard for me to judge. I look like a completely different person wearing this.

When I walk in the kitchen, Mom smiles at first and

then frowns. "Wait—really? Is that what you're wearing?"

At first, she was happy to have me taking dance classes with a friend. Now, I can tell she's not so sure. "Eileen wore it the first day. She's lending it to me. Do you think it's too much?"

"You look great, but are you supposed to go to class looking like a sexy twenty-year-old?"

She's trying to do her mom thing—*I'm not judging, I'm just saying.*

"No, but some people do." Eileen does.

"Is there a boy there and you want him to notice you?"

"No."

"Because he will, I promise you."

"It was nice of Eileen to think of it. I want her to know I appreciate it."

"Okay. Hopefully she won't regret it when all the guys ask you to dance."

I roll my eyes. "That's hardly going to happen, Mom."

Except it does in a way.

I feel a change the second we walk in the room together. Stenyak and Antonin stop talking to each other and stare as we walk past. It's disorienting. I feel like I'm wearing someone else's body. The attention isn't all directed at me. I assume most of it is for Eileen, who's wearing an even more attention-grabbing outfit—a bright red dress, with holes cut out in the shoulders and a scoop neck in the back—and heels I couldn't walk in, much less dance.

Before we sit down, Eileen snaps a selfie of us. "I'm sending this to David so he knows how hot you look."

I look at her. This whole time, we've hardly mentioned his name. Does she know about our lunch? Does she suspect something? Then I have the craziest thought: *Is she trying to set us up?*

"There," she says, sending it. "Now he knows."

After we sit down inside, she leans closer. "Did I tell you that Nicolai finally texted me back this week? He said he's bringing a surprise for me tonight."

"What kind of surprise?" I say nervously. I can't forget the awful things David told me about Nicolai.

"I don't know." Eileen smiles. "But I can't wait to see."

"I overheard some girls talking about him last week. They said he was a jerk." I sound nervous because I am. I don't want her to know that I'm supposed to be curbing her riskier impulses.

Instead of being mad, she grins. "You think I don't know that?"

The second Nicolai walks in the room, my worries double. He sits across the room and stares at Eileen the whole time, laughing and signaling in their secret language. Suddenly, these dresses feel like a huge mistake. Like Eileen wouldn't have worn hers if I hadn't worn this one. She knows what she's doing, and she also knows she shouldn't do it alone. It's like I'm the life preserver on the side of a dangerous pool she's about to jump into.

The first half of the night is a blur of attention. It's a heady and completely new feeling. Two younger boys come over to ask us to dance before the music even starts.

One wears braces with rubber bands that make him hard to understand.

He says, "Those guys over there are daring each other to ask you. I told them no one needs to dare me. I'm just *doing* it."

"Thank you," I say, taking his elbow. "My name is Jamie."

"I know," he says, as we walk out onto the dance floor.

It's hard to enjoy the attention I'm getting when I can't stop worrying about Eileen and Nicolai. I keep wondering if I should just come right out and tell her he was cruel to David.

At break, Eileen goes with me to the bathroom and shows me a text she's just gotten from David.

> David: You guys look great! Tell Jamie hi and have fun!

My chest squeezes seeing my name typed out by his thumbs. I haven't seen much of him since our lunch date. Today, I'd stopped by quickly to give him a movie he'd asked for a while ago.

"Stay, stay," he'd said, patting the chair next to his bed.

"I can't," I had to say. "I've got dance class tonight."

"Dancing, dancing, dancing. It's all you really care about."

I didn't want to tell him about the dress Eileen lent me. I didn't want him to think she was having a bigger influence on me than I was having on her. Now, he's seen the picture, and apparently he doesn't care.

When I come out of the bathroom, Eileen isn't there anymore.

I walk out in the hall. "Eileen?"

She's not in the main room, either. I check all the other places we're allowed to go on break: the lobby, the coatroom, the front vestibule outside, where some kids secretly check their phones. She's nowhere.

I pull my phone out and text her: *Where'd you go?*

In the main room I hear the music signaling that class is about to start. I text again: *Class is starting. You need to come back.*

I go back inside and realize my worst fear is true: Nicolai isn't here, either. I check my phone before class starts up. Nothing.

For the next half hour, I dance with whoever asks me to dance. I don't know what else to do. If Eileen is in Nicolai's car in the parking lot, or worse, if they left together, there's nothing I can do now. Even as I think this, though, I remember what David said. *Eileen doesn't have great judgment. She doesn't even realize the dangerous situations she puts herself in.*

We start learning the Viennese waltz the way they always introduce a new dance: with leaders on one side, followers on the other, and a demonstration couple in the middle. Each group watches the impossible-looking steps we'll be doing in a minute. Instead of watching the steps, though, I watch the door.

The longer they're gone, the more scared I get. What if they don't come back at *all*? What if Eileen is in real danger now and I haven't said anything because I'm scared to make waves or get her in trouble? I keep expecting the teachers to notice their absence and say something, but they don't.

Finally, I can't stand it anymore. I slip out of my seat and walk over to Tonya, our teacher, who is standing with one of the owners of the studio. "I'm worried about my friend, Eileen Sheinman."

"Why? Where is she?" Tonya asks.

"She never came back from break. I think she might have gone somewhere with Nicolai. He's not here, either."

The older woman takes a moment to consider this. "They're not allowed to leave during class."

"Right, but I think they have."

"They'll be in trouble then."

"Who's in trouble?" a voice says behind us. I spin around. It's Eileen, standing near the door to the coatroom with her phone in her hand.

"Here she is!" I say lamely. "Never mind! She's fine! Everything's fine."

"No it isn't, unfortunately. I'm going to have to speak to your parents about this, Ms. Eileen."

"Because I'm late coming back to class?"

"Forty-five minutes late."

"I got a text I had to deal with. I went into the coatroom to answer it. It was kind of an emergency."

I feel terrible. It's possible she went outside with Nicolai for a while, but it's also possible she's telling the truth and didn't go anywhere.

"There's a reason we ask you not to bring phones to

dance class. For two hours, we say you can live without emergency updates."

Does she not remember who Eileen's brother is? Doesn't she not realize this isn't true?

I say, "This was my fault. I shouldn't have said anything. I got worried, and it was stupid. Please don't blame Eileen. If she had an emergency to deal with, she shouldn't get punished."

It's too late. She tells us to go back to class. "I'm *sorry*," I whisper frantically to Eileen.

"Whatever." She shrugs.

For the rest of class, Eileen doesn't speak to me. She stays silent the whole ride home. It's the first time my mother has driven us, so it's the first time I've seen Eileen and David's house, which is enormous. Even at night I can see that it's beautifully landscaped, by the carefully angled floodlights crisscrossing the garden. Judging by the rotation of fresh flowers and the steady supply of expensive organic food David has in his hospital room, I've suspected they had plenty of money, but this house is more lavish than I ever imagined.

I imagine what my father would say. *They're not just rich, they're ostentatious, too.* Once upon a time, he went to cocktail parties in houses like these and sat on sofas underneath his own paintings. By the time I was old enough to realize what that meant, those days were over. I only heard about them occasionally when we sat outside houses like this one, eating sandwiches he'd packed while he told me sad stories about the people who lived inside.

For almost a month, Eileen's parents have given me rides both ways. They've been generous and kind, and no one has ever made me feel uncomfortable or said anything about our horrible apartment. Now I feel terrible. Eileen has been a good friend—the only new friend I've made this year if you don't count David, and I know I shouldn't—and I've wrecked it all by assuming the worst.

Before she gets out of the car, I turn around and say, "I'm sorry about tonight, Eileen. I got scared, and I shouldn't have."

"That's right" is all she says. "You shouldn't have."

I already know what will probably happen the next time I see Eileen. When I see her in class, she'll slide her eyes away from me and pretend she doesn't see me. At some point, I'll give her back her dress in a plastic bag, and she won't say anything. I'll want to say something stupid like, "You've been a better friend to me in the last month than I've ever had before," which won't make sense, because we're not really friends.

But I think about her noticing things about me I'd almost forgotten or else never knew. That I was artistic once. That boys notice me. That I'm different from other girls our age, but maybe it's okay.

I wish I could tell her all of this, but I won't, because even I know how awkward it will be when she doesn't say anything back.

CHAPTER TEN

DAVID

ME: Is it okay if I propose another outing? Bear in mind that after the last one, my PFTs went up to the best level I've had in over a month. Outings are good for me; the doctor can't exactly order them, but I know he would approve.

JAMIE: What's your proposal? I'm not saying yes. I'm just asking.

ME: I want to see a movie. In a theater. With popcorn and soda. I want to sit in gross seats where our feet stick to the floor. I want the whole experience.

JAMIE: No, David. Seeing a whole movie means being out of the hospital for at least two hours. There's no way.

ME: See, I knew you might say that, so as an experiment, I left my room for three hours today, and guess what? No one said a thing.

JAMIE: Are you serious?

ME: They think it's a good sign that I'm downstairs doing my homework. Nurse Nancy just told me she likes stopping by my room and finding me gone.

JAMIE: What if we go and something bad happens?

ME: Then you'll call for an Uber on my phone, and we'll come back to the hospital. Nothing will happen, I promise, and even if it does, it won't be a big deal.

For a long time, she doesn't answer. Then she sends this:

JAMIE: What movie would you even want to see?

ME: It doesn't matter. You can pick.

JAMIE: Okay.

ME: Thank you, dearest Jamie. You've made me the happiest patient on the fourth floor. And that's saying a lot, because someone just dropped off a case of Friendly's ice cream cups.

There's something I haven't told Jamie yet. I can't. It's too sad. Last night, I found out how her dad died. I knew he died last year, but she'd never told me how. I shouldn't have (of course), but I couldn't stop thinking about the mystery of it, so I started asking other nurses about her mom, because sometimes they don't mind talking about each other. I thought it was a smart strategy, except it didn't work.

"You know we can't talk about that, David," they all said.

Once, I asked Vanessa, one of my favorite nurses, "Is everything okay with Ronnie?"

"My God, can you tell? She seems like she's doing so well to the rest of us."

"I can tell," I said. "But what happened exactly?"

I thought that was clever, but apparently not.

"Nothing," she said, too quickly. "Come on, let's get your blood pressure now."

I'd almost given up, and then last night, a nurse I didn't know came with my evening meds. She had silver hair, and the first thing she said was that she'd come out of retirement to take this shift and it was just about killing her. She put the tray of meds down and sat in the chair next to my bed. "Sorry about this, but my feet are screaming."

I smiled and said it was fine. "A lot of nurses come in here and rest for a minute. I think this room is popular because I'm not a toddler and I don't cry unless something really hurts."

She smiled gratefully. "You're a sweetheart. I shouldn't let them talk me into taking these shifts. I'm too old is the truth."

We talked a little more, and then I asked her casually, "You don't know a nurse named Ronnie, do you? She used to work on this floor, and I was wondering how she's doing."

Her eyebrows went up in surprise. "Well, when your husband kills himself and your daughter finds him, you're pretty much just picking up the pieces, aren't you? I'd say that's left her a little distracted. I remember her from back when we both worked this floor. She's a sweetheart. Didn't deserve any of that."

"Her *daughter* found him?"

"Right. Then her daughter tried to do the same thing a few months later. They say Ronnie has to watch her all the time. That she doesn't want to leave her alone, even though the girl is a teenager. I think she's got her volunteering in the hospital somewhere. I don't know where—maybe the gift shop, I'd imagine."

Now I wish I could go back in time. I shouldn't have heard this story from someone else. I hate myself for asking. It breaks my heart to think of Jamie, who has been coaching me on staying positive and embracing life, and six months ago she tried to end her own?

I shouldn't know this story unless Jamie wants to tell it to me.

I want her to know that she *does* have real friends and she shouldn't go back to those awful ones she told me about. I also want her to know that what she's lived through has made her different but also stronger than most of the kids at our school.

I know what I'm talking about, I'll tell her. *Living on the edge between life and death isn't something most people our age can understand. They think if they get too close, they might catch what we've got or fall in or something. They don't see what matters. They don't see the strength that's needed sometimes to simply survive. I do.*

JAMIE

I was right. Eileen hasn't talked to me since class. Even when I stopped by her desk to say I had her dress in my backpack, she wouldn't look up. David says she'll get over it.

"Of course she left with Nicolai. That's Eileen. She doesn't understand why she does these things; she doesn't want to have to explain herself."

He doesn't think what I did was so bad, even though Eileen has been told not to come to class next week or the social dance the week after that. It makes me furious. "Why didn't Nicolai get in trouble?" I ask David.

"Because he sucks up to teachers and probably said it was her fault. He doesn't care about anyone but himself. It's okay, though. I talked to Eileen. She wants to go back to class after this little suspension, and she promises she'll be more serious about it."

"Really?" I laugh a little, I'm so relieved.

"Yeah. She liked going with you. I knew she would."

Is it possible that friendships can have misunderstandings and still right themselves? I wouldn't know. I've never experienced that.

In the meantime, I'd agreed to help David get to a movie theater. Which means bringing him clothes and calling an Uber. We end up choosing a romantic comedy, and he pays for everything—including the popcorn and soda that he doesn't eat at all. ("I was so excited I forgot my enzymes," he says. "You go ahead.") I know his pancreas doesn't work and he gets terrible stomach cramps if he eats without taking enzymes beforehand, but I don't know if that's just an excuse. He's not as thin as he used to be but he still needs a belt to hold up my father's pants. It's been strange going through my father's boxes, picking out clothes for David to wear. So far, I've brought him two different outfits, which means twice, I've gone on dates with a seventeen-year-old boy dressed in my dead father's clothes.

I know I shouldn't let myself think things like this, but they *feel* like dates to me. He pays for everything and says things like "Where would you like to sit?" when we walk in the theater, even though we don't have many choices. We have to pick an aisle seat for his oxygen tank, close to where we're standing because we've already walked a lot and I can see he's exhausted by it.

"How about right here?" I say, pointing to the seats beside us.

The movie is funnier than either one of us expected. We keep looking at each other and laughing like these are jokes only we understand. After it ends, we look at each other, smiling hard. "I think that was my favorite movie of all time," he says. "I'm serious."

"It wasn't *that* good, David. You might be a little light-headed. Or else you haven't seen very many comedies."

He laughs as hard as he did at some of the funny bits in the movie and touches my hand. "Maybe I need to see more."

There, I think. That's another reason this feels like a date. We haven't held hands, but he finds other excuses to touch my shoulder, or my elbow, or the back of my hand. Every time he does, that spot stays warm and tingles after his hand moves away. This time, to keep the date-like feeling going, I never mention Sharon. Or any topic that might circle back to her. Sometimes while I'm doing that, I worry that it's obvious: *I'm pretending you're my boyfriend because I like the looks we get from people who think we're a young couple on a date with our oxygen tank.*

"What's your favorite movie of all time?" he says.

There again. Isn't that a date question? Am I imagining this?

I must have waited too long because he adds, "I'm just wondering, with all these movies we've talked about, I've never heard what your favorite is."

"It's not Hitchcock, actually. In fact, you've probably never heard of it. It's from the late forties. It's called *The Best Years of Our Lives*. It's about three veterans returning from World War II and how hard it is for each of them to adjust to life back home. One of them had his hands blown off in the war and he's played by a guy who actually lost his hands in the war. He won an Oscar even though he wasn't a professional actor and that's the only role he ever played."

I keep talking because I know it's easier for him not to talk while he's walking. This way, he can concentrate on breathing.

"The no-hands guy isn't what makes it such an incredible movie, though. It's the best depiction I've ever seen in a movie of real people struggling with post-traumatic stress, and it was made seventy years ago. It gets everything right. How the family suffers, and how the person suffers watching the effect he's having on the family. For a long time, it was the highest-grossing movie behind *Gone with the Wind* and *The Wizard of Oz*, but you watch it now and think, 'I'm not even sure it would get made today.' It's like audiences were more intelligent back then, or else moviemakers had more respect for the audience's intelligence. I'm not sure which one it was, but watch it and you'll see what I mean."

It's been a long walk through a mall to get to the parking lot where our Uber is waiting. Twice, David has had to stop and sit down, which is two more times than he had to on our walk to Denny's.

"I want to see it," he says when we finally make it outside. He sits down on the side of a planter and smiles at me in a way that makes me wish I'd said a different movie. Something lighter and funnier, with Cary Grant. *The Philadelphia Story*, maybe. Or *Bringing Up Baby*. Why did I bring up a movie about families falling apart after trauma?

"You don't have to," I say. "It's pretty obscure. Whenever I mention it, no one's ever heard of it."

Suddenly, I feel nervous. I remember a scene where the man with no hands, only hooks, counts out pills because ending his life seems easier than starting it over.

"What's your favorite movie of all time?"

He thinks for a while, but doesn't say anything.

"Please don't say one of the Dark Knight Batman movies. I know they're supposed to be so great, but I never understood them."

"It's not. You're going to be surprised when I tell you. It's not a superhero movie, and it's mostly black-and-white, which probably shocks you, I know. It's called *Wings of Desire*, and it's German. You might not believe I've ever watched a foreign film all the way through, but I have. That one I love. You probably don't know it."

"Of course I know it! My dad was obsessed with it! He showed it to me about five times between the time I was nine and twelve years old. He was desperate for me to love it as much as he did."

"Did you?"

"No! I hated it! It was weird and slow and I never understood it."

"Okay. I can't believe I'm explaining a movie to you, but here's how I interpreted it. The angels spend the whole movie walking around Berlin, writing down their observations. I loved the idea that after people die, there might be an existence like they have—where you can still watch everything that happens, you just can't participate. The angels are there to comfort the living, but only the saddest people, or the ones closest to death, can feel them. And then it's super mysterious—just a touch on the shoulder of a man or a presence in a lonely house. For me, the point is: a movie about depressed people doesn't have to be depressing. It can be beautiful and say sad people have access to a world of angels the rest of us can't see."

I love that he's picked this movie, and it scares me a little, too. I think about my mother's warnings and Sharon and all the other reasons I shouldn't let myself feel this way, and then I think: *He loves a movie about people with depression?* My breath catches.

"Doesn't the main angel fall in love with the weird circus girl and decide to become a human again?"

"Exactly! He's spent a thousand years bearing witness to all the sadness humanity has to offer, and he still wants to join it! It's so profound!"

I laugh in surprise. "You sound like my dad."

"Do I?"

He looks beautiful right now—his cheeks ruddy from the effort of this walk, his hair longer and curlier than I've ever seen it. His face isn't puffy anymore, which means his eyes, behind his little round glasses, look huge and very hazel. I'm so used to seeing him in a hospital gown that it's almost overwhelming, seeing him like this. I can't look at him for too long.

"My dad loved it, too. He got mad at me because I didn't."

"I think you need to watch it again. It's also possible you need to have a high fever when you do, which is how I first saw it. That definitely helped."

We're back at the hospital now. I get out of the car first and come around to his side to help him with the tank. He's still a little unsteady. Every time he sits down, it takes him a while to stand up again. This time he looks sad. He asks if we can sit on a bench outside for a minute.

"Okay, but just for a minute. They need to hook up your evening IV pretty soon."

He nods. He seemed more nervous on this outing than

he did on the last one, but it's hard to tell what he's thinking except maybe the obvious: *I have a girlfriend, and I shouldn't keep pretending that I don't.* If we talked about it—which we don't—I might have tried to make a joke. "We can keep pretending you don't have a girlfriend! I don't mind!"

The truth is I *don't* mind. How could I possibly handle a real relationship when this crush is killing me? I can't say that of course, but it's true. Any time our bodies touch accidentally, I feel dizzy, like I might explode. What would happen if he actually kissed me? It would be too much. I'd break out laughing, or bite his lip. I'd do something horrible because I have no idea what I'm doing, which means I don't mind going on pretend dates where we don't talk about his girlfriend, and don't kiss at the end, or even look at each other. Anything more would be too much. But this isn't too much. This is great.

It seems like he wants to say something more, but I can't tell what it is. I don't want to sit here too long, near a door that staff members use. If anyone sees us outside, we'd both be in big trouble.

"We should go in," I say.

He swallows and doesn't move. It's like he hasn't heard me.

"I just—when you're as sick as I am, Jamie, it's hard to make sense of some things, and then it's easy to see a lot of other things. Like I keep thinking how amazing you are. It's so obvious to me now, and if I wasn't so sick, I never would have realized that. You would have been another tenth grader I smiled at, maybe, but never knew."

"That's okay, David." I look at the door. We really need to get inside. I can't tell why he's saying this now. "That's called being in high school."

The door opens. I stand in front of him so whoever walks out won't see David. I lean over and whisper, "Can you stand up? Are you okay?"

Once we get inside the building, I'll feel better. We can say we were taking a hospital walk. It won't seem so alarming if we're inside. I peek over my shoulder at a man in green scrubs who walks past us. He doesn't seem to recognize us, which is a relief, except that David still won't stand up.

"I know that's part of high school, but it's not okay. It's terrible. You've been a better friend to me since I've gotten to the hospital than any of my friends from school who I've known for ten years. I want you to know that."

"Okay. I do. Thank you. Now let's go."

"And I want to do one more outing. Just one. I promise. I won't ask again after that."

"I'll only listen to this idea after we're inside."

He looks up, surprised, as if he's just now noticing my panic. "Fine. Let's go."

We make our way to a set of chairs outside of radiology, where we aren't likely to see anyone we know. He can't walk and talk at the same time very well, so I wait until we're sitting. "Okay, tell me your idea."

He smiles. "I want to go with you to the social at Starlight."

"No. I don't even know if you're kidding, but no."

"You want to go, right? But now that Eileen can't, you probably assume that you shouldn't."

"What about Sharon?"

"Sharon's not interested in Starlight anymore. But I am. I miss it."

The social is next week and is open to the public. People are allowed to invite their family and friends. David's right: I assumed I wouldn't go—in part because of Eileen, in part because my mom is working and won't be able to drive me.

"It's nice of you, David, but I can't take you to a room full of people who know you're supposed to be in the hospital."

"That's just it. Nick and Eileen are the only people who know, and they won't be there. I haven't been there for more than a year. I won't know anyone very well." He holds up one hand in a Boy Scouts pledge. "I swear this is true, Jamie. Those parties get crowded. No one will notice I'm there or think anything of it. I guarantee it."

A nurse comes out and asks if we're waiting to get an X-ray, which makes me stand up. "No, we're leaving now," I say.

David gets up slowly.

"Are you thinking about it?" he asks in the elevator even though we're not alone.

I nod and stare at the numbers. Of course I'm thinking about it. Of course I want to go. If I thought going to the movies felt like a date, what will going to Starlight and dancing with him feel like? I look down at his hands and feel a little dizzy.

"Yes," I whisper. "I'm thinking about it."

I keep expecting something awful to happen, like running into my mom, who will smile at first and then recognize David's clothes and understand what I've done.

And then it doesn't happen.

It takes us about fifteen minutes to make it back to his room, and everyone we pass smiles and says hello. Even the peds nurses, who must assume he's coming back from a study session on the third floor, look happy to see him up. Maybe they assume I've been helping him catch up at school because one even says, "Good job, Jamie!"

After she passes, David looks at me and smiles. "See? Everyone thinks you're doing a good job. So do I."

All of this is confusing. Sharon is still his girlfriend. I'm scared to go to the dance with him and scared this might be my only chance. It's possible he'll get better next week and leave the hospital, go back to his old life of being Sharon's boyfriend and senior class president. He won't feel grateful to me the way he does now; or maybe he'll remember this feeling but by then it'll only be a source of guilt. Wasn't that what he was just trying to tell me? At school everything will be different. He knows our time is coming to an end. I know it, too.

"Okay," I say when he comes out of the bathroom wearing his hospital gown and shorts again, holding the plastic bag of clothes. "We can go to the party."

His eyebrows go up. "Are you serious?"

"Yes. But we'll only stay for an hour. We have to be back here by eight o'clock."

"That's fine."

I think about the rests he had to take walking from the movie theater to the parking lot. "If I think it looks like you're getting too tired or having trouble breathing, we turn around and come back. No questions asked."

"Okay."

His smile is so wide, I can't help smiling back. "Why are you so happy?"

"I'm going to dance with Ginger Rogers!"

"I'm hardly Ginger Rogers. I'm terrible."

"That's not what Eileen says."

"What did Eileen say?"

"That you're freakishly good."

"That's so not true."

"She also said you don't even know it. All the boys want to dance with you, and you don't realize that, either."

"It's not true, David. It really isn't."

"That's why I want to go and see for myself."

CHAPTER ELEVEN

DAVID

THE SUIT JAMIE BRINGS is amazing. Of course the pants are too big and I have to wear a belt, but the shirt is beautiful. It's the shirt of a man who knows materials and pays extra for nicer ones. Which makes him even more of a mystery. How did he get as sad as he did?

Pretend you know nothing, I keep telling myself. *Let her tell you when she's ready.*

I don't know if this is the right strategy. Some people might call it ignoring reality (which it is), but I prefer to think of it this way: I'm giving her her story back. I'm letting her tell me when she's ready.

The only problem with this is the stupidly hard time I have hiding my emotions these days. My oxygen-starved brain is ready to cry at a TV commercial. I feel everything too much. How can I look at her and not feel for what she's been through? I can't, really. But that isn't going to stop me. What I feel for her is completely different from what I feel for Sharon. With Sharon, everything is obligation and disappointed expectations. With Jamie, it's different.

I want this night. I want to be with Jamie and tell her what I've been thinking and feeling since we went to the movies. How much I admire her. How she's inspired me in ways that I never expected. I've spent a week composing the speech I started when I first asked her to help me leave the hospital. Tonight, I'm going to finish it.

But first things first: "You look beautiful," I say, because she does. She's wearing a simple, navy-blue dress that somehow manages to be both modest and sexy. "Where'd you find this?" I say, pinching the sleeve.

"Clearance rack at Marshalls. Do you want to guess how much it cost?" She's smiling infectiously. I know from comments she's made and where she lives that she and her mom don't have much money, but even so, she's smiling. "Guess high."

"Seventy dollars?"

"*Seven!*" She's beaming now. She spins around so the skirt flares out. "All this for the price of a sandwich!"

I don't know why it took me so long to see what's been obvious all along. Her strength. Her bravery. She told me once that I had to *choose* to live, and here she is, demonstrating how. With a clearance-rack dress and a big smile. I love that she has no idea how rare she is.

We're standing outside the side exit of the hospital. It's colder than I expected, which makes my teeth chatter for a second. That, or I'm nervous. She drapes the dark overcoat she's brought over my shoulders (also her dad's; also beautiful).

"Here. Hopefully this will help," she says, rubbing my arms to help me warm up.

I can't speak, I'm so grateful.

"Here's our car," she says. "Are you ready? Do you still want to go?"

I don't know why I can't move. I'm frozen for a moment, staring at her. I don't feel sick or short of breath. It's the opposite actually. For the first time in months, I feel like there's a chance I'm going to live. Like there has to be a future because I want more of this—more nights with Jamie, more chances to dance, more times when she surprises me with a dress. I want all of it so much it has to happen. I have to get better.

It's terrifying to realize this is more than admiration and friendship that I feel for Jamie. I wish I'd been able to talk to Sharon before tonight. On the phone with her last night, I thought about being honest and suggesting the break I'm almost sure we both want to take. And then I imagined being alone, and I got too scared.

"No, I'm fine." I smile. "Let's go."

I've brought my oxygen tank because I'm not so stupid as to think I can go more than an hour without it. I've already told Jamie I'm going to stash it in the bushes outside the back door of the dance studio.

"Are you sure about this?" Jamie asks. "Maybe we should just bring it inside."

"Absolutely not. I've been weaning myself off it. I'm

going to be fine. If I get light-headed, I'll come out here, I promise."

"I don't know."

"Jamie"—I take her hand—"I can't dance and roll my oxygen tank at the same time, okay. Trust me. I'll be fine."

The crowd is a little smaller than I remember from dance parties in the past, but that's probably good. I just want enough of a crowd that Jamie and I can get lost in it. I want her to forget about all her worries: my health, her dad, and everything else.

I smile and take a few of the shallow little breaths my lungs will allow. "Should we sit?" I whisper to Jamie, offering my elbow. I need to keep touching her. My fingertips are tingling from the lack of oxygen. If I'm not careful, I might stumble.

"Why don't we sit here," she whispers, steering us to the closest chairs available.

I need to catch my breath. I also need to get my racing heart to slow down. Jamie leans into my ear. "Are you sure you're okay?"

"Right as rain," I say, suddenly sounding like my grandmother. Another casualty when your brain isn't getting enough oxygen—any shred of coolness.

"Squeeze my elbow any time you want to go outside, okay?"

"I'm fine," I say.

Thankfully, there are some announcements to tune out and catch my breath during. By the time they're over, ten minutes have passed, and I have no idea what was said. The only thing I'm aware of is the warmth of Jamie's shoulder and her arm pressed against mine. It's calmed the constriction in my chest and the frantic spasm of muscles and organs gasping for oxygen.

Relaxing helps, and sitting beside Jamie relaxes me.

As does the word from the teacher that the first dance will be a waltz. I don't stand up right away. Instead, I lean over Jamie's shoulder. "Dance with me before I die," I say. In my mind, this sounded funny. Out loud, it doesn't.

"*David*," Jamie says.

"I'm sorry. I meant to say, 'May I have this dance, Ms. Turner?'"

"You may," she says, standing first so she can help me get my balance when I stand, too.

As the music starts, I have a strange thought. *I have to fit a lifetime into this dance.* My mind is veering in unpredictable directions. *I'm not going to die tonight*, I remind myself. Plus, we'll dance more than once. It's surprisingly comfortable to stand in front of her, our bodies aligned, one of my hands resting on the small of her back, the other raised to cradle her hand. Standing like this makes me feel strong, even though I'm not.

The music starts, and we move together, one turn, then another. We find a rhythm. She doesn't need to look down at her feet or count the beats with silent moving lips the way every other beginning student does.

Eileen is right; in a month Jamie's become a wonderful dancer. I go for a turn, and she follows beautifully. I turn her again. Soon we're moving in slow circles around the other couples, outlining triangles with our feet on the floor.

"You're quite the dancer, Ginger," I whisper.

"Thank you, Fred. You're very good yourself."

I press closer. "Maybe we should slow down. I'm a little dizzy."

"It's okay, I've got you," she says. I can feel her breath on my neck and her forehead on my collarbone. We're supporting each other.

Little black dots start dancing in my eyes, so I close them and breathe all of her in: her hair, her perfume, her seven-dollar dress.

Dancing can be as intimate as sex. More intimate if I think about all the towels and Kleenex Sharon always liked to have on hand.

"Is it a crime to want to clean up afterward?" she used to say.

It's not a crime, but this feels different and closer than sex on towels with Sharon ever felt.

I know from my reading that happiness is a physical thing. It comes from the automatic nervous system—the part of the brain that governs all basic nerve functions, that makes us blush when we're embarrassed and gives us goose bumps when we're afraid. Since we have no control over the automatic nervous system, we can't simply decide to be happy. Our bodies decide for us. Blood pulses faster, skin temperature rises, fingertips tremble.

With Jamie and me, it feels like our bodies are speaking quietly to each other. *This way*, my hand says. *You're okay,* her forehead on my cheek whispers. *No,* my closed eyes say back. *I'm not really.*

I can keep moving, though. I pull her even closer, so everything touches except our feet. Her father's beautiful shirt will be a ruin of wrinkles after this, but I don't care. I don't want to stop. I can't stop. I have to do this. I need to stay with this dance until the end.

When the music finally ends, I open my eyes and can't see anything. The room is black. "Are the lights off?" I whisper, squeezing Jamie's arm hard.

"Let's get you outside," she says, steering me.

I hear the door open. I feel the cool air. My lungs heave in anticipation of relief that doesn't come, even outside, with a world full of cool air.

I fall against the wall and shut my eyes again. It only takes Jamie a few seconds to hook the cannula around my ears and under my nose. It's a relief, but it's not enough. I need a mask and high-density oxygen to keep from crashing. With this tank, it will take me an hour, maybe more, to recover. I slide my back down the wall and sit in what must be dirt. I still can't see.

"It's turned up as high as I can get it to go," Jamie says. "Do you have a headache?"

As soon as she asks, I realize, yes, it's not just my lungs screaming in pain, my head is throbbing, too. It's too much pain all at once for my old tricks to work: pinching my leg, biting my cheek.

"Kiss me," I say. My voice is raspy, hardly recognizable. "Please."

She squeezes my hand. "I don't think this is the moment. I think right now, oxygen is more important."

"It's not. Something's happening. Kiss me now. I mean it."

I still can't see anything, but I feel her hands on my face. Two fingers on my lips. Her mouth on mine. Kissing her slows down my racing heart. It calms the frantic feeling that my body is about to shut down completely.

If I can stay calm, I won't die.

Kissing her calms me.

"You need to breathe," she says.

"No, I need to keep kissing you. No one will come out here, I promise." I don't know if that's true or if she's even worried about it. I just need her here, next to me. I pull her closer, so she's sitting, too.

"I'm sorry about getting your dress dirty."

"It's okay."

We kiss again and this time, I stop it. My head is clearer. It's strange how quickly I feel better.

"Are you okay?" I say. "Do you want to talk about this? You're probably thinking about Sharon right now, aren't you?"

"No, but maybe you are."

Everything feels clear to me now. "I want to break up with her, Jamie. I will tomorrow. I don't want to be one of those jerks who juggles two girls. I hate when really sick, hospitalized guys do that just because they think they can."

"Technically, they probably can get away with it."

I laugh. My head feels better. My chest, not so much.

"You're right, but not me. Total honesty from here on out. No bullshit from either of us. You can't bullshit me, either. If you have something you want to talk to me about, you have to say it, okay?"

"I do?"

"Yes. You can tell me anything. I won't be shocked, I promise."

I can see again, thank God. Going blind for ten minutes has had a weird effect. I want to tell her everything I'm thinking. I want to tell her that I never really loved Sharon and she never really loved me and I know it now. I'll call her tonight and the relief will be so huge we'll probably both cry in gratitude. *You don't have to feel guilty about not visiting me anymore!* I'll tell her.

Thank you! she'll say.

"I'm not thinking about Sharon right now, I'm thinking about you. You can't go back inside. We have to get you back to the hospital."

My head still feels floaty. "I hate to say it, but that's probably true."

"If you're okay, I'm going to borrow your phone and call for a ride. Will you be all right?"

"Of course. I'm good now. Better than good." I am.

Everything still hurts, but less than it did a few minutes ago. My mind is still racing. Why have I been so scared to acknowledge what's been obvious for so long? Jamie and I belong together. We understand each other. We've both lived in the gray area between life and death. For a month now, I've been readying for the end and bargaining with it at the same time. Now I think: *No, I'm not ready to die.*

I want my lungs.

I want my second chance.

Jamie has stepped away to the middle of the parking lot, where reception must be better. I can see her shape but none of her details. I can hear her calling, though it's strange; she sounds like she's speaking underwater. For a long time, I can't imagine what she's saying and then I realize all at once, she's not talking on the phone, she's talking to me. "I need your password, David."

I start to tell her, then stop. The asphalt she's standing on wavers. It's an earthquake, I think. Or else it's me.

I try to tell her my password—I know the numbers of course—but no sound comes out.

It's like I'm moving away from my body on the ground.

I'm leaving it, even though I don't want to. I need my body. I need my voice to tell her the password to my phone. I recognize all this, but I can't get myself to speak.

Two-one-two-three, I scream but nothing comes out.

I can see myself now, on the ground beside my oxygen tank. I'm falling over, but I don't even feel that part.

I must be dying.

What else could be happening?

I travel closer to Jamie and whisper in her ear: *Forget the Uber. Call an ambulance.*

Miraculously, she pulls out her own phone and dials it while she runs back to where I'm sitting. "I need an ambulance," she cries into it, checking the tank and all the dials.

I hover over her shoulder and realize what happened at

the same time she does: she turned the oxygen levels too high. I used it all up and now there's none left. That's why I felt so much better so quickly.

And that's why I'm lying in a heap right now, un-conscious.

PART TWO

CHAPTER TWELVE

DAVID

IT'S CRAZY THAT I'VE never figured this out before: *I can leave my body.*

One minute, I'm frantic and feel like I'm drowning, and the next, I can slip out of my pain and turn around to look at my body. It's thrilling and then it's terrifying. *Does this mean I'm dead?* Apparently not, because pretty soon an ambulance is here. I follow my body onto it, back to the hospital, watching the EMTs do everything they can to get it going again.

For now, it looks like their efforts have worked. I'm alive, at least, and stabilized, though I'm in the ICU and hooked up to a ventilator for the first time in my life. Whenever I've seen other people on ventilators, I've always looked away because it scares me so much. Now I'm surprised. I can't stop staring. They're loud and cumbersome, and no one looks good with their mouth taped around a hose, but they work. My chest keeps going up and down.

Deeper breaths than I've been able to take in a long time. I keep expecting to start coughing, and then I don't.

Here's the strangest part: I can't feel any of this. I must be in pain, but I can't *feel* it.

I know I *look* terrible: pale and ghostly, like the touch of a finger would leave a bruise. There's a little bit of blood crusted around my lips that I wish someone would wipe away, but no one does.

I don't recognize any of the nurses. They're all different in the ICU, which is too bad. I've worked so hard over the years to get every nurse on the peds floor to like me. I remember names and compliment scrubs. I never complain about things they can't help. It makes all of them nicer about things they can control. They sneak me extra ketchup and salt packets. They try not to interrupt when I have visitors.

But here, it's different.

Apparently, they've all heard the story of why I'm here—that I broke rules and snuck out—because they frown with irritation as they go about their work. The same irritation they must feel saving the life of a drunk driver or a stupid kid who rode on a motorcycle without wearing a helmet.

You'd better take care of yourself after this, their faces say.

One nurse tells another, "He had help, I heard. Someone brought him those clothes."

The other shakes her head and taps the numbers she's recording from one of my machines into her computer.

"Some people don't think they need to follow rules, I guess."

I wish I could tell her, *I always follow rules. That's all I've been doing all my life.* I only broke them this once, I want to say, except that's not true. I broke the rules three times. I had to if I wanted to spend any real time with Jamie. Now I understand: that's what I was doing. That's why I took such a risk.

JAMIE

I know he's still alive.

That's pretty much all my mom will tell me when she gets home from the hospital. The EMTs wouldn't let me ride in the back of the ambulance with David, and they were going to leave me in the parking lot, but at the last minute the driver said if I didn't have any other way to get to the hospital, I could ride up front with him.

Once we got there, they didn't let me stay with him. He was still wearing his hospital band, so they didn't need to ask me many questions after the first one: "If he's admitted to the hospital what was he doing outside?"

I had no choice. I had to tell the truth: I brought him clothes. I helped him leave.

After that much was clear, a nurse I didn't recognize told me I should wait in the lobby. Her voice had a warning undertone to it. Then she said, "If you leave, give the front desk a phone number where the police can reach you."

I understood what she wasn't saying but meant: *You're going to be in big trouble. Get ready.* I didn't stay. I left my name and phone number at the desk and walked home to call my mother and tell her what happened. She came home right away, and for the rest of the night, she called in to track David's progress, but she told me very little of what she learned.

Only "He's alive."

And later: "He's still alive."

Around midnight, she said, "He's in intensive care, on a ventilator. Stabilized for the time being, but that could change at any moment."

I knew what she wasn't saying: *I warned you about this. I told you it would be dangerous for both of you.*

She didn't even know yet that I'd given him my father's best suit to wear.

She asks me to sleep with her that night. I know she's scared of leaving me alone.

In the dark, we lie side by side, not talking at all. I've told her almost nothing about the night. What difference does it make that all of it was his idea? That we'd left the hospital twice before and he'd been fine? Better than fine—his numbers improved each time he got outside and glimpsed the world he was fighting to get back to. If I say any of this, my mom will point out all the flaws in my thinking. *Why do you think they were keeping him in the hospital? He'd been using oxygen the whole time you knew him—why did you think it was okay for him to leave the tank outside?*

She doesn't know that I've been watching him since the start of the school year and if I close my eyes, I can still see him healthy, the way he used to be, standing at the microphone in the cafeteria. If I tell her this, I'm scared I won't be able to stop. I'll keep going forever. I'll tell her how dancing with him felt different than any dancing I'd done before. I forgot about my body and my shyness and every impulse that has confused me and held me back in the past.

He might have asked for the kiss outside but I was already picturing it in my mind. I can still feel it now. I can smell him and taste him and feel his heart beating beneath my hand on his chest. It makes me dizzy to think about.

I take a deep breath—the kind I never take when I'm with David because he can't.

I know I shouldn't dwell on this part of the night. It'll only make the future harder, when I won't be allowed to see him at all.

I don't know how long we've been lying here in the dark, not speaking.

I thought she was asleep, but apparently not, because just as I'm reliving our kiss for the umpteenth time, she says, "You'll probably have to talk to the police tomorrow. There's nothing I can do about that."

DAVID

The ICU is crowded, but no one feels my touch or reacts if I stand near them. No one hears me say, "Excuse me."

I'm here, but not here.

I'm still wearing Jamie's father's suit, the one that was stripped off my body when I first arrived. It makes me feel like one of the angels in *Wings of Desire*. They both wear nice suits, which means that everywhere they go, they are both unseen and overdressed.

I figure out more rules to this new state I'm in. Though I have to wait for someone else to open the door, I don't have to stay with my body, which is a relief. It's hard to look at it for long. Out in the hallway, I see my mother, ashen-faced and stunned. I've never seen her look like this—not checking her phone, not issuing orders, not formulating a strategy or a list of to-dos. She looks paralyzed. As if even drinking from the cup of coffee in her hand is more than she can manage.

I sit down on an empty chair beside her. I think about the angels again and how only children and people in crisis can hear them. *It's okay, Mom*, I whisper. *I was so alive just before this happened that I can't die now. I'm sorry I took such a risk, but I was happier than I've ever been in my life. I won't die now, I promise. I can't.*

Her expression doesn't change. She breathes but doesn't blink. She can't hear me. Or if she does, her brain won't allow her to believe it. Feeling a presence beside her would be crazy, and whatever else happens, she can't be crazy right now.

I walk up the hall to look for my dad. I expect to find him crying, which he tries not to do in front of other people. Eileen and I have a joke about Dad's "pretending not to cry" voice. Hopefully, he and Eileen will be together, I think, comforting each other.

But no. I go up one hall and back and I don't see either one. Why is my mother sitting in the hallway alone?

I pass a clock that says seven forty-five, which confuses me at first. Wasn't it already seven when we got to Starlight? And then I realize—time has flown by. It's the morning, and more time has passed than I realized. Would Eileen have gone to school this morning? Did Dad take her?

Suddenly, I wish I'd talked to Eileen about Nick and whatever happened that night she left Starlight with him. For a day, I meant to, and then I put it off, because I wasn't sure what to say. But what if I come out of whatever state I'm in with too much brain damage to form a coherent thought? What if all I have are these *feelings* I should have expressed but never did? To Eileen, to our parents. Most of all, to Jamie.

It's too much to think about. I'm grateful when I spot my father through a window at the end of the hallway. He's standing outside the front door of the hospital, talking on his phone.

It takes a while to get down to him. I can follow other people onto elevators, but I can't push buttons, so I have to wait for someone else to hit Lobby. Eventually, I get outside, and he's still there nodding as he listens to the person on the phone. Who could he be talking to this long? Dr. Chortkoff? Eileen? I can't imagine him speaking for so long to either one. It also occurs to me: cell phones might not be allowed in the ICU, but the reception is fine everywhere else in the hospital, so why did he come outside for this call?

"Fine, yes," he says. "I appreciate your time. We'll get you that information as soon as possible."

As he hangs up, I touch his shoulder. *I'm going to be okay, Dad. I know I am. I had to leave. I couldn't make sense of anything in the hospital. I felt like I was losing my mind, but I'm better now. I promise I won't ever do anything stupid like that again. I don't need to.*

He holds the door for a woman coming out, which makes it easy for me to walk in ahead of him. Alone in the elevator, I keep talking: *DAD? I'M HERE! I'M WITH YOU. CAN YOU FEEL ME?* He watches the lit numbers as the elevator goes up. He's thinking about his phone call and what he'll tell my mother. He's obviously nervous, which makes me nervous.

"He needs some more information," he tells Mom as he sits down beside her. "But he promised he's going to get back to me this afternoon."

He gets no more response from my mother than I got twenty minutes ago. She doesn't look at him or seem to register what he's saying.

"Or someone from his office will. But I got a good feeling from him. I don't think he's giving us the brush-off."

Are they consulting a new doctor? Trying to get me moved up the organ donor list? Or worse—get me off it? I don't understand.

"I told him we're just investigating for now and neither

one of us is sure how we want to proceed from here. Linda? Can you answer me?"

She nods. Just as she opens her mouth to speak, there's a commotion across the hall. Two technicians push a crash cart over to the corner where my body is lying.

My mother stands up and moves toward my body. I get ahead of her because my first instinct is to block her from seeing something bad happening, but of course I can't. It's impossible to shield her. I wish I could look away myself, but I can't.

My body is convulsing. It looks like a seizure. My legs thrash, my arms strain against the straps holding them down. I don't feel the pain I must be in, but my face is red and covered in sweat. I've never heard anything like the animal cries coming from my throat.

I can't die now, I think. *I can't. Not when I've got so much I have to say to people.*

The doctors pull out paddles I've seen only on TV before. Bedding and gown are yanked away. Within seconds the paddles are on my chest.

"Ready . . . clear . . ." *THUNK!*

Everyone turns to one machine, bleeping chaotically a second earlier. After what must be a set length of time the doctor nods. "Again."

They do it twice more until finally they get the reading they're looking for: steady line . . . *BLEEP!* . . . steady line . . . *BLEEP!* Everyone relaxes.

The doctor wipes the sweat off his head with a bandanna he must keep in his back pocket for this purpose and leans over me. "Why don't you give yourself a break from these little dramas? You can't get better if you keep crashing, buddy."

I don't understand. Does this mean it's happened before? Have I been here longer than I realize? It's impossible for me to tell what day it is. No one leaves a newspaper lying around an ICU. Gradually, I'm beginning to understand the gravity of all this. I really might die.

Except I can't die yet. I have to talk to Jamie first. I have to see her so she knows that she did nothing wrong. Dancing with her clarified things for me in a way that reading a dozen essays on happiness couldn't.

I don't want to scare her with too much at once. I don't want to make her feel responsible, but I want her to know how much I've learned from her example about carving her own path. I want her to know that I meant what I said about breaking up with Sharon. That doesn't mean she has to start going out with me. It means that I see how much of my relationship with Sharon sprang from my fear of being alone. I want to be with Jamie, but if she doesn't want that or isn't ready, I'm not afraid of being alone anymore.

I go over to my body. Maybe there's some way I can force myself back into it—a scary prospect that will mean feeling all the pain of being on a ventilator with a tube down my throat and everything else I've just endured, but escaping that pain is leaving my body adrift. Maybe that's why it keeps giving up.

The problem is I can't do it. I can't get myself back into

my body. I touch my hand and feel nothing. I sit down on the bed. Nothing.

Can you hear me? I say to myself. Apparently not, but it doesn't matter, I keep going: *You have to stay alive to see Jamie again.*

Time warps in this strange state of half sleep.

I hear a nurse tell my mother, "It's only been two days. We wouldn't expect much response at this point. We have no idea how long his brain went without oxygen. There might be damage, but there also might not be. We just have to wait and see."

Another fear hits me, harder this time: What if I survive all this but have no ability to tell anyone what I've realized? What if I see Jamie and can't tell her how I feel?

JAMIE

I understand the mistakes I made were big enough that I can never work in the hospital or, for that matter, casually eat dinner there with my mother again.

My punishment was swift and unequivocal. I'm not only terminated from my position with the Smile Awhile group, I'm told that I'm not allowed to go to the hospital or visit David. I endangered a patient's life by violating policy and accompanying him out of the hospital without a discharge or doctor permission.

At that point, they didn't even know the full extent of it—that we'd left twice before without being caught. That comes out later, when I try to explain to my mother what I was thinking.

"We'd done it before, and he was *fine*. Better than fine! He was breathing better after we got outside. His numbers were up the next day!"

I watch my mother's face take in what I'm saying: That my lapse in judgment extends further and runs deeper than she's imagined.

She says, "He might have said that, Jamie, but it wasn't true. Kids as sick as David lie all the time. They can't control much in their life, so breaking hospital rules makes them feel like they're still in control of something."

I think about this. I don't want it to be true, but it's hard to argue against her point. Why *had* we risked everything for a bad lunch at Denny's?

"The point isn't the food," he'd said. "The point is getting outside."

He might as well have said, *The point is breaking the rules.*

I was wrong about a lot of things. Mostly, I was wrong to think I could help David the way I wanted to. I was coming back from a dark place that I was no longer in but had no perspective on. I gave him advice on topics I had no authority on. From G-tubes to college to not doing his homework and watching old movies instead. His health threw him off the course he'd lived his whole life on, but I stood in his room, wearing a stupid green smock, and welcomed him to the emptiness of my lonely world. You don't have to be ambitious anymore! Look at me! Taking non-honors classes and paper folding all day! Stay for a while and you'll see: you can fill up your days and survive okay, if surviving is all you need to do.

I see all my mistakes too clearly now.

I stopped seeing Rita three months ago, not because I was better or well, but because I didn't know what to say about my life. *I don't do art anymore. I don't work hard in school. I don't follow my passions because passions produce too many feelings, and I don't do well with those.* Therapists are tricky. They ask a lot of questions, and you don't do well if you don't feel like answering.

I thought not going to therapy would be fine if I stayed busy and filled my time with other things. Now I can feel myself going down again.

It's physical at first. A tinny taste in the back of my mouth. A tingling in my hands and the back of my neck. My vision shifts. Edges blur. I can't read more than a sentence before the letters start to move and lose all meaning. This time around, it feels like I'm having the panic attacks other kids in the hospital described. I have trouble breathing. It's like my body has internalized David's struggle for air and now it wants me to know how it feels. I can't take a deep breath even if I try.

I feel nothing except the weight of my responsibility for what's happened to David. I lie in bed and imagine him on a ventilator. My throat closes up, and I almost choke.

I know my mother isn't telling me everything. She's trying to strike a balance—protecting me from the worst news and still keeping me informed. She can't distract me, she knows, so most of the time we sit quietly, saying nothing.

After three days, she tells me I have no choice, I have to get in the car. She drives me across town to Rita's office. She must have called her ahead of time and told her more than I even know, because the first thing Rita says is, "I'm wondering if you can tell me what happened in your own words, Jamie. I want to hear all this from your point of view before we have to get into this business with the police and the lawyer."

CHAPTER THIRTEEN

DAVID

I DON'T KNOW HOW MANY days have passed. Daytime and nighttime are impossible to distinguish in the ICU. Nurses come on duty and leave. Their shifts are twelve hours. This is my only way to measure time.

I'm afraid of leaving my body alone for too long. If I go too far away, it seems to sense my absence. Every time I return, alarms are going off and people are clustered around me. I've experimented a little and discovered I can drift just as far as the lobby without causing a problem. On my first day in the ICU, the lobby was swarmed with kids from school. Most of student council was here—enough for a quorum, I tried to joke, but of course no one heard me. Some people cried, though it wasn't the ones I would have expected. Sharon looked stunned and numb but dry-eyed. Hannah kept reaching for a Kleenex box.

I stood there for a while trying to take it all in: *This is my world without me in it. These are my people.*

Then it was like my brain fragmented. I looked at some of the faces, and I couldn't remember their names. I *should* know them, I understood, but I didn't. Like my mom, Sharon was holding a cup of coffee, which surprised me. I'd never seen her drink coffee before. She won't even drink Frappuccinos. Hannah held her hand and rubbed her arm.

That first day, I stuck around the waiting room, not because I wanted to hear everyone talk about how sad they were, but because I needed information and I had so many questions. Who was my dad talking on the phone with earlier? What, exactly, was *going on*?

While I stood there, Ashwin walked in.

"What's happening now?" he asked.

Strangely, he was asking Hannah, not Sharon, though I didn't know why. Maybe they were trying to give Sharon space.

"He's still in the ICU," Hannah said. "Every time they try to wean him off the ventilator a little, he crashes, so they're not going to try that again for a while."

"Has anyone seen him yet?"

"No. They're saying they'll let us in soon, but only two at a time for five minutes each. He can't talk or anything, but we can talk to him. Supposedly, hearing voices helps when you're in a coma."

Sharon pulled her hand away from Hannah. "What are you talking about? He's not in a *coma*."

Hannah nodded. "That's right, not a coma technically, but what do you call it when someone's unconscious and they're on a ventilator that's breathing for them? It's not a coma exactly, but it's something else."

And then I knew. *I'm in a coma, but no one wants to say the word out loud. That's why I can stand here watching all of them, unseen and unheard. I really am like the angels in* Wings of Desire. *I'm hovering in between life and death.*

Everyone looked down at their phones or else at the door.

Suddenly, it was like I could hear what they were feeling and it was clear: they were all looking for excuses to get away. They thought they wanted to be here, but none of them wanted to see me hooked up to machines. Some started to make calls—to parents, to friends, to anyone who would give them a reason to leave. But how could anyone go with Hannah shooting looks and keeping a head count? Just when I thought the tension in the room couldn't get any thicker, the door opened up and Eileen walked in.

"You all have to leave," Eileen announced. "My mom and dad just talked to the doctors, and they say that only family can see him tonight, so—I'm sorry about this, but he'll still be here tomorrow, so you can come back if you want, I guess."

I laughed for the first time since this nightmare started.

Eileen could barely mask her disdain for my friends, though none of them saw this.

Hannah rushed over and wrapped her up in a hug. "How are you holding up, sweetheart?"

Eileen waited, stiff-armed, for the hug to be over. "I'm not the sick one, so I'm okay."

Behind them, people gathered their things. They all

looked grateful for this reprieve.

"Right," Hannah said, "but it's always hardest on the ones who are closest."

Eileen rolled her eyes just a little, not enough for Hannah to see. "I should get back to my parents. They just wanted to say . . . thanks for coming."

She spun around and left so quickly that it didn't occur to me until after she was gone: she and Sharon didn't say a word to each other. Which seemed odd.

Now, days have gone by.

I watch my parents whisper frantically to each other, snatches of a fight I don't understand. Every time I hover near them, they go quiet and don't speak. I want to know what they've been fighting about—it must be some decision they're making about my future—but there's another question I want to know even more urgently: *Where is Jamie?*

Every time I go out to the lobby, I expect to see her there. Maybe not sitting with my friends, but at least in the vicinity. I hover near Eileen whenever she's here. I try to read her texts as she types them to see if any are going to Jamie. So far nothing.

Every afternoon, the waiting room fills with a smaller group of students, and every day, I get more frantic. After a while, I can't help it; it makes me mad. Jamie must have known that I orchestrated all those outings as an excuse to be with her. I almost died trying to kiss her, so *where is she?*

I wish there was some way to ask Eileen. When she's here, she sits with our parents but stares at her phone

90 percent of the time. They ask her questions, and she answers without moving her lips. Even I get irritated by her, and I'm not the one asking what she wants for dinner.

When our parents leave for the cafeteria, I sit down next to her. I say, *I need to see Jamie. Can you ask her to come?*

My hope is that even if she can't hear what I say, she'll hear the suggestion and maybe she'll believe the thought is her own.

It might help me to hear her voice. I don't know how these things work or why I'm not waking up, but if anything is going to help me, Jamie would.

I wait. Eileen has a funny expression on her face. Even in this floaty state, it's possible to get dizzy, which I do. Her lips curl up. Her eyebrows crinkle.

Can you hear me Lee-lee? I'm shouting now because I think she can. *Don't say anything. Just nod.*

Nothing.

If you can hear me at all, tell Jamie to come.

I hold my breath. I wait. Nothing.

Eventually she opens Candy Crush on her phone, and I give up.

JAMIE

Rita says she's going to change my medication and add an emergency tranquilizer as a sleep aid.

"You want to be careful with these," she says, and then stops herself when she remembers that I know all about the dangers of prescription medication.

I was the one who found my father's stash two days after I came home from school and discovered my father "asleep" on the sofa in his studio.

In theory, my change to public school was meant to free my dad to focus on his work and return to painting again, which he'd gotten away from. Before I was born, all his success had been with his paintings. He was profiled as an up-and-comer in *Art World* magazine and had a gallery rep who sold his pieces to some of her wealthiest clients. He'd dropped out of art school, believing the narrow aesthetic of the faculty limited students and made them all produce cloned replications of one another's work, so maybe what happened with his work was inevitable. After a few years of success with his painting, he shifted his focus into an obsession with trying new formats. By the time I joined him in his studio, he no longer painted at all. Instead, he made himself a beginner over and over—printmaking one year, graphic collage the next. As the projects got more experimental, he grew more insistent on defending their value.

The first time I ever saw my father cry, I was ten years old. He'd brought me with him to a meeting with Lorna, his gallery representative, along with three new pieces to show her. They were just a sample, he told her. He had fifteen more at home, finished and market-ready. I liked his new work, but I also knew they were unsettling pieces to look at for long—abstract woodcut prints with slashes of red and orange paint bisecting the canvas, as if the artist had changed his mind halfway through one work and decided to do something else completely.

I knew the meeting wasn't going well, though I pretended to look around the gallery, as if I couldn't hear what was being said.

"I don't understand these, Leo," Lorna said. "People love your paintings; they don't know what to make of these. No one understands why you don't go back to painting."

I knew what he'd told me: That a true artist must push himself in new directions. That fear fuels creativity. That repetition is the path to entropy and death.

Alone in the car afterward, my father broke down. Weeping, he apologized and said I shouldn't have to see him like that, that he didn't want to scare me away from becoming an artist myself.

"That's the most important thing, Jamie. I don't want to scare you." He seemed to have a bigger point he wanted to make. It was the first time he said that I had more talent than he did, a terrifying thing for a ten-year-old to hear. "You're not better yet," he explained. "But you will be soon. You mustn't let what's happening to me stop you."

I didn't understand, but I'd already seen many things that scared me, even before that gallery visit. The way he talked to himself while he worked. The way he'd stare at a piece for long stretches of time, not moving a muscle or doing anything to it. The way his anger grew, anticipating rejection that hadn't even happened yet.

After that day, he started paying more attention to my work and finding reasons to prove his point, that I had a God-given talent. I don't know why he used that phrase when we had never been churchgoers. I didn't understand what it meant except that he didn't sound like himself. I was probably better than most people my age, but I assumed that was only because I'd spent more time doing art than other children.

"I've practiced more, that's all," I would say.

He insisted: No. My understanding of color and form was eerily sophisticated and had nothing to do with my education.

I wanted to say, *Color and form is pretty much all we talk about, Dad.* I felt the weight of his expectations, but I also understood that he had to put the burden of his own disappointment somewhere.

For two years, I worked in my corner of the studio and watched his corner carefully. I knew he wasn't producing much new art, but was he making *any*? Were we spending hours down there with one of us only *pretending* to work?

When I finally approached him about wanting to go to regular school for eighth grade, I knew he would talk about my "talent" and his fear that going to public school would waste it. I was right.

"Art teachers only teach conformity," he warned me. "But go ahead. See for yourself. I'll still be here, waiting, when you're done."

I wanted to say that I was partly doing this *for* him. That maybe focusing on my potential had taken him away from realizing his own. Whatever my intentions were, they didn't work. In his last year, we knew my father had started drinking more and spending money inexplicably.

On art supplies he didn't use. On clothes he didn't need, for events he didn't go to. It was as if he were rallying himself to start a life he couldn't get to.

The day I found him was the first time I'd been down to his studio in weeks. It was too filled with memories for me. Plus, I didn't want to see how little he was producing. Seeing him stretched out on the sofa, asleep, didn't seem so unusual at first. The surprise was finding a new canvas on his easel, and fresh paint squeezed onto his palette. For a moment, my breath caught. What he'd painted looked like a good start—darker than his old work, perhaps, but still reminiscent. Then I looked closer at the canvas and I realized it wasn't newly stretched. I turned it over and looked at the back. He'd whitewashed over an old painting that Mom and I loved called *New Life*. It was the first thing he painted after I was born. My mom told me he was once offered four thousand dollars for it, and she asked him not to sell it. It reminded her of the sweet, early days of my infancy. Now an abstract red pulsed at the center and exploded out over layers of green and yellow.

That's when I knew something terrible was happening.

This wasn't a return to painting. He was so tortured by the past, he was trying to erase it.

That's when I tried to wake him up and couldn't.

Two days later, as I went through the basement studio to figure out how many of his old paintings he'd painted over, I found a stash of empty liquor bottles. Above that, in a cupboard that once held our most expensive oil paints, was another stash of pills—some in labeled prescription bottles, some in Ziploc bags as if he'd bought them on the street. The bottles were a shock, but the pills left me reeling.

Now, I tell Rita that I'll take a prescription for Xanax, but I don't think I'll use it. "I know the dangers," I say.

We talk about strategies for the next few days. She goes over the importance of exercise and sleep to keep depression at bay. "Get out of the apartment as often as you can. Exercise. Go for a walk. Make sure you're sleeping well and eating okay."

I nod because I know all of this. In the hospital, I learned that doing a lot of little things really does make a difference. Getting out of the apartment and walking over to see David every day for six weeks probably helped my mood more than any antidepressant. Now that I'm banished from the hospital, though, it's hard to imagine where else I might go. Denny's? The strip mall?

"Okay." I nod.

"Ruminating is a danger," she says. "Being alone too much leads to ruminating."

She doesn't answer the obvious questions: How can I avoid being alone if David was my only friend? Who will I talk to at school if my only conversation in the last week has been with Eileen and it lasted less than thirty seconds?

"I'm so sorry, Eileen," I said.

"You should be" was all she said.

There was so much more I wanted to say but couldn't. So many questions I wanted to ask, but the words caught in my throat.

Since then, I've moved in a deeper silence, more alone than ever during my school day. At home, there's no reason to turn on the computer. For days now, I've sat on the sofa and waited all afternoon for my mother to come home and tell me news about David.

So far it's been the same. "No change today," she says, and then, because there's nothing else to talk about, I stand up and retreat into my room.

"Are you staying active?" Rita asks.

No.

"Are you making sure you're not spending too much time alone?"

No.

"Are you eating and sleeping appropriate amounts?"

No.

I can't do any of those things now. I also can't tell her the truth: this was all my fault. David was reaching for happiness in spite of his illness and picked the wrong person to help him find it. I couldn't help him. I was only pretending to know what happiness was.

DAVID

I start taking a few more risks. I leave my body alone and wander down to the cafeteria. Not that I'm hungry—in this bodiless state I have no bodily needs—but I need the distraction of seeing people going about their lives. In the ICU, everything moves at one of two speeds: crisis or lull.

It jangles the nervous system after a while, being on high alert or bored most of the time. It helps to see normal things, like plates of food under warming lights. Like a salad bar. This is what I tell myself anyway, even if it isn't true.

I'm here to find Jamie. If she won't come to visit me, I assume she's still meeting her mother here for dinner. I want to make sure she's okay. Is that worth risking my life for? I don't know. It must be, because here I am.

Only she's not here. I've timed it exactly when she used to meet her mom—five forty-five—but I don't see either of them.

I look hard at everyone—the cafeteria workers, janitors, doctors—as if Jamie might be hiding in someone else's clothes. But no.

She's not here.

On my way out the door, though, I see a surprise.

My parents are here. Sitting with a man I don't recognize. He's balding, red-faced, wearing a suit with a yellow legal pad in front of him. A briefcase sits on the chair beside him. I walk closer and slide into the empty chair at their table for four. They seem to have just gotten started. The legal pad is empty.

"Let's start with this," the man says. "Was David ever a risk-taker in the past?"

"Absolutely not," my mother says.

"No." My father nods. "Not that we've ever seen."

"Had he ever disobeyed doctor's orders before?"

They look at each other. "No," they agree. "Never."

"Would you describe David as someone who was easily influenced?"

They exchange another look. Why is he asking these questions? What's he getting at?

"Before this hospital stay, was he easily manipulated by certain people?"

My mom nods, and my dad says, "Occasionally we thought he was a little too quick to go along with some of his girlfriend's demands. They've been dating for a long time, and he was scared of that relationship ending. So we thought he allowed her to manipulate him a bit."

Why are they are telling a stranger this?

The man writes for a while, more than their answer warrants, and then flips a page and asks: "Had David ever suffered from depression in the past?"

"No," they both answer simultaneously.

"Has he ever mentioned suicide, even in passing, with either of you?"

"No."

"With all his health issues, he never said, 'Maybe dying would be easier'?"

"No, never."

He pulls a file folder out of the briefcase sitting beside him and flips through a few pages. "There's a note here that you recently asked the doctor about putting David on Prozac."

"I can explain that," my mother says. "He's always dealt so well with the challenges that came with his condition, but this was a lot for any seventeen-year-old to cope with.

We knew it was taking a toll on his spirits, so we asked for that as a preventative measure. We were trying to stay ahead of any mood swings he *might* have! The important point, though, is that he stayed incredibly positive and was never depressed. In fact, he'd recently made a project out of researching what philosophers have to say about happiness."

Why are they even debating this?

"Regarding the girl who helped him leave the hospital, were you aware of the history she had with depression?"

A chill travels down my spine.

"No, of course not."

"Was David aware?"

"Not that we know of."

"Did you know how frequently she visited David? Staff members report that she'd recently been visiting him every afternoon."

"We weren't aware, no. She usually came before we got off work."

"Did David talk about her with you?"

My dad leans in. "Only recently. In the last few weeks, we saw a real personality change in David. He told us he wasn't sure whether he wanted to apply to college at all. He couldn't explain himself very well, and then he said there's a girl here who was homeschooled most of her life. We'd given her a few rides with our daughter, but that's when we understood that she'd had some kind of influence on him."

"Would you say she was one of the factors that made him want to change his plans?"

"Yes, definitely. Before this hospitalization, he was planning to apply to ten schools. He's president of his class, with excellent board scores and a good GPA. He'd have no trouble getting in. It's what he's worked for his entire life. But suddenly, he was telling us he wasn't sure he wanted to go to college at all."

My mother leans in. "We didn't understand how he could change so dramatically—one day, he's filling out college applications, and the next, he's not interested in applying anywhere. Then a few weeks later, he's endangering his life by sneaking out of the hospital. None of these things reflected the David we know."

I can explain. *I was dying, Mom. It turns out that changes a person pretty quickly. It means you don't have the time to explain every little thing. You have a lot of feelings, and this urgency to act on them.*

The man clicks his pen and flips back a few pages through his notes. "All right, this is a good start. It's possible the hospital may have some culpability in allowing this girl to volunteer on a pediatric floor, but I can't guarantee anything. It sounds like her recent visits were outside her work shifts, in which case there's no responsibility on their part to monitor who visits him as a friend."

"But they were never friends from school. He met her here. Because the hospital employed her."

"Utilized her services. She was a volunteer. But I'll look into this. It's clear she shouldn't have been working on this floor. No question about that. Her age, her past."

Now I understand. This man is a lawyer, and my parents are trying to sue the hospital by blaming Jamie. Now I understand why she hasn't come to visit.

I have to make sure Jamie never finds out about any of this. I have to figure out a way to warn her.

CHAPTER FOURTEEN

JAMIE

"**D**ID YOU ENJOY BEING one of David's only visitors?" the lawyer asks me.

"I wasn't. He had lots of friends from school visit him. They might have visited a little less after he was quarantined, but only because they were afraid of bringing germs in."

My mother is sitting next to me for this interview with the hospital's lawyer. I told her she didn't have to come with me—that if I had to tell him the whole truth, it might be hard for her to hear. She didn't care. "There's no way I'm leaving you alone," she said.

"Did you feel like you had a special friendship with David?"

"Yes."

"Did he feel the same way?"

"I think so. We watched old movies and talked about a lot of things young people usually don't talk about."

"Like what?"

"Being sick made David question whether he wanted to apply to colleges, the way all his friends were doing. He was trying to look at the bigger picture. If his life expectancy was going to be shorter, he wanted to make sure he was doing things that really made him happy. Most teenagers don't talk about stuff like that."

"You didn't mind?"

"No, of course not. I like being friends with him. I was happy to talk about whatever he wanted to."

"Did you like having David all to yourself?"

I don't answer for a moment because I don't understand the question. "I didn't. His family was always here. And he talked to his friends a lot, even if they didn't come to visit him much after the first few weeks."

"With him having so many friends at school, did you worry that if David got well again, you might not see him so much?"

My mother squeezes my hand. We both understood what he's implying.

"No," I tell him. "That wasn't how I felt."

"But he had a girlfriend at school who couldn't visit for a while because she was away for a time, and then she got a cold and didn't want to bring germs in. Were you trying to make sure David remained sick enough to keep them apart?"

"*No.*"

"If he was the one who suggested leaving the hospital,

as you say, why didn't he ask his girlfriend to take him out?"

"I don't know. I never asked that question. We didn't talk much about her."

His eyebrows go up, as if this sounds surprising to him, but I'm trying to tell the whole truth, as completely as I remember it.

"But surely you thought about her. She and David had been dating for a year. Maybe you knew that she would probably say no to such a proposal. That she would recognize the risks to David. Maybe you recognized them as well but didn't mind the idea of David staying in the hospital for longer."

"No."

"Did David know about your history of depression?"

I look at my mom. "Some of it."

"Did he know that you spent three weeks in a psychiatric hospital after a suicide attempt?"

I look away. "No."

"Did the hospital know of this history when you applied to volunteer with the Smile Awhile office?"

My mom got me the job. Betty, who runs the Smile Awhile office, is her old friend and a nurse she worked with early on. I never filled out an application. I don't know how much my mom told her.

"I'm not sure."

"You're not sure? Do you realize the liability the hospital has with an answer like that?"

DAVID

Because my own status doesn't change much, I've started following some of the other patients in the ICU. I'm beginning to see things I didn't before. If I squint into the spaces between the equipment and the people, I can see other figures like me. Most of them are older, and more faded than I am. They hover in corners, uninterested in talking to anyone else. Some are so ready to move on, they don't even look at the bodies they were once part of. Others are like me. They hover close and read over doctors' shoulders. They study their charts to figure out their odds. They want to survive.

I've never tried to talk to any of them until this afternoon, when a new admission comes in, fresh from a car accident. He looks as young as I am and terrified. He can't figure any of this out. I leave my corner of the ICU and go over to him.

His body looks terrible. One side of his head is swollen and completely black and blue. The eye on that side looks strange—swollen shut and empty at the same time. I overhear a nurse tell another that his pupil blew out, which is a bad sign for brain damage. They're talking quietly to themselves, assuming no one can hear them.

It's worse when you first get here, I say to the guy.

I assume he won't be able to hear me, but talking is a hard habit to break. Even after all these days, I keep trying. I feel like I have to say something. Compared to this guy, I'm an old hand. When I got here, I recognized these machines; I knew what a ventilator was. He must feel like he's woken up in a science fiction movie.

They'll stabilize you. It'll get better.

After the doctors stop by, we know a little more: he's got internal organ damage on top of whatever's happened with his brain. It looks like the problem is mostly with his liver. I'm not great at reading charts, but I recognize bad-liver-function numbers when I see them.

Your lungs look good, I tell him, trying to sound positive. *My lungs were in terrible shape when I came in.*

I watch his face. He can't take his eyes off his shattered body. He looks like he's only a year or two older than I am. He also looks like he might be an athlete—tall and lanky, like a basketball player.

They keep saying there's no sign of brain activity, but what does that mean? he says, and it takes me a minute to register. I can hear him! Which means he can hear me! We can actually talk! The relief of this is huge, until I see his face and realize what he's asked me.

I don't answer. We both know what it means.

Do you have brain activity? he asks me.

They weren't sure at first. You don't really know until you wake up, but there's certain signs. Breathing without the ventilator. Pupils dilating. Do your pupils dilate?

He looks down and says nothing.

I don't know what I can say to help. Then he surprises me.

What happens to us when they turn off the machines?

He means our spirit selves. I have no idea. I assume

that if your body dies, this form we're in now doesn't stay around the hospital.

Maybe you go home with your family and watch over them for a while.

Like an angel?

I think of the angels from *Wings of Desire.*

Maybe. I don't know.

Do you think you still feel the same things when you're dead? I spent all last week mad at my dad. I was driving too fast because he told me not to take the car, and I had to get it back before he got home from work. I'm still sitting here, mad at him. I wish I didn't feel that way.

I wonder if this is why I feel so frantic to see Jamie. Because the thrill of kissing her was the last emotion I felt.

I don't know, I say softly. *Maybe. I still feel the same things I felt before.*

Do you think we're stuck? Can you change your feelings?

I don't know. I should probably go. You can't leave your body alone for too long. I've figured that much out.

What happens when you do?

My heart stopped for a while. I almost died.

He nods and looks at his own body, as if maybe this is good news. A way to take charge of a situation if his parents can't. *Good to know,* he says.

JAMIE

It's hard to hear what my mom is saying. Since my interview with the lawyer, it's hard to hear anything.

I haven't been able to go back to school. I also haven't been able to do anything Rita suggested: walk outside; read; eat; exercise.

Talking with the lawyer from the hospital, I could defend myself against only one charge—I never meant any harm to David, and I never wanted him to get sicker than he was. I couldn't deny anything else he suggested: I liked my visits alone with David. I wanted to be more than friends. My fantasies clouded my judgment. I believed leaving the hospital wouldn't be harmful to him because I wanted to believe it.

When he said, "You understand that just because you want something to be true doesn't make it so, right?" I knew there would be no escaping the vortex I was slipping into.

David's crisis is my fault. If he dies, I'm responsible.

It's impossible to make sense of anything else.

I tried going back to school for one day and it was a disaster. I got lost between classes. I went to the office. When the nurse asked me where it hurt, I couldn't say anything. An hour later, my mother picked me up. When we got home, she called work to say she wouldn't be coming in that night or the next day, either. She steered me to the sofa and sat down next to me.

She didn't speak.

She knew no words would help me at that point.

She was reminding me with her presence that however bad it got—and it would get worse, we both knew that— she would be there. I'd been in the hospital for three weeks and that whole time, we hadn't fought once. We were shy and careful and we squeezed each other's hands. We whispered, "I'm sorry," and "I'm sorry, too." We cried and then apologized for crying. We talked about other people in the hospital—how crazy they were, as if I had nothing in common with them. Whatever had happened when I took the pills from my dad's stash was a one-time event, not a permanent condition. Not a life sentence.

In the car ride home, when I got out of the hospital, I told her, "I feel guilty."

"Guilty for what? What did you do?"

Did she really not see it? I left Dad alone. I saw his sadness, and it scared me. I couldn't deal with it. Every choice I made when I first started school pushed him further away. I kept all my art at school; I showed him none of it, even when he asked. Once, when he questioned an assignment, I actually said, "You're not my teacher anymore."

I might as well have said, *You're not my father.*

In the car, my mother got so angry she pulled over to the side of the road. "Your father didn't kill himself because of you. He allowed grudges and anger to get in the way of doing his work. He built them up in his mind, and they became so destructive he couldn't make art any longer. And he was depressed! You were too young to see any of that. I did. It was *not you*, okay?"

Now it's different, though.

I *am* responsible for what happened to David. One of Rita's favorite things to say when I was in the hospital was, "Remember, depression lies. It makes your brain think certain things are true that aren't true." She might have been right back then, but she's not right now. It's not just my depressed brain thinking this. His family blames me. So does the hospital. So does the lawyer.

When I was in the hospital, my mom and I pretended that I wasn't as bad off as the other kids there, but that was never really true. I know that now because I can feel it coming back, swallowing me up.

CHAPTER FIFTEEN

DAVID

I'VE ONLY MET JAMIE'S mom twice. I know she works as a floater nurse, filling in all around the hospital when other nurses are out. Taking this position means she works more hours but also has more flexibility than she would have if she stayed on one floor.

It also means she's almost impossible to find.

I remember Jamie saying her mom's favorite floor to work on was the renal unit, where patients get dialysis, then go home at night. The same people come back two or three times a week, and she liked getting to know them.

Twice now I've made it up to the sixth floor, where dialysis is done—a complicated business of riding elevators and waiting until someone gets on and pushes the right button—but I didn't see her either time. It's a risk, I know. I time my trips away from the ICU when extra nurses are on duty but no doctor is due. That way I won't miss any information, but I also know my body is covered if something happens. I don't know if this is the wrong risk to take, but I have to do something.

Watching my body hover in limbo for hours on end is too much sometimes. It makes me restless. I want to tell myself to either wake up or die already. Which isn't the answer.

The answer is somewhere, and I have to keep looking. I keep thinking: The answer is seeing Jamie. My body is waiting to see Jamie again.

This time I get lucky. I get to the sixth floor, and Jamie's mom is there, sitting at a nurses' station at the end of the hall. She looks so much like Jamie my breath catches. The same curly brown hair, the same big brown eyes. This is what Jamie will look like when she's middle-aged. She's beautiful, I think, even though she looks exhausted, like she hasn't slept well in days.

A few things I've figured out since I entered this state: I can't pick up a pencil or any object with any weight. Nor can I press a keypad to type a note. I've strategized and tried every option I can think of for communicating with the people who come to see me and sit in the lobby for hours on end. The only physical impact I've managed to have so far has come—ironically—when I've blown on a piece of paper and seen it move. My greatest weakness in life is my superpower in this state. Last night I managed to blow a Kleenex to the floor, which felt triumphant and also pointless, because no one noticed.

I've figured out something else, though. I can slow a computer down by putting my hand on it. It doesn't work with phones, but with the friends who've brought their laptops to the waiting room, I've tried it. I touch the back of their screen, and they look up a moment later. "Is there something funky with this Wi-Fi?" Ashwin said yesterday, looking at Hannah, who wouldn't look back at him.

"No," she said, and I touched hers, too. "Wait—what's going on?"

Look at him, I said, which she did. *Talk to each other. You've been sitting here for hours, and neither one of you cares about what you're reading on your screens.*

"I hate this hospital," Hannah said. "It's like they can't do anything right."

Ashwin nodded with his nervous, *I can't believe I'm talking to her* expression. They've been friends for four years, and he's always had a crush on her. "Except keep David alive. I mean there's *that*."

"Right." She rolled her eyes and smiled. "There's that. But their coffee and their internet, not so much."

They both look at the wheel-spinning frozen state of their screens and then back up. "Hey, can I ask you a question?" Ashwin said.

I almost took my hand off his screen, but I knew if I did, the conversation would end.

"Okay."

"Why are you here more than Sharon these days? I mean—it's nice of you. I just wondered if Sharon was okay."

"It's been really emotional for her. She's already been here so much over the last eight weeks. She thought he was going to be better by now. I don't know—it's hard for her to see him in this state. It freaks her out a little bit."

Ashwin looked at her. "It doesn't freak you out?"

"No. I don't know why not. My brother was in the hospital for a while when he broke his femur. Maybe I'm used to it."

"Was the coffee bad then, too?"

"I was only eight, but . . . yeah, I'm sure it was."

It was a nice conversation, but I took my hands away from their screens so they could both relax back into their mindless scrolling.

Now, I go to Ronnie, Jamie's mom, seated at the nurses' station, and put my hand on her monitor. She looks up. Not at me, of course, but to the right of me.

I need to see Jamie, I say.

"What's going on?" she asks the other nurse, seated behind her. "Are we having a server problem?"

I don't touch the other computer because I don't want them to start talking to each other. I want to try to get through to her by myself. *Tell Jamie to come see me.*

She looks up. She hears something, I think.

I'll wake up if she comes. I will. I promise.

How can I promise this? If I could wake myself up, I'd do it now and start breathing on my own. I'd sit up in bed and type Jamie a note. I can't control my body, and I shouldn't promise this. But I can't think of anything else.

I know my parents have started some kind of lawsuit where they're blaming Jamie for what happened, and I need her to know it's not her fault. She didn't make me sicker; she made me better.

Ronnie hasn't moved since I started talking. It feels

like this is as close as I've gotten to communicating with someone in this state.

"Nancy?" Ronnie says. "Do you hear something?"

"No," she says.

Yes! I say. *It's me, David. Don't be scared. I need to see Jamie.*

"That's strange. I thought I heard something."

I'm so happy to hear her say this, I do something I haven't done before. My feet leave the ground. I float a little. She's different from the others! She can feel my presence, which means maybe Jamie will be able to feel it, too!

It's me, David! Tell Jamie I need to see her!

Just as I say this, though, I feel a prickle in the back of my neck. Something is happening. I'm not just floating, I'm being pulled away.

I try to hold on, and I can't. I'm traveling without elevators back to the ICU. I try to stop myself, but it doesn't work. I can't put my feet on the ground or touch anything.

I don't understand.

And then I'm back in the ICU, and I'm terrified. My body isn't here anymore. I'm not in the corner where I left myself a few minutes ago.

What's happened? Have I died? Have days slipped by the way they did in the beginning without me realizing it? In the corner, I hear nurses whispering. The beeping of machines seems louder suddenly. How can I be dead and hear so much? That's when I hear someone say my name.

"Is David in pre-op already?" a nurse asks. I don't know her name because I haven't been able to ask, but she's one of my favorites. She does little things when no one is looking—opens my hands across my chest in the morning. At night, she tucks them under the blanket.

"They just took him over. They're sterilizing and prepping. We're still waiting for the go-ahead."

"Did they schedule an OR?"

"I think so, yes. The request is in."

"And they're shaving before they get the approval?"

"Yes. They have to. No time to spare."

It sounds like I'm going into surgery, but what could they be doing? My chest is already intubated; my airways are open. Did my heart stop?

Then I look over—at the empty bed across the ICU. The boy who was here a few hours ago is gone. I don't see him anywhere. After our one conversation, I looked for him a few times but could never find him. I know his body was still here when I left a little while ago.

I look around for other spirits—anyone who can tell me what's happened here in the last hour. There's one older man who's hardly visible anymore, singing to himself. When I try to get his attention, he disappears.

I go out in the hall. In the chairs where I first found my mother sitting, a family is huddled—two parents, with their arms around two younger girls. This must be the boy's family.

I sit down near them. I think about Damiel, the angel in *Wings of Desire*. I reach out and touch their shoulders and heads. They're warm. It feels like I'm touching their spirits within. Bodies connect in myriad ways; in sex and touch and blushes and goose bumps, but this is how spirits speak to one another: in light and silence. We sit side by side and be with each other.

I'm so, so sorry, I say. I touch his father's shoulder. *I'm sorry you were angry with each other, but he's not angry anymore. It's over now.*

His father sits up and blows his nose. They look at each other, all of them red-faced with wet cheeks. They laugh for a moment, at their red faces and their tears. I feel the laugh in whatever I have instead of bones. It makes me shiver.

I remember the last question the boy asked me: *What happens if you leave your body alone too long?*

I didn't know, of course, but I took a guess.

"I keep thinking, *where is he?*" the mom says. "Where did he go?"

"I don't know," the dad says, shaking his head. He has a British accent, which is a surprise. I feel like I know them, but I don't, of course. "His body's in surgery. They're fetching his organs right now, I expect."

I feel a prickle on my neck. The same feeling that carried me in a whoosh back down here. The pieces of his story and my own fall together.

He's donating organs, and I'm in pre-op now, getting sterilized and shaved.

I don't know why, in all this empty time, this possibility hasn't occurred to me. I'm getting my lungs.

I race back to my own body. On my way, I pass Eileen sitting in the hallway with Ashwin, of all people.

"They're deciding all this today? Isn't he still too weak for this surgery?"

"He is really weak, but he already passed their brain-function tests, so the main thing they care about is whether he has any infection. If he has any temperature or sign of infection, they won't do the surgery and they'll give the lungs to someone else."

I feel a prickle in my neck at this: my brain function is fine. I just can't have an infection.

"What about the pseudomonas bacteria? I thought testing positive for that meant he'd have a harder time getting new lungs."

I'm touched. I can't believe Ashwin knows this stuff. It means he's quietly been going home and researching the updates I've mentioned. I thought my school friends weren't interested or couldn't deal with what I was facing, but no.

"Yeah, I guess they changed that rule. It turns out the best thing you can do to move up the transplant list is look like you're going to die if you don't get a transplant. That's what the doctor said. The other stuff, they can treat. If you die, they can't do much."

Ashwin nods. He looks around awkwardly, the way he always does when he's alone with a girl. Even Eileen makes him nervous.

"Plus, it helps that some lungs are being donated and they're a blood-type match."

"Where did they come from?" Ashwin asks her.

"We're not supposed to know, but we're pretty sure

they're from a kid who came into the ICU a few nights ago after a car wreck. His parents have been keeping him on machines because they wanted to donate organs. Which is nice and sort of weird, because we're not supposed to know, so we don't say anything even when we're all passing each other in the hallway."

Eventually, I find my body. I'm in a pre-op room, lying naked on a gurney, covered loosely by a blue hospital sheet. Two nurses stand on either side of me. A portable ventilator is next to the gurney, doing its job, moving my chest up and down. One nurse is shaving my chest; the other is washing it. I don't have much chest hair, but there's enough that she clears what she gets into a silver bowl next to me.

They lift one arm and then the other. "Here," one nurse says, pointing to a spot she missed.

"Thanks," says the other.

A door opens behind them, and my parents come in with Eileen, everyone wearing face masks. They look like a trio of surgeons, searching for someone who will let them operate.

My mom says, "We're all going to be right here, David, the whole time. We're not going anywhere."

I can tell my parents have both been crying, even though they're trying not to let it show. They've got big phony smiles behind their masks and bloodshot eyes. They look terrible and fragile, but there's also something different about the way they're standing. Dad has one arm around Eileen and a hand on Mom's back. They're leaning on each other.

I've never seen this before. It's nice.

They all move closer to the bed together. Mom takes my hand, and Eileen touches my arm. Dad says, "We know how strong you are, son. We know you can get through this."

I've never heard Dad call me "son" before. I wonder if they've been told my odds of surviving surgery are bad enough that they need to come in now and say goodbye without letting on what they're doing.

Tears spring to my eyes. I know I'm going to die at some point soon, I just don't want it to happen in the next few *hours*.

Mom drops the act first. "You're our beautiful boy!" she says, and starts to cry. "You've got to get through this! You've got to be okay!"

I stay in the operating room as they cut open my chest and lift up my rib cage a few inches. I can't get over the way they work in unison, without talking about what they're doing. I also can't get over how little I feel, watching my body get cranked open and dug into. I peek under the hood of my rib cage at what might be my heart, or maybe a lung, I can't tell. I feel so distanced from the whole matter that I don't even think of it as myself on the table.

I'm free to drift away, out to the waiting room where my family is gathered and too many of my friends to even count them all. It's nice to see everyone here, not arguing or competing—just waiting, together.

I drift over their heads and see that from above, a light pulses off each person. Their auras touch each other. It's as if their spirits are reaching out to comfort one another, the way I did earlier with my donor's family. It's a relief to see. It makes me think they'll survive even if I don't.

I leave the hospital because, at last, it feels safe to do so. My body is in a state of suspended animation. I can't crash now if I'm already being kept alive by machines.

I move without thinking about where I'm going. I've been stuck inside for so long that when I breathe in the fresh air I'm reminded of the best thing about being in this state: My lungs work fine! I'm not alive exactly—I haven't eaten anything, and I haven't been hungry—but I've been breathing this whole time, better than I ever did before, and I didn't realize it until now!

I pass the Denny's I went to with Jamie and then, a few minutes later, the movie theater where we came by car, which makes me think I'm not traveling geographically but through a different dimension of memories and time.

I look through the windows of the restaurant, but I don't see Jamie or myself for that matter. I find the bus stop where I sat down and Jamie joined me with the sweater, but we're not there, either.

It makes me mad. If I'm traveling through my own memories, why can't I see her again? Why can't I watch us laughing and eating at Denny's? Why can't I spend the next two hours reliving our last night at Starlight? I remember it all so well now: the dance, then the kiss. If I could, I'd go back and watch us dancing again. I'd follow us outside and watch us kiss, too—like our bodies understood what our brains hadn't allowed ourselves to think. We weren't just friends.

If I could go back anywhere in time, I'd relive that whole night over and over, even though I know how it ends.

It's not here, though.

I float forever and can't find that night. It seems so unfair that I can finally move freely but not go where I want. Just as I think this, though, I'm caught by surprise. I'm standing outside Desert Paradise apartments. This isn't a memory, because I've never been here before.

I move through the parking lot, toward the entrance, where the paint is peeling and whatever garden was once planted has long ago gone to weeds. I never asked Jamie too many questions about living here because I didn't want her to feel self-conscious. It looks terrible from the road, with piles of garbage and old furniture left in a trash area to rot. Up close, though, it isn't quite so bad. A few apartments have potted plants out front or decorations taped on the door. Signs of life. Of real people behind them.

I don't know which apartment is Jamie's. It might take me hours of window peeking to find her, but I'm close enough now that my heart is beating.

I'll stay all night and look in every window if I have to.

Unfortunately, almost all the apartments have window

shades down or curtains drawn. It's impossible to see inside. The only thing I can do is stand close to the window and use my other senses. At one door, I close my eyes and smell—curry, cinnamon. At another, I listen closely. At one, I think I might hear her voice. I hold my breath and wait, then realize it's someone watching television.

I get a little frantic. Every sound and smell is almost Jamie and then it's not. I can't get this close and then not see her after all this time waiting.

As I move around the horseshoe of apartments, I hear a thread of familiar music. I move toward a faint glow two windows down so I can hear it better. At first, I think it's a woman singing, and then I smile. I know who it is. It's not a woman, it's Fred Astaire: a thin, agile man, with a surprisingly high voice. "Heaven. I'm in heaven. And my heart beats so that I can hardly speak."

He's singing "Cheek to Cheek." I float over to the window, where the curtains are sheer enough for me to see Jamie inside, watching Fred sing and dance with Ginger Rogers.

"And I seem to find the happiness I seek, when we're out together dancing cheek to cheek."

I'm not sure how it happens, but it feels like my heart moves ahead and carries me inside. Suddenly, I'm standing in the tiny living room, alone with Jamie. It smells musty and a little like BO. I'm so happy to be near her, but even I can see—she hasn't showered in a while.

For a long time, I stare at her. I don't know what to do.

I sit down beside her, a few inches away. She can't see me, of course, and I'm scared to touch her. I don't know what effect it will have. It might feel scary—like a chill, or goose bumps.

Instead, I lean away and watch for a while. Ginger is wearing a dress made of feathers that move on their own, like the auras I saw earlier around the people in the waiting room. I watch Fred and Ginger dance, their magical and mysterious synchronicity. Then I turn and look at Jamie. She looks heartbroken, sitting on the sofa, with tears rolling down her cheeks, one after another. In all our time together, I've never seen her cry.

Supposedly, those dress feathers drove Fred crazy, I say. *They went up his nose in rehearsal and made him sneeze. They got in a big fight over the feathers, and Ginger put her foot down. She said the feathers stay or I go.*

I know Jamie can't hear me, but it seems like she senses something. She's not crying anymore. And there's a tiny smile in one corner of her mouth.

Sitting beside her after all this time, I want to tell her that at last I've figured out why I love *Wings of Desire* so much. I love it because it's about living in two worlds: the visible and the invisible. The visible is everything we can see and touch; the invisible is what we experience with our hearts. I've been living in this invisible world for months, hovering between life and death. She knows this world; she's lived here, too.

I think about Damiel, the angel in the movie, entering

the world he's only been observing all his life. How he has to fall into it. Experience pain. Taste blood. I try to imagine what this has been like for Jamie—watching my body get loaded into an ambulance and then coming back here to wait for news alone. I think about the lawyer's questions to my parents.

I don't want you to blame yourself, Jamie, I say. *None of this was your fault. I'm the one who made all this happen.*

I move over to the TV screen and touch it with my hand to see if it has the same effect as touching a computer. I don't want to scare her, but I want her to feel me. I want her eyes to drift off the screen the way her mother's eyes did earlier today. I want her to know that I'm here—but the hand trick doesn't work. The movie keeps playing through its silly final dance number on the canal boats in Venice. I move around the room while I wait for it to finish.

It's a tiny apartment with depressing brown shag carpeting, but on the walls is some of the loveliest artwork I've ever seen. Small oil paintings, mostly abstracts, that look like moody skyscapes and then, when you look closer, they have tiny, realistic objects floating through them: a teddy bear, a picnic basket, a child's shoes. They almost remind me of the *The Wizard of Oz* tornado, except everything seems to float happily in its darkly colored patch of sky. Some items are connected. In one, a dog chases a ball down a slide of dark red. It looks ominous from afar, but funny close up.

I try to remember what Jamie told me about her father's

career as a painter. How he was successful when he was younger, selling his paintings to high-end clients when he was in his early twenties. Then something happened that made him retreat from his own success. She never told me what it was, only that he hadn't sold anything since she was a child.

Knowing that he stopped working makes it all the sadder to look at these beautiful paintings now. I squint down at a date in the corner and am surprised. It looks like these are only two years old. Then I look at the initials beside the date. JAT.

I spin around and look at Jamie. It doesn't seem possible, and yet it must be. These aren't her father's paintings.

They're hers.

I turn around and look at her in the dying light of the movie. The reflection of the credits rolls over her face. I remember her telling me that she used to paint, too, but it got harder and sadder after her dad died. I remember her saying, "Passions are tricky. They can take over and suddenly, in your mind, nothing else matters."

I go back to the sofa and sit down beside her. Sitting this close is enough for me to feel her spirit and remember more: How sick I was when I first got pseudomonas. How I thought I was going to die. How her voice in my ear kept me alive.

You won't always feel this way. You'll get better. You can't see the future yet, but it's there. Just hang on.

I whisper those words now. *You won't always feel this*

way. You'll get better. You can't see the future yet, but it's there. Just hang on.

Just hang on.

JAMIE

This is stupid, I know.

It's my second viewing of this movie, but it's making me feel better. I like the way no one gives up in this story. The characters are all completely wrong about each other in their assumptions (absurdly so, really) but they forge ahead with their blind convictions. They barrel into parties and hotel rooms, wearing ball gowns and tuxedos, creating awkward situations they have to tap-dance their way out of.

Who am I kidding? I love it because it reminds me of David, and I feel like he's here, watching it with me.

He isn't. Any minute, my mom is going to call and check up on me. I'll need to mute the TV and pretend I'm not crying. I'll need to make a joke so she knows I'm okay for another hour.

I push Pause and stand up. I go to the bathroom and splash water on my face. When I come out, it's strange—I notice the paintings on the wall that my mother hung up months ago, while I was in the hospital. I did them in eighth grade, my last burst of creative fervor, after the show downtown and my dad's devastating reaction to my *Runaway Bunny* paintings.

It's not you I have the problem with, he kept saying. *It's the assignment. So derivative. Asking for young people to paint imitations.*

In the month I had left before the end of school, I wanted to produce work that was entirely, unequivocally my own. I also wanted the pieces to connect. Three paintings that told a story, though I didn't want the story to be too obvious. I put realistic toys in a maelstrom of color because that's what growing up had felt like to me—pieces of childhood still in sharp focus; everything else, prismatic and confusing.

What I never realized (how could I not?) was how close the abstract backgrounds were to my father's paintings. Once my mother pointed it out, I couldn't believe I hadn't seen it for myself. It was like I'd taken sections of his old, most successful work, re-created them exactly, and littered the canvases with my childhood belongings.

Later, when I brought the pieces home and compared them, it was obvious how I'd internalized his swirls of color. It was mostly true on the one I'd titled *Youngest Child*, that included a sippy cup and stuffed bear. With the others, the items aged upward until they included a dog we never had chasing a ball. By the third one, it's as if I'd left my father's influence behind.

I haven't looked at these for years—I didn't understand why my mom hung them at all, with all the complicated baggage they represented. Now I look closer.

They aren't terrible.

The hardest one to look at is the first one. It's the least confident, the most tentative. The other two have—I can't believe I'm thinking this—an exuberance to them. A joyful quality. I remember how it felt to work so intensely for a short period of time. How it took me out of myself, almost out of my body, and made me feel older, like I was floating above middle school and all its disappointments.

Like being good at this might save me, or at least get me through, until the end of high school. Back then I believed such a thing was possible.

PART THREE
FOUR MONTHS LATER

CHAPTER SIXTEEN

JAMIE

THE FIRST TIME I see David again, I almost don't recognize him. He looks like he's put on at least thirty
pounds, though he doesn't look fat the way some people
do when they're taking steroids. He looks like himself,
but fuller. More solid. His cheekbones aren't so promi-
nent. His hair is much shorter. All the curls are gone.

I'm sitting in the cafeteria where I always sit now, at
the same table with Missy and Bethany and the rest of
the crowd.

I watch David walk slowly up to his old spot at the
microphone with Sharon on one side and Ashwin on the
other. Apparently, the other seniors weren't expecting this.
When they see who it is, they all go quiet.

Ashwin looks at Sharon, who nods okay. He leans into
the microphone. "We have a surprise for you, everyone. As
most of you know, David's been out of commission for a
little while, but today we're super excited because he's back

at school to make our first announcements about senior-week activities!"

The whole place goes crazy, hooting and shouting and stomping their feet. David leans into the microphone and tries to say something but gets drowned out. He smiles at first, then laughs awkwardly, looking a little flustered by it all.

He holds up his hand, flat like a policeman stopping cars.

"Thanks, everyone," he says. His face is red. "Really. Thanks."

They still won't stop. It's awkward. He looks at Ashwin and tries again. "I have some announcements. You need to listen."

They finally quiet down, and he leans into the microphone. "It's great to be back, you guys. Thank you for the nice welcome. The main thing I want to tell you—" He looks down at the piece of paper in his hand. He doesn't sound short of breath, just nervous and flustered. "Is that we really need people to buy senior class T-shirts. They're great-looking and this is our primary fund-raiser for senior-week activities. We can have a really fun grad-night party with entertainment and good food, or we can have a not-so-great grad-night party with a few bowls of pretzels and Brian here, singing karaoke. It's your choice! Buy your T-shirts!"

This doesn't sound like David's old announcements. It sounds like he didn't even read what the paper said before he got up there. He shakes his head sheepishly. I think he's trying to say *I don't really care if you buy T-shirts or not*, but it's hard to tell, and it's not my place to guess. I haven't spoken to or communicated with David or Eileen since he had his operation, so I can't possibly guess what he's thinking.

For weeks, I've been trying to imagine what it'll be like to see David again. Rita even gave me exercises where I visualize this moment so I can plan what to say. *It's good to see you. I'm so happy that you're better.* When I practiced this in my mind, he looked the same as he did in the hospital. Now he looks so different, I don't know if I can say it. He doesn't seem like the same person.

He goes to sit down, and the applause starts again.

"Shine on, David!" Missy yells, so loud, he looks over at us. I scrunch behind a backpack so he won't see me.

I don't know if this will work. There are two months left of school. I don't know how I'm going to get through them if he's back for good.

Sharon's back at the microphone, smiling at David, who's sitting in his old spot at their old table. "Thank you, David! Just a reminder: you can buy T-shirts at the table in the corner or with one click on our web page. Do it for David!"

Another resounding cheer rises from the crowd.

"Did you ever run into him when you did that weird hospital job?" Missy asks when the announcements are over. "You couldn't have, right? Because you worked on the kids' floor."

I'm surprised. Ever since I started eating lunch with them again, Missy has tolerated my presence, but she hardly ever says anything to me. She never asks me a question. They know I left the job, but they don't know anything I did there or why I left.

I'm not sure what to say.

She turns to Nicki. "Can you imagine changing David Sheinman's bedpan? That would be wild."

"I never changed bed—" I start to say. I stop because they're not listening anyway. They're imagining some fantasy version of meeting him alone in a hospital room, just like I'm imagining my own version, which is obviously just a fantasy, too.

DAVID

The weirdest things happen when you're taking steroids. To your body obviously, but also to your mind. At first, I didn't understand, then I googled around and asked my friends on the CF chat boards: "Do you guys feel like your personality changed after your transplant?"

"Oh God, yes," Joyce answered within seconds. "I got really depressed for a while and then kind of manic. Is that happening to you?"

A few minutes later, Calvin Richard weighed in, "I was the opposite. Super mellow, like I was on drugs, and then I realized: Oh right, I'm on drugs."

For me, it's been a roller coaster of mood swings that started about a month after the surgery, when I was well enough to sit up and walk to the bathroom a few times a day. I felt better—I was definitely breathing better—but

I was still too weak and too vulnerable to do anything I wanted to. Suddenly, I couldn't stop shopping online and ordering things I didn't really need.

A few weeks after I got home from the hospital, Eileen came in my room and stared at the unopened boxes in one corner. "What's with all this shopping? You're acting like me all of a sudden."

I knew it was stupid, but I couldn't stop myself. I ordered weird food that I thought would taste good, but didn't. I ordered clothes because nothing I owned fit anymore. When I walked into my room again and remembered how I'd left the bed covered in vomit months earlier, I ordered new sheets.

"You can't just wash everything and expect it to be fine," I told my dad.

"You also can't keep spending money like this," he said gently.

I ignored him. It was Eileen who finally got me to slow down. She was poking through a box of Harry & David fruit. "You remember that we still have grocery stores, right?"

"You can't get good pears at the store. Dad just bought a bunch that were mealy and disgusting. If you want decent ones, you have to order."

"Oh my God," she said, grinning. "You sound crazier than me."

I'd been home for two weeks at that point, and I still hadn't left the house. One condition of my release from the hospital was that I not expose my precious new lungs to predatory germs for as long as possible. "It might be a month before you can go outside," the doctor told us. "Maybe more. Are you ready for that?"

"Yes," I said, because I would have said anything to get out.

My last night in rehab, I lay awake late and made promises to myself: *I won't be moody and irritable with my family. I'll remember how grateful I am to be home. I'll remember how hard all this has been on them.*

It only took a day to break that promise. My dad had bought a new router in my absence, and for some reason my computer wouldn't recognize it. I was the only person in our family with enough tech savvy to solve a problem like this, but either my brain wasn't functioning well enough to do it or the glitch was real.

"It's strange," Dad said. "Our computers all work fine."

"Well, mine's fucking not fine, Dad, and I need to get on! I can't be stuck at home for a month with no way to talk to people!"

He took a deep breath and nodded. "No, of course not. We'll figure this out. We'll get someone out here."

Since then, I've had a blowup every two or three days. I try to control them, or at least vary my targets, but I can't stop.

"Buying a lot of stuff won't solve your problems," Eileen said, unwrapping the tissue around one of my pears. "I should know. I've been doing it my whole life, right? Then it turns out nothing's ever as good as it looks online."

She was right. The food I ordered online didn't taste

much better than whatever my dad was buying at the grocery store. I hadn't tried on most of the clothes, so I didn't even know how they looked. Everything was waiting for my great new life to start. The life where I could finally keep up with my friends again and go to a party without having a coughing fit at a tiny thread of smoke. Where I could laugh without losing five minutes to coughing; where I could spend time—real time—with Sharon again.

She's the only person I haven't gotten mad at these past four months. When I first came out of the surgery fog, I remembered nothing about the week before the surgery and the whole month before that is hazy and confusing. I remembered becoming friends with Jamie and going on two outings with her—to the movies and Denny's—but I had no memory at all of going to Starlight, where they said I collapsed.

The first time we talked about it, Sharon was upset, but mostly at herself. "I should have been there. I should have taken you myself. I didn't understand why you were thinking about Starlight so much, and I'm just so sorry!"

I thought about the whole summer I spent waiting for Sharon to get off work and call me: it was gratifying to have her feel a little guilty for being so busy. But no matter how hard I try, that whole week is a blank to me. I remember getting the idea that Eileen should sign up for Starlight; I remember thinking, *Jamie'll love it, too*, but I don't remember why.

I wish I could recall more about my friendship with Jamie beyond this vague feeling that she was easy to spend time with and I liked talking to her. Eileen told me our parents filed a complaint against Jamie and the hospital, along with the outcome: the lawyers read all my emails and texts where it was clear that I'd been the one who asked her to help me leave the hospital twice before and they dropped the lawsuit. Apparently if you knowingly violate hospital rules, you don't have a great case for suing the hospital, surprise, surprise.

Eileen shook her head. "It was all pretty moronic, even for Mom and Dad. They're just freaking out. They think we're going to need all this money to take care of you, but they're forgetting that we have money."

When I finally got my internet working, Jamie was the first person I tried to get in touch with. I pulled up our old threads and read through them, which only reminded me of how endless that time in the hospital felt. There's a lot of talk about the movies that I watched and the origami I was working on. Now that I've returned to my real life, that one seems surreal and almost like a dream. Did I really spend hours folding origami? *Why?*

I tried writing different notes to Jamie. The first one was casual with a general thanks.

Just wanted you to know I'm home now. Feeling okay except for having a fat face, mood swings, and Eileen around all the time complaining even more than usual. I wanted to say thank you for everything and sorry about my lame-o parents. Nothing was your fault!

I never sent that one because I knew what my parents had done deserved a bigger apology. A few days later, I wrote a different note.

I've been home for a little while now, wanting to get in touch with you, but I haven't been sure what to say. I have a feeling there's a whole story I don't remember very much of. I'm worried that you got blamed for things that weren't your fault, like me insisting that I had to leave the hospital or I'd go crazy. I told my parents none of that was your idea. No one in my family still blames you for anything. You were a good friend when I needed one. I wish I could repay you somehow, but I have a feeling that staying out of your life might be the most helpful thing I can do at this point.

I waited a day before deleting that message.

Maybe I was taking it all too seriously, I decided. She's probably moved on and put the whole episode behind her.

In the end, I took the coward's way out. Afraid of saying the wrong thing, I never wrote her at all.

Instead, I've been concentrating all my new moody energy on making things right with Sharon. She told me she was "confused and hurt" that I never asked for her help leaving the hospital.

"Did you think I would never break the rules? That I'm too much of a goody-goody?"

No, I wanted to tell her. *I knew you'd never break the rules.*

I told her, "Jamie knew that hospital inside and out. I wanted to ask you, but I knew we would've gotten caught, and I didn't want to get you in trouble, baby."

All things considered, Sharon and I have actually been doing surprisingly well. Much better than we were last summer when she worked ten-hour days at her mother's real estate office and I sat around all afternoon and evening waiting for her texts. I remember feeling panicky back then that she was going to break up with me and less panicky this fall when she didn't visit for days on end. *Maybe it's for the best*, I actually thought, when I was in the hospital, watching Jamie's movies and folding origami. *I'll see Sharon later, when I'm better.*

I was right, as it turns out. In the three months since I got home from the hospital, Sharon's been stopping by every afternoon on her way home from school. Sometimes she'll bring me funny things, like a terrible oatmeal cookie from the cafeteria. Last week she brought a flyer the student council had just put out.

"Here's what a bad job we're doing without you," she said, pointing to a typo. "This is why we need you back."

Technically, I was supposed to wait five months before doing anything strenuous like go back to school. "Four months, give or take," the doctor said.

"Could I give or take a month if I'm feeling okay?"

"A week maybe," he said. "And small doses at first. Go to school for an hour. Believe me, that'll be enough."

He was right. I haven't even been to a class, and I'm wiped out. Sharon picked me up an hour ago so I could come for lunch and make the cafeteria announcement about senior-week activities, and, already, I'm exhausted. Lunch isn't even over yet, and I've talked to more people in the last thirty minutes than I have in the past four months. Most of the conversations are two seconds long.

"Great to see you, man."

"You look amazing."

"We've all been rooting for you."

Everyone is so nice that I worry I'm going to lose it. This is what happens when you can't control your moods. Someone says, "You look good," and your mouth wants to say, "Fuck you, I'm fat and I've got acne I never had in puberty. I look terrible." Your brain doesn't consider the wisdom of saying something like that out loud. Instead of a man with an ice pick in my chest, I have a drunk, angry stranger in my head.

Smile, I tell myself. *Don't worry if you talk to people you don't care about for a long time and hardly at all to people you do care about. Just get through this. There'll be time.*

By the end of lunch, I feel like I've been here for six hours. How do people do this all day long—talking and smiling and not saying anything *real* at all?

It's completely exhausting.

I keep signaling to Sharon, who doesn't register what I'm saying. When I finally catch her eye, I point to my wrist, which of course has no watch, just the medical alert bracelet I'll have to wear for the rest of my life declaring that my body contains transplanted organs.

Sharon smiles and waves back like I'm saying, *Isn't this*

fun? She even mouths, "I told you."

I try to remember what she said: That people would be happy to see me? That everyone would clap? I don't know if I'm just having a mood swing, but to me, it doesn't seem hard to get a round of applause if you've spent time in a coma and almost died several times since the last time you've seen these people. In ninth grade, Jeremiah, a mean boy no one liked, got hit by a car and when he finally came back to school with his leg in a cast, everyone politely stood up and clapped. It's an automatic response. I wonder if I should explain this to Sharon when she says, "See? Everyone is so happy to see you." I'll remind her of Jeremiah, universally loathed until his brush with death got him a standing O. Maybe I'll also point out that I didn't even get that—just a lot of foot stamping and noise, the same as a dropped tray or a food fight might get.

I keep smiling back at the people who walk up to me. I don't want to be in a bad mood when everyone is being so nice. It's not that hard to say, "It's great to see you, too." Which is what I say to everyone who files by me and touches my shoulder or shakes my hand.

Then one voice makes me look up.

"I can't believe how different you look."

It's Jamie. The sun is behind her, so it's hard to see her face.

"I mean, good. You look good."

I remind myself to breathe. This is what happens when you get new lungs. You can never be sure they'll work when you need them. But they always do. They work perfectly. I breathe in and breathe out.

"Jamie," I say, and hold out my hand. I need to say something more so she knows that seeing her again is different for me than seeing all these other people. She deserves more than "thank you," and I never even told her that much.

She looks down at my hand and doesn't take it. Instead, she steps backward. "I should go," she says.

Say something, the angry voice in my head screams. *Say something, you moron. Tell her none of these people were as good a friend to you in the hospital as she was.*

My mouth opens, but nothing comes out.

I can't even manage one of the throwaway lines that I'm giving everyone else. "We should catch up," or "Text you later."

I don't understand this.

I sit with my hand outstretched, untaken, and I stare into her eyes and say nothing at all.

Hannah barrels up behind her and throws her arms around my neck. "I've got some great news! We're throwing you a party! It's going to be at Suze's on Friday, and it's in honor of you, which means you're not allowed to back out last minute. That's why I'm telling you now, so you can sleep and do whatever. But you have to come, okay? Say, 'Yes, Hannah, I'll be there.'"

"Yes, Hannah," I hear myself say, even though I can't stop staring at Jamie. "I'll be there."

"Perfect! See? It's not that hard."

In the course of this thirty-second exchange, Hannah

has touched me more than I remember Jamie and I touching in our whole hospital friendship. She's taken the hand I was holding out for Jamie, ruffled my hair, squeezed my neck, and kissed my cheek.

It's enough for Jamie to shake her head and walk away.

What is the matter with me? I can breathe better now than I have in ten years, and I can't exhale a few kind words for someone who actually means something to me?

When Sharon comes over and whispers in my ear, "Isn't this nice? Don't you want to stick around for the afternoon and come to the student council meeting?" a black anger has already boiled up in my chest. I can taste it in the back of my mouth.

"Fuck no," I say. "I need to go home."

To really make my point, I start walking toward the parking lot, but then I remember I need a ride from Sharon because of course I'm not well enough to drive my own car yet.

JAMIE

Well that was a mistake. I have so much trouble measuring the size and proportion of my social missteps that I don't let myself think about this one until I get home that afternoon and then I feel so icky about the whole thing I have to take a twenty-minute shower to wash the feeling away.

When I get out, I feel a little better. I stare at my face in the circle I've wiped clean in the mirror. *That wasn't your fault*, I tell myself.

It's taken me a long time to say this and mean it. None of it was easy, and nothing happened quickly.

It took a long time for the new dosage of medication to feel like it was working. Before it did, this depression felt different and scarier than the one after my dad died. This time it was even more physical. I felt it in my bones and in the back of my neck. In the mornings it was a vertigo that made it impossible to get out of bed. It also felt—at times—like I was just plain crazy. More than depressed, I was delusional. I kept thinking David was in the room with me or hovering somewhere, just outside my window. Like he was in the air around me, watching me fall apart.

I only told my mom once, "I hear his voice sometimes. Like he's here, talking to me."

"He's not, sweetheart. That's your brain playing tricks. I had the same thing with your dad. Memories surface, and you feel like they're real."

These weren't memories, though. If I held my breath and listened carefully, I could hear snippets of what he was saying, and they weren't things we'd already talked about.

It was impossible to put it all in perspective. The best I could do was be as honest with Rita as I could possibly be, and the rest of the time, put David out of my thoughts. It's taken months of seeing Rita twice a week for an hour and going over the facts—or at least my interpretation of the facts—to settle on what is probably the truest version of what happened.

I am, according to Rita, an "unusually mature tenth grader" who stumbled into a friendship with an older boy at a crossroads in his own life. We connected on topics most teens don't grapple with. Because it felt real and powerful at the time, he convinced me to help him take risks he shouldn't have. Just because my judgment is "usually quite good" (Rita's words, not mine), that doesn't mean I'm not still a fifteen-year-old capable of making mistakes.

"Your friendship wasn't a mistake, your actions were," Rita says. "Important distinction."

My mom also helped.

"Let's make a list of everything you think you've done wrong, so we can put it all in some perspective," she suggested at the end of my second week seeing Rita again.

The list was easy at first: "I broke hospital rules. I endangered David's health. I pretended I was on dates with someone else's boyfriend. I liked pretending that, and I indulged in imagining that he liked me back. I never gave Bethany or the other girls much of a chance to be friends again. I once loved art but don't do it anymore because I'm scared it will make me sad. I've gotten sad again and can't stop it."

"It's a good list, sweetheart," my mom said, writing it all down. "Now, let's go over it and see what's fair and what isn't."

The more I thought about it, the more surprised I was at how badly the second to last one made me feel: not making art. After spending two weeks at home, Rita asked me a surprising question: "Is there something you wanted to do at school but didn't get a chance?"

I thought about the art room. About the nice teacher

saying he'd consider letting me work there after school. "Maybe," I said.

About two weeks after David's surgery, and after two weeks of sessions with Rita, my mother was clear—she wanted me to go back to school. She couldn't take more time off from work, and she didn't want me home alone. "I think you'll be okay this time," she said. She sounded sure of herself, even if she wasn't.

She reminded me that I'd always held it together in school pretty well. I wanted to tell her that was part of the problem. I didn't fall apart right after my dad died; I fell apart seven months later. Seven months after I first told my best friends that he'd died of a heart attack.

At the time, it seemed like an easy lie to tell. What my friends knew of my dad didn't fit the other picture. They all thought he was funny and cooler than most dads. Bethany always said I was lucky, having the parents I had.

"I wish my dad was an artist," she said.

After he died, I had come back to school in a state of hyperawareness. My skin prickled with self-consciousness. *Everyone knows*, I thought. *Everyone is watching me.* Bethany hugged me with tears in her eyes. "It's so unfair. Your dad was so awesome."

The prickling sensation turned into a hot wave through my body. "Yeah," I said. "There wasn't much we could do. That's what happens with heart attacks."

At lunch that day, I told the lie again. Only Missy cocked her head, looking skeptical. "Really?" she said.

"Yes," I said. "He had an undiagnosed heart condition."

I expected the lie to bring me relief from the awful feeling that I was being watched all the time. It didn't. I still wonder how things would have been different if I'd told them the truth. If I'd found a way to say "My dad killed himself," maybe I would have figured out how to understand it all better. As it was, the secret became a black hole I fell into.

I started saying things that didn't make sense. I talked about him too much, mostly about his old success. I told people I couldn't get together on weekends because we were putting together a retrospective show of his work. I lied about the show for months, until finally I had to pretend that it had happened and had gone really well.

After that, I had no excuses. I had to go to Missy's house for the boy-girl party. It was the first time I'd been to her house, and I couldn't get over how phony everything seemed. Bowls of plastic grapes next to potted plastic plants. Even the sofas looked fake to me, which made no sense.

A few weekends later, Missy invited us all back. I said nothing the whole night until I couldn't stand it anymore, and then I screamed at all of them. "You guys are so phony. . . . You don't understand anything. . . . You think we're all friends but we're *not*. . . ."

I rode my bike home in the middle of the night.

There was only one week of school after that. A messy week of silence and finals and eating lunch by myself in the school library. At the end of the last day of school, I sat on a nearly empty school bus and watched my friends pile into Missy's mother's car. In that moment, it seemed like maybe Bethany had been right. It was better to have a big group of bad friends than no friends at all.

I'd made a terrible mistake, I thought. I'd destroyed my own life. I was no different than my father, self-destructive in ways I didn't understand. I had no summer plans. No money for arts camps or even supplies to carry me through the next two empty months. I remembered the pills I'd found months earlier in my father's basement studio: prescription sleeping pills, fourteen left. I didn't know what I was saving them for, and then suddenly I did.

I didn't take the whole bottle. I only took four in the distorted logic that I'd save some for next time, in case this didn't work. It didn't work because within ten minutes of swallowing the pills, I called my mother in a panic, and told her what I'd done. In the ER, they made me drink a terrible-tasting charcoal liquid so they wouldn't have to pump my stomach. The doctor said I had to spend thirty-six hours on the psych floor under mandatory observation.

In the end, I was in the hospital for three weeks. When I got out, I spent the rest of the summer in my mother's constant company: at the hospital, at home, watching old movies. Having spent so much time with my dad growing up, it was nice to learn new things about my mom. She once dated a woman named Georgia. She once thought she didn't want to get married and have kids.

"Why not?" I asked.

"I thought it would make me too vulnerable to getting

hurt. Now look at me. Here I am, a puddle of pain. The most vulnerable human being in the world." She smiled as she said these things and squeezed my hand so it was clear—she was half joking, half not.

When I came back to school this time, after David's surgery, the first person I talked to was Bethany.

"Are you okay?" she said softly.

"Sort of," I said. I was surprised—I didn't feel so vulnerable, or so confused. "I had another bad patch for a while, but now—" I look around. "Well, I'm here again."

She gave me a hug, which surprised me so much I started to cry. Then I stopped myself and said, "Thank you, Bethany. That's all. Just thanks."

I walked up to David today because I wanted him to know that I was happy to see him well. I also wanted this much to be clear: I never wished he would stay in the hospital or get sicker. Of course, maybe I was hoping for more. Maybe in the back of my stupid mind, I thought he might say, *Jamie! I've been watching a bunch of Hitchcock movies! I want to talk to you about them.* Maybe I wanted some acknowledgment that our hospital friendship might not survive the fluorescent glare of our school status differences but still, we could say, *I remember it all. It was real to me too.*

But no.

He looked up from his chair, said "Jamie" once, and nothing more. Yes, he held his hand out, but I don't really count that. He did the same thing the first day I met him in his hospital room after he'd gotten his pain medication.

I could have even said, *We've held hands when it meant something. I don't want to do it now, in front of all these people, when it obviously doesn't.*

Now that I'm home again, I've tried to shower all these thoughts away. We were friends—more than friends, really, I know we were—but we're not anymore.

I started eating lunch again with Missy and the other girls because Bethany asked me to and I have to admit, it hasn't been awful. I've even learned a few things in the last few months that have made these girls seem more interesting than I once thought. Nicki wants to get her GED at the end of this year and start taking classes at the community college where my mom got her nursing degree. She says she wants to become a physical therapist, so why waste time sitting around high school . . . ? She leaves the rest of the sentence unspoken: being miserable. Or: feeling bad about herself. For the first time, I remember Nicki coming to my defense that night at Missy's house. Not in any big way, but quietly, from the corner. I remember her saying, "She's got a point, Missy."

Hearing her plan made me happy. She already knows what I need to remember: *We aren't going to be here forever. There'll be a life after high school, where girls like us will be able to follow our interests and have a better time.*

I also kind of like the new girls who've joined us. They aren't the silent Missy minions I assumed they were from afar. One, named Mary Ann, is actually very funny. She transferred from Catholic school at the start of this year, she told me. "That's why all my clothes are new. I've been wearing a uniform for years. It turns out getting dressed every morning is *hard*."

I laughed because I knew exactly what she meant and felt the same way when I started eighth grade after so many years of homeschooling. Some nights I spent an hour figuring out what to wear when it shouldn't have been complicated because I always ended up with jeans and a T-shirt. I remember thinking: *The possibilities make it harder.* I had funkier clothes I'd bought with my dad, but did I dare try for a scarf or a skirt tiered with mirrored chips? Did I dare be myself and wear clothes I loved but couldn't explain?

Mary Ann seemed stuck in the same conundrum: "I have this whole funny T-shirt collection, but I'm not sure this school is ready for it."

I told her if she wore one of her T-shirts, I'd wear my scarf that looks like a tablecloth and, surprise, surprise, we both did! Hers was a math-nerd joke: *Dear X, Forget finding Y. She's not coming back.* When we saw each other we both laughed and flashed a thumbs-up.

I realize wearing a scarf isn't a giant achievement, but it's not nothing, either.

Now David has been back for a week, and I've had the funny feeling that maybe Eileen wants to say something to me. I've caught her looking at me in class, though not for long. When I catch her eye, she quickly looks away, but I can't tell if it's anger or regret that's fueling these looks.

Even though David said she wanted to go, neither of us

has been back to dance class at Starlight. I've tried to tell her how sorry I was a few times, but the closest she's come to acknowledging me or the friendship I thought we had was when we were alone in the hall and she said, "I can't really talk to you. I'm not allowed."

As far as I understood, the lawsuit was over but maybe that wasn't the issue. She walked away too quickly for me to say any more. I've thought about writing her an email or a text, but how can I possibly express my regret in a handful of words? I know that she sometimes made fun of her brother, but I also know that she loved him and depended on him more than anyone else—even, in many ways, her parents. I know this because he felt the same way about her.

They might not have seemed close to outsiders, but they were. What I did with David scared her, more than any of her own risky stunts. If I tried to explain—we thought we were being careful, we brought his oxygen— none of it would matter against the simple fact that she almost lost him.

She was standing outside the art classroom the one time I thought we might speak to each other. Then she moved really quickly up the hall away from me, like she was scared that I was coming to confront her. I wanted to reassure her—*I have to be in this hallway. I'm taking classes here now.*

CHAPTER SEVENTEEN

DAVID

IT TAKES ME A week to figure it out because I don't let myself look around the school cafeteria too much. I still go into sensory overload every time I walk in—the smells, the noise, all the people. Usually I don't do too much more than grab my lunch and walk to my old table where my friends make more room for me than they technically need to because they're all still a little nervous around me.

I keep my eyes on the ground, so I won't see people staring or notice anyone whispering to their friend. "There he is. The guy who almost died."

That's why it's taken me so long to notice: Jamie is sitting with the old friends she hated.

I watch for a few days to be sure I'm right, and I am. I can even guess which one Missy is: slightly heavyset, louder than the rest, being watched by the others. The only one not watching Missy is Jamie, who eats quietly and stares into her reusable lunch bag.

How can she be sitting with girls she hates? Like so many other things these days, it makes me mad. I remember one of my favorite things about Jamie being how little she seemed to care about appearances. *I didn't say I was looking for friends, I said I don't have any. There's a difference.* Her sitting with these girls makes me sad until it occurs to me: maybe I can help, or at least make sure they appreciate Jamie. If there's one good thing about the phony popularity of an elected student council position, it means maybe I can shake up a table of wannabe, uncool tenth graders.

Before I think about it too much, I get up from my own table and walk over.

"Where are you going?" Sharon calls behind me. "If you need something I can get it."

I shake my head without answering. *No, thanks, Sharon. I'm fine.*

"Hi, girls," I say, sliding into an empty spot at the table, across from Jamie.

She looks up, surprised at first and then something else. I'm not sure what comes over me, but I know this much: Jamie is smarter, braver, and more original than all these girls combined. They need to know it. She needs to know it.

"I'm sorry to interrupt, but I just wanted to talk to Jamie for a second." I make eye contact with each of them. I save Jamie for last. It's impossible to tell what she's thinking. I used to be able to read her expressions, but I can't anymore. Apparently, in this setting, our personalities are reprogrammed. I'm only just becoming aware of this fact, with the help of my new lungs and my new lease on life.

"I didn't get a chance to thank Jamie for all her help while I was in the hospital, and I want to do it now. She is pretty incredible. I don't know if you guys realize that or not. She's really smart, and I don't know if you've had the chance to talk about old movies with her but you totally should. You should also watch some of her recommendations. They're awesome. No comparison to the crap we're watching today."

Judging by the silence that follows this little speech, it's possible I'm not helping her at all. It's possible I'm making her life worse.

"We like Jamie fine," Missy finally says. "There isn't any problem, so we're not sure what you're talking about."

The "we" is kind of sinister considering no one has said anything.

"Great then!" I say. "As long as you all know you're lucky to have her as a friend, I don't need to stay."

I half stand from the table, except I can't go. The angry, drunk man in my head will punch me out if I walk away now. I lean across the table so my face is inches from Jamie's ear. "I'm sorry if I've embarrassed you, Jamie, and I'm also sorry I haven't thanked you before now. I'm on a bunch of medications at the moment. They screw up my concentration and my ability to modulate my emotions. I can't seem to say what I want to these days. I'm not even sure if 'modulate' is a word. Do you know? Is 'modulate' a word?"

"Yes," she whispers. "It is."

She's mad, I'm pretty sure. I want to ask her if she'd

mind leaving this table so we could talk privately some-where, but I'm not sure where we'd go, since no place in this whole school is private, the way the hospital was. I'm also not sure she would even go. Suddenly, she seems *really* mad.

I lean even closer. I can smell her hair and peanut but-ter on her breath. I need to say something more before I walk away, but I'm not sure what it is. "Can I email you tonight?" I whisper. "Or message you. Would that be okay?"

My brain is so messed up I can't remember if we texted or emailed or what we did when we joked around online at night.

"Yes," she whispers. "But you should leave now."

Every girl at the table is staring at me. Not in a good way. They aren't impressed that the senior class president, the guy who got a round of cheering last week for being alive, has come over to endorse Jamie.

"Fine," I say, too loud. Now I'm mad, too. "I'll leave, but, Jamie, I have to say, I hope sitting here is just a tempo-rary arrangement for you. You're better than these people. Way better."

That's when I feel a hand on my back and hear Sha-ron's voice behind me. "It's time to come back to our table, David. Ashwin has something he wants to talk to you about."

I swing around and face her. The angry voice in my head is getting louder because this is what she's been doing ever since I came back to school. *It's time to go to class, David.*

Do you remember where you're going? Have you taken your pills? Remember, you don't get so cold these days. You don't really need to wear that sweater.

When your brain is wrapped in a fog like it's wearing the sweaters that Sharon keeps insisting I don't need, your first response is gratitude. Thank you for explaining what I should be doing. Thank you for updating me on cool clothing choices and my body temperatures. It's a lot to keep track of when my thoughts feel like they're trapped in Jell-O cubes these days.

All last week I thanked her. Now I say loud enough for everyone to hear, "Fuck off, Sharon. Give me a break. I'm talking to a friend for one more minute and then I'll come back."

She laughs as if this is part of some inside joke we have—her bossiness, me snapping back—but it isn't one of our jokes. She and I both know it. I've never said anything like this to her before.

She moves away with a smile still frozen on her face. I don't know what I just did or how many more enemies I want to make.

I turn back to Jamie. I realize what I've really wanted to say to her—the truth that I'm only just now unearthing from the fog and the confusion it's been hiding behind. I whisper, "I need to talk to you, Jamie. I don't remember what happened before my surgery."

She looks surprised. "You don't?"

"I remember going to the movies but nothing after that.

I know we went to the social, but after that, it's all gray."

She stares at me. "You want me . . . to tell you?"

"Not here . . . but yes. I want to know."

JAMIE

I have to wait for our movie to end before I can go online and look to see if I have a message from David. I'm not being paranoid. My mother has been very clear: I am really and truly not allowed to communicate electronically with David.

"I mean it," she said the first time she laid down the rule, in the same conversation when she told me he was recovering pretty well from his transplant and would get released to rehab soon. "Recovering from surgery like this will take all his energy. He can't have any drama in his life. He needs to concentrate on himself and not worry about anyone else, including you. I'll worry about you. And you can worry about you. But the most important thing for you to do to help his recovery is to not complicate his life. That means no emails or texts. Nothing. Understand?"

I told her I did.

For four months I haven't done anything more than scroll through Instagram updates from Sharon and his other friends, tagging pictures of him:

First walk after surgery!

First meal!

Coming home!

In most of the pictures, Sharon is by his side. Eileen is in only one, but that's also the only picture where David is laughing. She's sitting on his bed beside him, showing him something on her phone, and they're both laughing.

At eleven fifteen, when the movie is finally over and my mother is in bed, I open my laptop and find an email written at four this afternoon.

From: sheinmand@northwoods.edu
To: turnerj@northwoods.edu
Subject: You

Dear Jamie:
First of all, I'm sorry for ambushing you at your lunch table like that. I know I keep mentioning these medications I'm on, but they mess with my brain, and it's hard for me to have normal conversations. I came over there wanting to say hi to you and apologize for being so lame the first time you came up to me at school. I promise I didn't mean to yell at your friends or embarrass you the way I probably did.

I just kept thinking, these girls don't deserve to be your friend. They really don't. Not that I know them well, obviously, but I remember what you told me about them at Denny's, and I just keep thinking, "Why is Jamie sitting here pretending to like these fucking people?"

Because I have to sit somewhere, David.
Because being alone all day, every day, might seem

intriguing or romantic in your mind, but it's really not.

Of course I can't say this. I also can't say, *Because I can't figure out how to talk to Eileen.* I see he's online and IM him back:

> **ME:** Does this medicine make you swear more or something? You sound like a different person.
>
> **DAVID:** I hope I'm not a different person, but yes, it makes me edgy in a way that some people are having a little trouble with.
>
> **ME:** Like who?
>
> **DAVID:** You can probably guess.
>
> **ME:** Your parents?
>
> **DAVID:** Among others.
>
> **ME:** Sharon?
>
> **DAVID:** Yes.
>
> **ME:** Eileen?
>
> **DAVID:** No, interestingly. Eileen loves my new gutter mouth.
>
> **ME:** You shouldn't have yelled at my friends at lunch. I understand why you did, but it was embarrassing for both of us.
>
> **DAVID:** I was trying to help you. And save you from years of soul-destroying fake friendship. You're better than those girls.
>
> **ME:** Thank you for that, but it's better to let me decide these things. Some of those girls are a little toxic, but not all of them. I'm trying to change my ways and not judge everyone by association. I like some of them. You coming over and saying all that stuff made them think I'm still obsessed with something that happened last year. It also made them think I've been talking about it with everyone, which isn't true.

DAVID: You're right. I'm sorry. Have I mentioned this medication makes me do crazy things?
ME: Yes.

Neither one of us types anything for a while. I'm not sure what else to say, because nothing is simple. He says he doesn't remember what happened at the social, which means even if he says he wants to be friends the way we were in the hospital, we can't be really, because our friendship changed that night. I wanted to kiss him. I still do. Pretending I don't will never work. I'd feel hurt every time I had to watch him sit next to Sharon, which would happen every day, because she never lets him out of her sight.

I might not have much experience to draw from, but I know a no-win situation when I see one. Every time I watch him climb out of Sharon's car from my seat on the school bus, I understand that our differences are greater than whatever bonded us for six weeks. He has two months left of school. I have . . . the end of this year and two more years after that.

He's already gone, and I'm still here.

Even if he writes me charming, funny notes, I don't want to go back to the friendship we had. I don't want to wait for emails to come in. I don't want to check my phone every two minutes. I don't want to care the way I once did, when it only got me in trouble.

Even as I think all this, though, I know the real reason is scarier and hard for me to consider. I don't want to go back to that place where I cared about him so much I wanted to die.

> **ME:** So how are you doing? Is it nice to have new lungs?
> **DAVID:** It's great and strange and overwhelming and scary. It's a lot of things at once.
> **ME:** Why scary?
> **DAVID:** Because I keep thinking they'll stop working. It took me a month to go outside without an oxygen tank even though the doctors kept saying I didn't need one. I just didn't feel safe. I still don't, really.
> **ME:** You will. You have to push it a little so you keep surprising yourself.
> **DAVID:** Is that what you've done?
> **ME:** Actually yes. After you got so sick and all the lawyers were saying it was my fault, I got depressed again. I couldn't go to school for two weeks. It was pretty bad.

This is the first time I've said this to anyone besides Rita or my mom. Not that I was depressed (I've told Bethany and my new friend, MaryAnn, at school), but that I feel okay now. Like maybe that episode might be behind me. I know my depression won't go away. It's a matter of containing the episodes. Saying this helps me feel like I've done that with this one.

> **DAVID:** I know. I'm so sorry about all that. None of it was your fault. My parents never should have hired that lawyer. They're worried that my expenses will keep going up and

we'll need money. It's not a good excuse, but that's the only one they have.

ME: It's not a terrible excuse. It sucks sometimes, having no money. And worrying about it.

DAVID: Did your mom have to spend money hiring a lawyer?

ME: No. It got dropped pretty quickly when they read our threads.

DAVID: Did they ever apologize to you?

ME: No, but that's okay. They need to think about protecting you. I understand that.

DAVID: They have no clue what I really need, though. They still think I should go to college next year.

I think about how much school he missed.

ME: Are you still graduating on time?

DAVID: Yeah. It turns out I almost had enough credits to graduate at the end of last year. Weird but true. You don't need as many as you think.

I already know this from hearing Mary Ann's plans to graduate early. It's a good option to keep in the back of my mind.

ME: What will you do next? Do you know yet?

DAVID: Turns out my parents sent my college applications in while I was sick.

ME: Didn't they know you wanted to wait a year?

DAVID: They thought I shouldn't limit my options.

I remember how determined he seemed about waiting on college and "charting his own path." It seems a little sad that he's forgotten that now.

ME: Have you heard back yet?

DAVID: Yes. I got in everywhere. I guess being in a coma gets you points with the admissions people.

ME: Wow. Do you know where you'll go?

DAVID: Sometimes I feel like starting a big trash can fire at school so I'll get expelled and I won't have to go anywhere. I'm telling you, these mood swings are intense.

ME: I should probably go. My mom really doesn't want me messaging with you. She thinks you need to concentrate on getting well and you shouldn't worry or feel guilty about me.

DAVID: Funny. I don't feel guilty about you. Should I?

ME: No. That's exactly her point. You shouldn't.

DAVID: Mostly what I feel is that I miss our chats. Is it okay to feel that?

ME: Probably not, since I'm not supposed to chat with you.

DAVID: Does she check your phone?

ME: No.

DAVID: So maybe texting is okay once in a while.

ME: Maybe.

DAVID: Can I ask you one more question?

ME: Okay.

DAVID: What happened that night we went to the social?

ME: You got really sick. It was terrible and scary.

DAVID: But what about before. Did we have a good time?

DAVID

She doesn't answer for a while. Finally, she types, *I really have to go*, and signs off.

That night I have a dream where I'm wandering around the hospital, trying to talk to people who can't hear what I'm saying. I scream to make my point, and they look right through me. I'm not sure why it's so terrifying, but it is. I wake up in a sweat.

I know it'll be hours before I fall back asleep. I go to the kitchen and stand in the dark, trying to remember what I came in here for. Eileen turns on the light and screams. "Oh my God! Were you standing here, waiting to scare me?"

I don't tell her *No, I'm standing here because I forgot why I came in*. That's another thing that happens with these medications. You can't sleep, and you can't remember anything. You stand in dark rooms, trying to remember why you walked in.

"Yeah Lee-lee, I've been standing here for three hours waiting to scare you. It was worth it, right?"

"Shut up."

She opens the fridge to take out a yogurt and unpeels the lid.

"So why *were* you standing here?"

"I don't know. I don't remember. I'm losing my mind, maybe."

"Too late. You already did that today when you screamed at those girls in front of everybody."

Oh God, I think. I was hoping only a few tables around us noticed. It's bad news if Eileen has heard about it. "Is that what it looked like?"

"That's what it *was*. Senior class president yells at random table of tenth-grade girls. No one's sure why."

"They were being mean to Jamie. If you knew the whole story, you'd say I was right."

"Now suddenly you're friends with Jamie again? I don't get it."

I know why she's saying this. I don't get it, either. For three months I've been home and recuperating—plenty of time to get in touch with Jamie—and I never did. Instead, I focused all my energy on Sharon.

"I never stopped being friends with her."

"Yes, you did. What you did was sort of the definition of not being friends with someone. You never even wrote her to tell her you were out of the hospital."

"I know. It was complicated. But I told her I'm sorry. That's what I was doing at her table today. Why were you even watching us? Don't you usually sit across the cafeteria?"

"Not anymore."

"What do you mean? Why not?"

"Because my friends are idiots, and I hate them. But I have to tell you, you're the bigger idiot. You don't see anything."

"What do you mean?"

"Never mind. Just—never mind." She's only eaten a few bites of the yogurt, but she opens the trash can and drops it in.

"No, tell me. It's like ever since I got home you've been avoiding me, and I don't get it. You're mad at me, but I don't see what I've done to you."

I can tell she doesn't want to have this conversation. She's already at the door when she spins around. "I'm not mad at you!! I feel sorry for you! You don't see what's going on!"

"Like what? What am I not seeing?"

"Like Sharon isn't really your girlfriend! She's been going out with someone else for months! Since last summer, at least."

I gasp. This is one of those times where I expect my lungs to fail me. I wait for the coughing to start, or the constriction in my chest to get so bad I have to sit down until the room stops spinning. It doesn't happen. I keep breathing in and out.

"What are you talking about? Who is she going out with?" This makes no sense. After my operation, Sharon visited me every day, for at least an hour, sometimes more. Since I went back to school, she spends all her free time making sure I'm okay. If anything, she pays *too* much attention to me.

Eileen hesitates. It's obvious she doesn't want to tell me. "Nicolai."

"Nicolai?"

I think back to the end of our dancing-school days. After the one episode where I had to sit out most of the night, Sharon went to one lesson without me. I remember her saying she didn't like being there by herself, and a few days later, she said we shouldn't take classes anymore. That it didn't make sense when we had so many other responsibilities.

I remember saying, "We've always been busy, and it doesn't take that much time." I wanted to keep going; she didn't.

"It just seems silly to me now," she said. And that was it.

I ask my sister, "How do you know this?"

"They were at that party I went to in August. She didn't see me. I was hiding in the pantry while they were in the kitchen making out."

The room starts to spin, but it doesn't have anything to do with my oxygen levels. "Why didn't you *tell* me?"

"You were sick all summer. I could tell something weird was happening. What was I supposed to say: 'Sorry your lungs suck and, plus, you have this other problem you don't even know about yet'?"

She's right. Last summer was pretty bad for me. I think back to when I waited for Sharon's calls and she apologized every day for working so much. I don't know why this possibility never occurred to me.

"Who else knows?"

She shrugs. "A few people. She's not that careful. You haven't been able to go to a party for a long time, so I think she meets him at those and pretends it's a coincidence."

For a long time, I sit, breathing in and out.

"I didn't want to tell you. That's why I agreed to go to Starlight. I wanted to find him and tell him to leave Sharon alone until the end of the school year."

It takes me a minute to understand what she's saying. "So in case I didn't make it, I could die thinking Sharon and I were fine?"

"Well—I mean, you were really sick, and everyone kept saying you wouldn't handle a breakup very well."

"Is she still going out with him?"

Eileen doesn't want to answer, which should be answer enough, but I want to hear her tell me the truth.

"When you talked to Nick, what did he say?"

"That he loves Sharon and he won't stop seeing her. He was pretty dramatic about it. He said he's loved her for a long time."

I think back to the kids we once were, inexperienced and awkward, equally dazzled by the new girl from Texas who arrived with new moves we'd never seen before. Geography was on my side—Nick went to the high school across town—but time was on his. Apparently, he's been working this whole time to win her away from me.

I can't sleep after this, so I spend the rest of the night stalking everyone's Instagram feeds for picture proof. Pathetically enough, it's not hard to find. He's in a few of the summer pictures of our group hanging out at cookouts and pool parties I didn't go to. There's Nick floating on a raft in one and standing behind a grill in another. By the fall, I see him in the corner of a homecoming dance picture.

It's one o'clock in the morning, and I feel like the biggest loser on earth.

For an hour I feel sad and then, almost without any warning, I'm furious. WHY DIDN'T ANYONE TELL ME? I'm angry at Sharon, of course, but also with everyone else. I don't know how much they know or just sensed, but it makes every friendship I have feel even phonier than it did four months ago. Why did I get out of surgery and think the most important thing I had to do was get back to school and all my class president responsibilities as soon as possible?

It's two thirty when I finally turn my phone off. For the first time in months I wish I had a nebulizer treatment or a vest session to get through. Those used to calm me down when Sharon had done or said something that made me mad. The buzzing/breathing combination always soothed my nerves. Which now makes me wonder: Did some part of me know the truth all along?

Eileen asks if she can get a ride with me to school in the morning. I can tell she feels bad.

"If it makes you feel any better, I hate Sharon, and I haven't spoken to her once in over six months. Even if she says hi, I don't say hi back. It's a point of pride."

"That doesn't make me feel better, sorry. I mean thanks,

but this is kind of my whole life that sucks right now."

She makes a face. "Should I not have told you? Would it have been better to not know and get through prom and graduation and then find out the truth and break up?"

I haven't thought about prom. Weirdly, I haven't thought about breaking up, either. For this whole sleepless, horrible night, I've assumed it's already happened. That I'll get to school and Sharon will know that I know and we'll never talk about it and never talk again except when we have to for public events like, well, everything coming up over the next two months.

"I don't know," I say honestly. "It would have been easier not to know."

Eileen gives me one of her sideways looks. "But would it have been *better*?"

"No. I guess not."

Suddenly, it feels like I don't have any real friends. I have a bunch of people who like the idea that we're all friends—that we're all headed to great schools and we'll always be close—but none of it is true, really. We don't know each other very well. We're not there for each other when it matters. I hate realizing this. I don't like hating all these people. "I don't know what to think about my old friends."

"How about this? Who *has* been a good friend?" Eileen says.

"What do you mean?"

"Think about it. Who was a good friend while you were in the hospital?"

"You know the answer to that. Jamie."

"Right."

"What are you saying? That I should go sit with her friends at lunch today?"

"You should think about the things you did with her. Like the origami and the old movies. You kept saying you wanted Jamie and me to be friends, but I think you're the one who really liked her and wanted to be her friend. Maybe you wanted to be more than friends and you didn't want to admit it."

I remember this thought crossing my mind, but I never let it linger for long. She was too young, I told myself. I had Sharon; the situation was too complicated. "She's in *tenth grade*, Eileen."

"Yeah, but she doesn't act like it. I don't know what you'd call her. An old soul or something. She's also a pretty good dancer. A lot of guys really liked her in class. She probably got asked to dance more than I did. I know, shockingly hard to believe, but true."

Suddenly, I'm flashing on a memory. Or a dream maybe. Where she and I are dancing. "Do you think I danced with her when we went to the social?"

She stares at me. "Do you seriously not remember?"

"None of it. I don't remember asking her to take me there, or any of it. Did she tell you what happened?"

"No, of course not. She doesn't talk to me because our family is so screwed-up."

"You haven't talked to her this whole time?"

"No. I assumed she hates all of us. Then I saw her go up

to you that day you came back and I watched your freaky little scene with her friends and I thought, wait a minute here. I wonder if David needs a little help getting in touch with some of his feelings."

"Shut up. You're the freaky one."

"Fine, you're right. That was completely normal, you going over to her lunch table and telling all her friends they should love her because you do."

"That's not what I *said*."

"Yeah, sorry, but it kind of was. 'You should watch old movies with her sometime'? I think what you meant was 'I want to watch old movies with her again.' Even though I'm not sure there's any left that you haven't watched."

This is kind of crazy what she's saying, and it's also kind of not. I did love watching old movies with Jamie. It was by far the best part of my hospital stay, but I never thought of her as more than my hospital friend, did I?

"We were friends, Lee-lee. That's it. Apparently, I needed friends, and I didn't even realize it."

"Yeah, so if this never occurred to you, why did you ask her to take you to the social?"

I don't know the answer to this. I really don't. I remember being in the hospital and hearing the Smile Awhile cart in the hall and always hoping it was Jamie. I remember when she started stopping by more often, on her way to have dinner with her mom. I remember messaging her and laughing at night over things she wrote. I remember getting closer and talking about what I wanted to do with my life if it was going to be over soon. I remember feeling thankful that those conversations didn't freak her out.

We pull into the school parking lot. Eileen gets ready to fly out of the car as soon as it stops. "Look, all I'm saying is, you should think about it. But don't screw with her head. Our family has already freaked her out enough."

With that she's gone.

I look up and see Sharon's blue Elantra pull into a space ahead of me. She toots her horn and waves, but she doesn't get out of her car. She must be reading a message on her phone, because she's looking down and laughing even though she's alone in the car.

It's strange, though—even as I wonder if she's texting with Nick, I also realize that I really don't care if she is.

CHAPTER EIGHTEEN

DAVID

I DON'T KNOW WHY IT'S taken me all this time to see it and remember. I also don't know why *Eileen* had to remind me of everything Jamie and I wrote to each other. I know. I reread it all after my surgery. But I go back and read it again. And the more I read, the better I remember everything. How funny she was. And honest. How I could tell her what I was really thinking. How she was the only person I could do that with.

Maybe I was scared to look too closely, afraid I would discover someone I liked more than my supposed girlfriend, but it's as if getting new lungs returned me to the person I was before I got so sick. But that's not who I want to be. I know that statistically I've extended my life, but not by that much. Five years, maybe. Ten if I'm lucky. Eileen is right. I don't want to waste another minute pretending. I want to know the scary bottomless, crazy feeling of real.

I read through the messages I wrote with Jamie and I

think, *This is the person I want to be for whatever time I have left with these lungs.*

I ask Sharon to meet me at morning break. She's studying for a quiz this afternoon in AP Spanish. Our grades don't matter anymore, and still she's got index cards with vocabulary on them that she's shuffling through.

"Why didn't you tell me about Nick?" I say.

She looks up from her cards. "What do you mean? Who told you? No one knows except Hannah, and she swore—"

"It doesn't matter who told me."

"We broke up after your surgery. I swear. I told him it was wrong—" There are tears in her eyes. I'm not sure who they're for.

"Maybe you shouldn't have. Maybe you've wanted to break up with me for a long time and you just didn't know how, especially after I got so sick."

The tears spill over and run down her cheeks. I realize— in the years I've known her, I've never seen her cry.

"I don't know what I wanted. I still don't," she says.

"Maybe we're both in the same boat. Maybe we have to figure this out by ourselves."

She looks away. "It's impossible to imagine going to prom without you. Everyone will be so confused."

I can't help laughing. Is this really her first thought? What everyone thinks? "Why don't we not worry about what other people think and do what we want? Do you want to go to prom with Nick?"

"I don't know anymore. What do you want?"

"I definitely don't want to go to prom with Nick."

She laughs a little.

"I think we've both been afraid of being alone and maybe we shouldn't be so scared of that."

She narrows her eyes. "Are you having a weird medication mood swing?"

"Not at all. It's like my brain is finally clear. I feel like I pushed us to stay together because I was scared of looking too closely at my own life. I shouldn't have done that, and I'm sorry. Now we can stop all that. We're free."

It feels great, I have to admit.

I think this was Eileen's point all along. A little rebellion doesn't have to be scary. It can also be freeing. My new exuberant mood is only shadowed by the fact that I haven't seen Jamie all morning. I keep expecting to catch a glimpse of her in the hallway. I'm ready to run over, grab her by the hand, and tell her we need to talk.

At lunch I ask her sullen-faced lunch table if they know where Jamie is, and none of them do. She's not responding to texts, and Eileen hasn't seen her since first-period life science.

"Did she say anything to you?"

Eileen rolls her eyes. "We don't talk, remember?"

Oh, right.

The secretaries in the main office let me look up Jamie's locker number and schedule, which surprises me at first, and then I remember, as student council president, I'm given certain privileges like this. I'm tardy to all my own classes because I spend all afternoon walking back and forth to Jamie's locker.

I need to talk to you, I text. *Did you leave school or something? I can't find you.*

I get a little frantic.

This is what happens when you realize what you want in life and you're also taking thirteen different mood-affecting medications. Everything is heightened.

I need to find her.

I check my phone every thirty seconds. Nothing.

When the final bell for the day rings, I stand next to her locker for twenty minutes. "Who doesn't come to their locker at the end of the day?" I ask Eileen, who has apparently missed her bus and needs a ride, because she's appeared out of nowhere and is standing beside me, reading her phone.

"You need professional help," she says, rolling her eyes, forgetting that I do see a psychiatrist once a week. "Two days ago, you were all, 'I have to make this work with Sharon.' Why don't you give your love life a rest for a while? Calm down a little."

"Because I can't. When you don't have as much time as other people, taking time off doesn't make a lot of sense, okay? I need to find her."

Even I'm surprised by how frantic I sound. It's like I'm back in my dream, wandering the hospital corridors, only this time people can hear me, thank God. Maybe I am losing my mind, but I want Eileen to understand why.

"When I got so close to dying, it's like everything was clear—who I was and what I wanted. The person I wanted to be with. Then I woke up and I forgot all of it. I went back to my little cocoon of safety. I don't want to do that anymore. I don't want to be scared of having something real. And I don't want to wait anymore. I'm sorry, I just don't."

Eileen smiles.

"Why are you smiling?"

"You sound like me."

"No, I don't. I'm not that crazy."

"You know you do. It's like you're trying to sound like me, but usually I'm acting, and you really mean it."

"I do really mean it. Maybe you've been right about a few things."

"I'm right about everything." She's really smiling now. "Just say it. You know you want to say it."

"I want to know why Jamie's not texting me back. That's what I want to know."

"I think it's because she probably has a new boyfriend."

"Shut up."

She's really laughing now. "She had enough of waiting around for you to have your little revelation. She's found someone new to fold her origami with."

"I'm begging you to shut up."

"Fine, okay. I actually saw her just now going into the art room. I guess that's where she spends most of her time these days."

"Why didn't you tell me this five minutes ago?"

"Because I like watching you freak out. Plus I was waiting for you to calm down, but obviously that's not going to happen."

"Okay, so I'm going to the art room to find her."

"Can I come and watch?"

"Absolutely not."

"If I promise not to laugh?"

I'm already running backward. "You're a terrible human being. . . ."

"That's what makes me such a great sister."

Eileen's right. Jamie's here.

My breath catches when I see her in the corner near a window, in front of a canvas that's painted in geometrically divided shades of the same color—a beautiful pale green, shaded darker in some triangles and lighter in others. Her back is to the door, so she doesn't see me. I walk in quietly so I can stand behind her and study the painting she's working on. It's simple and beautiful. At first it looks abstract and then, after a minute, I realize what it is.

"A piece of folded origami paper?"

She gasps and spins around. "You scared me! What are you doing here?"

I smile and stare at her wonderful face. Her beautiful brown eyes. Her freckles. "I was looking for you."

It's almost too much to take in all at once. While I was regaining bodily functions like the ability to breathe, she has started painting again. Even with an idea that's seemingly simple—painting a piece of folded paper—I can tell she's good. There is light on her mountain folds and shadows in the valleys. Almost as if the canvas has been folded, but it hasn't.

"It's a frog base, unfolded."

"Really?" My eyebrows go up. "Isn't that what a geisha would give to a man to say, 'Come back'?"

She doesn't turn around and look back at me. This isn't going to be easy. She isn't painting this as a message to me.

I start over. I say, "I'm sorry to interrupt you here. I've been looking for you all day."

"What for?"

She starts painting again.

"I wanted to talk to you. About how stupid I've been, forgetting . . . what happened between us. Going to the social. All of that."

She peeks over at me. "You remember that now?"

"Not all of it. But enough, I think. We danced, right?"

"Yes."

"And then we went outside."

"Yes."

"And did I collapse right away?"

"No, you put on your cannula, and I turned the oxygen up too high. You felt great for about five minutes, and we thought everything was fine, but it wasn't."

I don't care about that part. "Did we kiss? I'm sure I wanted to. I remember wanting to, but did we do it?"

She looks away again. "Yes."

I close my eyes for a second and try to imagine it. I'm glad it happened. I'm sad I don't remember. "Was that my only chance, or is it possible you might give me another?"

She waves a hand that's covered in green paint. She

doesn't want to talk about this right now. It takes her a moment to gather her thoughts.

Finally, she turns around. "Why are you saying this when you have a girlfriend?"

"Sharon and I just broke up."

She nods and takes a deep breath. "Okay." She turns back to her painting. "I have to tell you, these last four months have been really hard for me. I felt very guilty about what happened to you, and then I had lawyers saying I *should* feel guilty, I *was* guilty." She shuts her eyes. "The only way I got through it was to go on a kind of autopilot where I don't think too much and I don't feel too much. I've told myself that if I can do that, at some point I'll wake up and high school will be almost over and I'll have survived."

"That's not really a great plan."

She spins around, her eyes flashing. "Yes it *is*, David. It's the only plan that will work for me. I can't kill myself, because that would destroy my mother. This is the only way I can think of to not want to die most of the time."

"I don't think you could be painting like that if you wanted to die."

"Don't, David. Don't come in and say you're so happy to be alive and everyone else should feel the same way. It's not really fair."

"I'm not saying that."

"What are you saying?"

"I'm saying that I stayed with Sharon for way too long because I was scared that if I met someone who I really connected with, being sick would be ten times harder and dying would be unbearable. Then I met that person, and it happened, and I figured out that it didn't make my life scarier or worse. Being with you made my life easier."

"Because I said you should forget college and watch movies and do origami instead?"

"No. Because you write your own rules. You make decisions for yourself. Most people never do that. They're too scared to take a risk. They've never done it. It's not easy, carving out your own path. Just ask Eileen, she's carved out fifteen of them."

She laughs like she's grateful to change the subject. "How is Eileen?"

"She's okay. I think she'd like to be friends with you again. She feels terrible about what our parents did. We both do."

"That wasn't her fault. Or yours."

"Still. She's not as ridiculous as she seems sometimes. She helped me see a few things."

"I never thought she was ridiculous."

"It turns out she did all that stuff with Nicolai because Sharon's been secretly dating him for a while and she wanted to get him to stop seeing her. Even though she hates Sharon, she wanted me to think I still had my girl-friend while I was dying."

"That's weird but nice."

"Exactly. 'Weird but nice' is the right description. Now she's saying I should forget about all that and go out with you."

"She *said* that?" Jamie's obviously surprised.

"Yeah. She was never really mad at you for getting her in trouble. She felt bad about a bunch of things and didn't know what to say to you."

JAMIE

Eileen *doesn't* hate me? Is that even possible? For some reason this is easier for me to wrap my mind around than David standing here saying he wants to kiss me again. The second thing is terrifying and real. The first is a relief. I liked Eileen, and I wanted to be friends with her. I thought she wanted to be friends with me, too. Realizing I was wrong about that made me feel like I was wrong about a lot of things.

"I'd like to be friends with her," I say. "Real friends. Not friends where I'm meant to be babysitting her."

"Yeah, that was a bad idea on my part. I'm sorry about that."

He looks so different than he did in the hospital. His face is full; his curly, overgrown hair is gone. He sounds like the boy I visited every day for seven weeks, but he doesn't look like him. It scares me to imagine him saying, *Okay, yeah, let's pick up where we left off at the social. I'm pretty sure we were kissing and I was talking about breaking up with Sharon.*

Maybe that's my problem.

"Did you really break up with Sharon?"

"Yeah. I'm pretty sure both of us felt relieved."

"Sounds like you're having a busy day."

"Very busy, because I've spent most of it looking for you. I've been to your locker about eight times. Why don't you ever go there?"

"I've never figured out how to open it."

"Are you serious?"

Of course I'm serious. "Yes, David. I'm a sophomore who has never used her locker because it's embarrassing to stand in a hallway and not be able to open something for ten minutes. That's not the only embarrassing thing about me."

"Do you want to tell me the other embarrassing things?"

"Not really."

"Okay. Maybe I could help you with your locker then?"

"I don't know about that. Wouldn't everyone wonder why you're opening this random tenth grader's locker?"

"We could pretend I'm conducting a random locker search. Hopefully you don't have any contraband in there. No, Jamie, on second thought, let's not pretend anything. I don't care what anyone else thinks. I care what you think. I want to try going out with you. What do you think about that?"

The problem with him saying something nice like this is that he hasn't been listening to what I'm saying. He doesn't know what depression is like and how you have to think about it all the time. He doesn't have to make sure he's not alone too much and also not around people who trigger bad feelings. He doesn't understand that it's always here, waiting to sneak back into your life.

I tell him all of this. "I can't take risks, David. I just can't. That's all."

"Going out with me would be a risk?"

"Are you kidding?"

"What would be so risky? I don't understand."

"You're about to graduate and go off and start a great new life. You're a hundred times more experienced than I am in every aspect of socializing, including dating and sex, which I can hardly bring myself to say, and I certainly can't look at you when I do. No. Just no, David. You're not listening when I say I can't do this."

DAVID

She turns around and looks at me. She still looks beautiful to me, but I understand I shouldn't tell her that right now. I hold up both hands.

"Fine," I say. "But just so it's clear: I've only kissed one girl before you in my whole life, and yes, we've had sex, but not very much and we've always had towels around so we can clean up right afterward. It's always struck me as a little bit . . . not the way it's supposed to be. I wouldn't mind going back to the start and going slowly with someone . . . more right. That's it. That's all I'm saying. I'll leave you alone now."

I don't want to leave, but now that I've said this, I have to.

I walk out into the hallway and, a second later, walk back in.

"I don't want to leave on that weird, creepy note. This isn't about sex, which I'm not supposed to have. For a while anyway. Eventually, I can. This is about realizing I came close to dying and now I've got a new lease on life and I want to make some changes. That's all. That's it. I want to spend more time with people I actually like, not people I feel like I'm supposed to spend time with, okay?"

"Okay."

I haven't made a dent, I can tell. I take a step back. "So now I'm going to leave, and the last thing I'll have said will not be about sex."

"Okay."

"Okay."

CHAPTER NINETEEN

JAMIE

IT DOESN'T HELP TO obsessively replay conversations in my mind, but it also doesn't work to tell my brain not to. I spend all evening going over everything David said. With every replay, I can't help it, my armpits tingle and my heart speeds up a little.

David is still David.

I didn't imagine our connection or fabricate some bond that I wanted to believe was true. It was true. Then I remember what I wanted to say in my speech about my struggle with depression. *Sometimes people can feel a connection, but acting on that feeling isn't good for either one of them. It just isn't.* Did I say it, or did all those words get caught in my throat? I'm not sure anymore.

I'm almost sure I'm right about this. David needs to go off to college without feeling tied to anyone back here, and, more important, I need to figure out how to get through the rest of high school without getting depressed.

With an objective like that, you can't add other people into the equation. It makes you too vulnerable. They leave and then what?

I check my messages all night not because I want to see one from him but because I want to make sure I don't. *There*, I think, each time I look and find nothing there. I was right. If I'd said okay, I'd be spending all next fall doing just this: waiting for messages and texts that wouldn't come.

Over dinner, my mother asks me if I'm ready for this weekend. She was the one who pushed me into entering the same citywide art show I did in eighth grade. The one I'm working after school every day to get ready for. Six schools participate, and four students are selected from every school. I almost didn't tell my mother when Mr. Standish told me I'd been chosen. I didn't think I deserved it, for one thing. I'd only been in his class for two months, though I'd started going to his room when I first returned to school after two weeks at home. It was the only place I could think of to go after school when the hospital wasn't an option anymore.

The first day I went, I was shocked at how comfortable it felt. I'd been so scared doing art would carry me back to memories of Dad, and it did, but not in a way that made me sad. Instead, I remembered the hours we spent together: my dad squeezing paint from tubes, washing brushes, adjusting lights, and setting us up. I remember how, in the years before he became unpredictable and hard to be around, it was surprisingly easy for us to spend hours alone together working on art, not talking at all. Now that I look back on it, I can hardly believe that I had the attention span to work as long as I did without getting restless. We didn't even listen to a radio, which Mr. Standish had playing in the corner the first afternoon I stopped by.

I don't know if Mr. Standish knew anything about me or who my father was. I couldn't look him in the eye when I asked about working after school in his room. I was so nervous, I stammered.

"I'd be happy to clean up . . . or wash brushes in exchange for supplies. I want to try painting . . . and I can't at home."

He said it was fine, with a surprising stipulation.

"I'd like you to sign up for an art class next semester."

When had a teacher ever noticed me enough to ask me to take a class of theirs? Never. Maybe he could see how shocked I was because he said, "For my more parsimonious colleagues, that would help me justify giving you supplies."

"Of course," I said. "I want to take art." I stopped myself from saying anything else that might lead to over-sharing. *I've wanted to paint again for a while. I've been scared. It's complicated for me.*

Since then, I've gotten to know Mr. Standish better, and I've told him a few things. When he asked how I knew so much about art supplies (where to buy them, which brands I liked best), I told him the truth.

"My dad was a painter. We worked together a lot."

When I said his name, he raised his eyebrows. "Oh

my gosh. I remember him. I had some friends who used to know—" Then he remembered. "I'm sorry about your loss."

Mr. Standish didn't ask too much of me at first, but after I finished my first painting, he put his hand over his mouth and shook his head, as if he wasn't sure what to say. Then he smiled. "Well, I see talent must run in the family. It's great to have you in the fold, Jamie."

I replayed his words in my mind a lot. It was just before Christmas break—our second holiday without Dad and our first in the new apartment. We had to spend Christmas Day with my aunt who is high-strung and hard for my mom to be around for more than a day, but the rest of the time we were on our own, which wasn't as hard as I thought it would be. Mostly we watched movies. And in between, I thought about Mr. Standish's expression when he looked at my work. I thought about what he said. *It's great to have you in the fold.* It made me think about origami and see it for what it really had been all this time: a replacement for doing art, which scared me too much.

I've learned that I can't bear not creating. It soothes me to look at colors and study the way they change in different lights. I love the magic of transforming paper from a flat one-dimensional object into an animal or a piece of art. It taught me things I'd never learned in all my years of painting and drawing with my father. Paper has a life of its own. I'm interested in three-dimensional art, something my father always dismissed as belonging in the realm of craft shows. Mostly I've realized it's okay to think about my father's ideas and disagree with some.

Mr. Standish was careful when he asked if I'd like to represent my class in the citywide art show. "I wanted to ask you first because you're the most obvious choice, but I also understand if you'd like to wait until next year. It would mean working intensively over the next two months to create three works you'd feel good about displaying."

I wanted to say yes right away.

To my ear, "working intensively" meant I'd have permission to come in at lunch and during study hall. Maybe even before school. It meant filling my days (and my mind) with something besides worrying about how David was recovering and what would happen when he came back to school. I'm glad I had this pressure. In the week since he's been back at school, I've been too busy to think much about him until today.

Now it's hard to think about anything else, and the show is five days away. I have two pieces finished and a third one I can't get right no matter how hard I try. It helped that he recognized what I was painting right away, but it also confused me. What if I couldn't finish this one because it was too tied up with memories of David?

Spotlighted artists must have three finished pieces in order to participate. It's too late for Mr. Standish to ask another tenth grader to replace me. I've been working toward this for two months; backing out would be crazy. But crazier still is what I keep thinking the whole next day when I go into school early, work all through lunch and class time: I still can't get this right.

Finally, I break down and go to Mr. Standish. "I can't do this. I've tried. You've seen how many hours I've been working on this. I don't want to disappoint you, but I also don't want to be part of the show with work that isn't ready."

He pulls a chair close to his desk and suggests I sit down.

I don't want to sit. I don't want to talk about this any more than I already have.

He waits and points to the chair again. Apparently, I don't have a choice.

"Sometimes when I get in a tight spot like this—and trust me, Jamie, all artists go through this before most shows—taking a step back helps. Think about what you were trying to achieve with this painting and ask yourself, is there a different way you can do that."

It's hard to talk about this.

But I try anyway. I tell him in pieces: It was hard for me to do art after my father died, I say. And I made this crazy discovery, origami. It wasn't art the way my father defined it (one of his first rules: art had to be original, not replicable). Still, it was soothing to me.

He looks at me and nods as if this doesn't sound so crazy to him. "'Soothing' is an interesting word. Why do you think it felt that way?"

"Because—I don't know."

He nods again but doesn't say anything. It's as if he already knows my answer, because I do, too. "Because you know when it's finished. It's supposed to look a certain way, and when it does, you're through."

I laugh because it sounds silly. *I like origami because it's easier.*

"What if you tried to do something with that idea? Capture the beauty of what you discovered and loved about origami this year? Only not with a painting?"

What are you talking about? I want to say.

He stares at me like I'm missing something obvious. Finally he says it: "Three-dimensional art is allowed in this show. Why don't you try something that stays true to your original inspiration?"

What he's saying is clear: *Why don't you make some origami?*

My heart is racing by the time I rush out of there. It's hard to tell if it's the idea, or the freedom from having to finish the other painting that has energized me. It doesn't even matter. He's right: it's a great idea! I've seen photographs of beautiful origami art displayed in museums in Japan and around the world. I don't have the skills to make a single piece my finished work, but I could arrange smaller pieces—in a scene maybe. I think about Ms. Yu, the art therapist in the hospital, setting up our houses on a small table and clapping her hands. *We made a community! Right here!*

I wish I had a picture of that ragtag row of paper houses. Some had pink roofs or daisies drawn in instead of windows. A few were all black, but next to others, they didn't look so bad. In fact, they made the others look brighter and stand out more. I wish I could go back to the hospital and find out if that woman had saved five months' worth of origami houses made by teens who'd lost their place in the world. Creating little houses out of paper helped us find that again. Or it helped me, anyway.

I can't go back, though. There isn't time, and it's doubtful she's saved anything.

I run through other ideas. What if I made a mobile of birds—different kinds, flying in harmony? If I balanced it correctly, it would respond to the movement of viewers walking underneath so the birds would "fly" when people came near.

The more I consider this idea, the more I like it.

That night I IM David:

ME: If I have a project that's important and is due on Monday, could I ask for your help as a friend?
DAVID: As opposed to what? As an enemy?

I try to think of a funny retort and I can't. Hopefully, he understands what I mean: *I'm not trying to send mixed messages or date you after saying I couldn't. I really need help, and you're the only person who can do it.*

ME: I've been chosen as a finalist for an art show, but I need one more work to include. I've been trying to finish a painting for weeks, and I can't get it to work, so I've changed my mind. I want to do a mobile of origami birds. But to get it to work, I need a lot of them. A whole flock. Hundreds. And I have to finish by Monday.

DAVID: You want me to meet you somewhere and fold cranes with you?

ME: Not just cranes. I need swans and gulls, too. Every flying bird we can think of.

DAVID: Do you remember who you're asking? Stubby-fingers Sheinman?

ME: You're good at origami.

DAVID: You don't need to lie. I'm not dying anymore.

ME: Okay, you're fine at origami. The important part is quantity, not quality. I want it to feel like a cloud of birds. I want them to hang perfectly still until someone walks underneath and the slightest movement—a breath even—will stir them. The person will look up and breathe more, and they'll start to take flight. Hopefully the person won't even realize they're the ones doing it.

DAVID: Kind of like you did for me?

ME: What do you mean?

DAVID: They'll bring something back to life by just standing there, being themselves and looking.

ME: That's kind of stupid, David. I mean, I'm sorry—it's sweet, but it's also not what happened. New lungs brought you back to life. What I did got in the way of all that. Just saying.

DAVID: Oh, right. I forgot. It just FEELS like that.

ME: Can you help me?

DAVID: Of course. Sharon and I decided we shouldn't be on any of the same committees, which means she's on all of them and I'm on none, so I have a lot of extra time now.

ME: Isn't that a little unfair?

DAVID: No one trusts me to get anything done. If I volunteer to do something, they secretly assign someone else to do it.

ME: Are you sure you're not being paranoid?

DAVID: Just because you're paranoid doesn't mean everyone's only been pretending to be your friend for a pretty long time. But never mind all that. I appreciate the genuine request for help. I'd be honored. Where should I meet you?

I hesitate.

ME: Do you mind coming to my apartment? I have all the stuff here.

DAVID: Not at all. That makes sense. What's your apartment number?

CHAPTER TWENTY

DAVID

T HIS IS EERIE. I feel like I've been to this apartment
complex before, but I know I haven't.

Maybe it's because I could see it from my hospital window. But why do I know which door is hers before I even
see the number? It feels like I *have* been here before.

Jamie opens the door wearing sweatpants and a T-shirt,
holding an elaborate contraption of what looks like twisted
metal wire hangers. "I keep screwing up the base. This
is my third try. Hi, by the way. Come on in. Thanks for
coming over."

She spins around and returns to the corner of the living
room, where she has a pile of hangers and wire cutters and
two other tangled versions of the base she's holding.

"It turns out there's a lot more to a mobile than you'd
think. It's all about physics and balance, but some of it is
counterintuitive. I put more weight on one side, and it goes
up. I don't understand why."

She's completely focused on this problem. She's not nervous like I am, standing here alone in her apartment. My palms are sweaty, and my heart is beating. She's just staring at her wire hangers and venting.

"What do you want me to do?" I ask.

She looks up, surprised, like she almost forgot why she asked me to come over. "Oh, right! Fold birds! I've got the box of paper over there. And a book with the different birds for you to make."

She waves her hand in the direction of the only table in the place—a small metal one in the kitchen, big enough for two people. I have to admit, I imagined this differently. I pictured Jamie and me sitting at a table, bumping knees and locking eyes as she zipped through three birds for every one that I finished. "Alone?" I say. "You trust me?"

"Of course. Plus, I left the abalone folder out to help with your creases."

I sit down and flip through the book. "Should they all be flying birds? No penguins, I assume?"

She's so absorbed in her pile of hangers, she doesn't even look up. "That's right. Flying—with open wings, if it's possible."

It's hard not to look at her. She's got her hair pulled into a ponytail, which I've never seen before—a curly bush in the back with escaped curls framing her face. I fold for a while, but I keep sneaking looks. Concentrating furiously, she hacks and twists and yanks at her wires. Every ten minutes, she holds it up to test the balance. From where I'm sitting, it looks good.

Her focus makes me focus more. I'm not sure how long we've been working when the door opens and Jamie's mom walks in. She's obviously surprised to see me. "David? What are you doing here?"

Jamie says, "You remember, Mom? I told you, David's helping me on this project. He asked if he could help, and I said yes."

There's a whole silent conversation between them that I can't follow.

I'm guessing her mom doesn't like this idea for any number of reasons. I'm too old, maybe, or I'm too fragile. Or I strung Jamie along in some confusing way while I was in the hospital. Or else she just doesn't like me.

She narrows her eyes, like she's trying to figure out if Jamie's telling the truth.

"I like Jamie's art," I say. "I want her to do well in this show. I really do. I just want to help, and she said she was a little behind on this last one."

She studies my face as I say this—really looks in my eyes—and it's strange. I feel as if we've done this before. I have the same déjà vu feeling I had coming to this apartment. I try to convey the simple truth: *I care about her. I'm not going to hurt her.*

It must work, at least to some extent, because after a moment, she says, "Well, okay then. Maybe I should order a pizza?"

It's a long afternoon, but I stay the whole time. I want to see if Jamie can get her idea to work. Constructing the metal skeleton is one challenge. Hanging all the birds is another. Some are too heavy and throw the whole thing off. It's so tricky, we start to laugh. "Here, let me try. I'm in AP Physics, I should be able to figure this out."

Jamie hesitates. "What grade are you getting?"

"Never mind that. I have great intuition about spatial placement and balancing."

I retie some birds and bend some wires. It turns out I don't have great intuition. It flops to one side. Her mother holds her hands out. "David, you hold the thing while Jamie and I fold some more birds and tie them onto the other side until it balances."

It takes another hour, but eventually it works. We celebrate with iced tea. I'm the tallest one in the room, so I've preserved our triumph by stringing it up to the light fixture in the middle of the room. We sit down on the sofa, glasses in hand, and stare up at it.

"What does it suggest to you?"

"A lot of things. Birds mostly." I smile at Jamie.

She squints up at it. "Do you get a sense of freedom and possibility? That's what I was going for."

"Sure. Birds always seem free, don't they?"

I remember one day in the hospital when two pigeons landed on the ledge of my window. They sat there forever, cocking their heads at each other.

Jamie does that now. "Do they?"

I cock my head back at her. My chest hurts, sitting so close to her. Wanting to touch her. Wanting to say something and having to remind myself: *You're not what she needs right now.* "I don't know. Maybe not. Maybe birds would like to stop flying and put down roots somewhere and they can't."

Jamie's mom stands up. She says she can't wait to see Jamie's other pieces in the show. "Have you seen them, David? Do you already know what a wonderful painter Jamie is?"

She's heading to the bathroom, but on her way, she touches one of the paintings on the wall. I hadn't noticed it before, but now I have the same déjà vu. I do know these paintings, but I don't know how.

When we're alone, I ask Jamie why this all feels so familiar. "Being here in your apartment. Sitting on your sofa."

She gives me a funny look. "Maybe you were poor in a different life?"

"I'm serious. Did you ever bring me here?"

"Of course not. Though I'll admit I thought about it. I used to have this stupid fantasy about watching movies with you here."

"We could still do that, couldn't we?"

"No." She stands up so there's no more temptation for our bodies to fall together, side by side on her sofa. "I think it's better for me to say, 'Thank you so much for your help, David, and it's time for you to go home.'"

"Okay." I stand up so she knows I'm not going to push anything or make her uncomfortable. "Then I'll be on my way."

"Oh, I almost forgot. Before you go—I have something for you."

She disappears and returns holding out a green plastic box that I recognize but forgot all about. I laugh. "My happiness quotes!"

"When I left the hospital that first night you were in the ICU, I stopped by your room on the way out. I'm not sure why I took these. I was scared someone might throw them out. Or maybe I thought I might need them. I don't know—but I definitely shouldn't keep them anymore. They're your project. I'm sorry I held on to them for so long."

I open the box and pull out the first card.

"'The deeper that sorrow carves into your being, the more joy you can contain.' Kahlil Gibran. Wow, did I really write quotations on all of these cards?" I flip through the box. There must be at least a hundred in here. I don't remember writing that many, but they're all in my handwriting. "It seems like kind of a strange thing to do."

"You were in a strange mood. Illness does that."

I pull out another. "'Action may not always bring happiness, but there is no happiness without action.' Disraeli. Who is Disraeli?"

"You don't have to read all of those right now. In fact, you probably shouldn't. But you should definitely hold on to them. I read through a lot of them, and I might have changed my mind a little. It wasn't such a bad project."

"Really?"

"I still have a few issues with it. But it got me reading some new writers who I like."

Her mother comes back in the room. I'm dying to

know which writers she liked, but I can't ask her now. We've finished the project I came to help her with. I have to go now.

JAMIE

I wasn't sure about returning David's box to him. The whole time he was in the ICU and after his surgery, I kept it next to my bed, refusing to open it. *Aphorisms won't help me*, I said to myself, every time I was tempted. When he got worse, my inner monologue grew crueler. *You don't deserve any comfort. Especially not from him.*

And then about a week following his transplant, after I'd seen a picture of him on Instagram, sitting up in bed, drinking a milkshake and smiling, I let myself open it. I reached in and pulled out a card from the middle of the bunch. It was a quote from the Archbishop Desmond Tutu: "Our greatest joy comes when we seek to do good for others. We are bound in a delicate network. We learn to be a human being from other human beings."

I had to admit: I liked that one.

It made me look up Tutu's writing. Eventually I found where the quote came from: *The Book of Joy: Finding Lasting Happiness in a Changing World*. Even though I didn't love the title, I checked it out of the library. It was based on a conversation between Desmond Tutu and the Dalai Lama, and a lot of it made sense to me.

I go online and tell David about the book.

ME: It got me reading about Buddhism, which is pretty interesting actually.

DAVID: How so?

ME: Well the first Noble Truth of Buddhism is that life is filled with suffering. They call it "Dukkha," which is roughly translated to the stress and anxiety that arises from the attempt to control what fundamentally can't be controlled. Frustration is the core of all our created suffering.

DAVID: So what are you supposed to do about it?

ME: You accept. Or you pretend to accept. I think pretending is a big part of Buddhism. You pretend to be super calm about whatever's happening. You also can't be too ambitious. Buddhism says that in order to be ambitious you have to define yourself as distinct and better than other people, and that erases the love and connection that you really need.

DAVID: So I guess that means you enter an art show but you don't try to win it.

ME: Oh no, I want to win. I'm just saying the idea is interesting.

I can't bring myself to tell him what reading through his box really made me think about. Being happy takes work. For some people it takes a ton of work. If this isn't how you're genetically programmed, it takes therapy and medication and living with the side effects of medication and the stigma if anyone finds out you're taking medication. I wish I could tell him: *For some of us, it sometimes feels like it might be easier to just be sad.*

I also wish I could tell him: *I don't want to be. I'm trying.*

Even though I joked with him about Buddhism and pretending, one of the main things I learned from my old friends is that being fake is a terrible mistake. It puts you in a battle with yourself, where you're trying to sound one way so no one will suspect anything is wrong. I couldn't do it. I exploded and yelled horrible things at the only friends I had. I was furious at them for making me feel like such a fake, but it was my fault, not theirs. Or maybe some of it was their fault, but no one forces anyone to be phony.

I wish I could tell David this is why being with him scares me so much. With him, I couldn't pretend. I also couldn't be sure I'd always be happy. I'm not made that way. I don't want him to feel like he has to run over to my apartment with books and quotes every time I get quiet or discouraged. Aside from everything else, it won't work. Not really.

Depression can happen when everything is good. You wake up one morning so scared of losing it all you can't get out of bed. I learned this in the hospital, listening to other kids. One boy had his worst episode after he got in to his first-choice college. It's irrational and unpredictable.

He has a chronic condition he's living with, and so do I.

I don't expect anyone besides my mom and Mr. Standish to come to the show. For one thing, it's hard to get to—across town, which means it's a forty-minute drive after school. My mom has taken the day off work to help me transport my mobile to the event. Mr. Standish is bringing the other pieces from school.

When he meets us at three, I realize he must have skipped his afternoon classes. He's also carried two canvases from four blocks away, which apparently was the closest parking he could get. His face is still sweating a little. "Thank you so much for all this," I say.

"My pleasure," he says. And then, after we find my spot and set up the paintings on the easels with my name, he adds: "It really is my pleasure, Jamie. It's lovely to have such a talented student. I even told my wife about you."

He seems embarrassed to admit this, which makes it feel all the more sincere.

I don't know what else to say except "Thank you."

"Just make sure you stick with this. That's all."

"I want to stick with this. I really do."

Mr. Standish can't stay for more than an hour, and the whole event goes until seven. There are judges and panels and a medal ceremony at the end. It seems to take forever, and I still love every minute of it, even when my mother gets so tired from standing and smiling at people walking under my mobile that she pulls a chair over and sits down so she can point up and make sure everyone sees it.

I have to admit, the mobile works beautifully. My mom even seems like part of the work after a while. Everyone looks up and smiles as she shows them what to do: blow a little.

She demonstrates, and they do. And all the birds take flight.

It works like I wanted it to. Like I imagined but hardly dared hope, it might.

In the end, I win a silver ribbon, which isn't first prize, but it's still more than I expected.

The much bigger surprise happens at the end of the medal ceremony when I get back to my seat and find David sitting beside my mom.

"I'm sorry I'm late," he says. "But I got here in time to see you win!"

My heart is beating crazily. I can't believe he's here. He even looks like he showered and changed his clothes before he came, like he thought this was something he should dress up for. He looks wonderful, in a button-down shirt and nice jeans.

"I didn't win. The gold ribbon is the winner. Silver is second."

"So it's like the Olympics?"

"Right. Except none of us are athletic."

He laughs and leans toward me. "Eileen is here, too. She thought there would be more fashion, I think. She doesn't realize most people don't do art on their T-shirts."

We're sitting so close our arms brush each other. "Some do. There's other shows for that."

"Maybe you can talk to her about that. On the drive here, she told me she wants to be an artist."

"*Really?*"

"I said she should probably take an art class before she decides something like that."

"Most people do, but it's not a requirement."

I'm surprised that my mother doesn't seem nervous about David's being here. When I catch her eye, she leans across him and asks if she can see my ribbon. I hand it to her, and she holds it up, letting it dangle and flutter, the way our birds did earlier. "Well, I like this better than the gold one, actually. I think it's classier," she says.

David gives it a twirl. "I do, too. Definitely."

I laugh and grab it back. "I'm shooting for gold before I finish high school."

My mom squeezes my arm, and almost without realizing what I'm doing, I take David's hand. I think I'm going to just squeeze it, to thank him for driving all the way here, and then it feels so nice I leave it.

Maybe this is okay, too, I think. Maybe I can handle this.

Maybe a little bit of happiness doesn't mean I'll be sadder, later down the line. Maybe it means I'll know what the real kind is like.

Eileen's voice materializes behind us. "Oh my God, your stuff is so much better than the girl-who-won-the-gold's is."

I laugh and spin around. She's not even trying to keep her voice down. "Thanks, Eileen. And thanks for coming."

She leans closer. "You're welcome. So I have to say, I've been looking at the others, and some of them aren't that great."

"Every school in the city is represented. Some don't have very good art programs. We're lucky. We do."

"Yeah. I'm thinking I might check it out."

It seems funny that she's had a locker on the art wing of our school for almost two years and it's never occurred to her to sign up for a class. I think about the drawing she does in life science instead of taking notes.

"You definitely should."

David squeezes my hand. Our fingers are laced now. It's hard to look down and take this all in. So many times, he's held out his hand, wanting me to take it, and so many times, I've refrained. Because I'm scared. Because he'll know what he's doing and I won't. Because I haven't let myself imagine any of this.

Now it's happening, and I don't feel panicky or over-whelmed. My mom is right here, seemingly unfazed. Eileen is, too. I have a weird thought: *Maybe they're even rooting for us.*

Afterward, I ask my mom if I can get a ride home with David and Eileen.

"Of course." She laughs, rolling her eyes, like this is something that happens all the time. Me acting like a teen-ager who'd rather be with other teenagers than with my mom.

"Thank you," I whisper as I kiss her cheek.

In the car, David starts by announcing that he's still a little rusty. "I'm told that I'm a little heavy-handed on the brake. I apologize ahead of time if any airbags are triggered."

"Gee, that's not unsettling at all," I say.

"To be fair, I was never a great driver, even before the

transplant. In fact, it's possible I'm better now."

Eileen leans in between us from the back seat. "You've always been terrible. You always will be. Stop apologizing and go."

He does. It turns out he's not a terrible driver, just slow compared to others, especially on the highway, where all the cars fly past us. "I just don't see what the big rush is," he says, when he notices me checking his speedometer. "I think driving fifty is fine, don't you?"

"Let's talk about something else, Grandpa," Eileen says from the back. She asks about a few cute boys she noticed who were also in the art show. I tell her I don't know them.

"See this is what we're going to work on with you. You have to learn how to do this thing where you say hi to people and introduce yourself. After that, you say, 'Have you met my friend Eileen?' and I'll do the rest."

"Okay," I say, laughing.

"Next year, I'd like to come earlier to this show and work the room more. I think that might make a difference for you, prizewise."

After a while, Eileen gets out her headphones and tells us to "talk among ourselves." She leans back and closes her eyes. When I look back, her lips are moving to the music, which makes me laugh.

We drive in silence for a while, and then David says there's something he wants to tell me. I look at him and wait.

"Okay. I've been having these dreams. Where I'm back in the hospital, but I'm not sick. I'm just walking around the hallways, trying to talk to people, only no one can hear me."

"That's weird."

"Some of the nurses are in it. And my family is there and a few of my friends. But the strangest part is that no one can see me. I'm screaming at the top of my lungs, I'm frantic, and they all keep having their own conversations."

That actually sounds less like a dream and more like the busiest times at the nurses' station—call buttons going off and no one responding because there's too much work and not enough coverage.

"Maybe you spent too much time in the hospital," I say. "It's haunting you."

"It's not that. Because every dream is the same—I'm looking for you. I'm asking everyone, 'Where's Jamie?' In some of them, I'm even talking to your *mom*."

He reaches for my hand. "I think it happened. While I was in a coma—that whole time, I was wandering around looking for you."

"David—" I don't know what to say. Should I tell him the truth? "Sometimes I felt you. Or I thought I heard your voice."

We sit with this for a while. There's no way to know what fevered dreams mean or what truths might be revealed in the fog of depression.

Instead of saying any more, he changes the subject. "I'm not going to go away to college next year. I've already told my parents. It doesn't make any sense. My doctors are all here; there are too many unknowns. I need to keep my variables to a minimum."

"Won't you need fewer doctors now?"

"No, the opposite. You get new lungs and you trade one condition for another. CF isn't the main battle now—I still have it, but the bigger danger is chronic rejection. It can happen anytime, and it can make me really sick, really quickly. I might feel better than I have in years, but the reality is I'm still limited. I still have to think about it most of the time."

I don't know what to think. I'm thrilled that he won't be disappearing off to college next fall, but the health news is scary.

"What did your parents say?"

"They weren't happy. They think it's a mistake. I told them it's my life and I've got to be able to make my own mistakes. I think they were surprised that I held my ground."

"What will you do?"

"I promised them I'd take some classes at the community college. I just want to make sure they're ones that are interesting to me."

"Happiness studies?"

"Film history, actually. I spent a lot of my recovery watching more movies. I should warn you, I don't agree with all your opinions. I'm developing some of my own, believe it or not."

"Like what?"

I dare myself to turn and look at him, even as he holds my hand. Though he's driving one-handed, he doesn't look away from the road. He's too cautious for that, too aware of the risks. Just like I am.

"Well, for starters you have a pretty superficial understanding of Hitchcock. I'm sorry to say that, but it's true. He's far more screwed-up than you ever realized."

I smile. "I never said he wasn't screwed-up."

"Maybe, but you implied that it wasn't a big deal. That given the artistry of camera angles and shot composition and all that, the psychology was secondary. I'm sorry, but it wasn't. The guy was a nutjob. Brilliant, but a nut."

For the first time, I let myself form the complete thought in my mind: *Maybe this could work. Maybe we might stay together as long as possible and be as happy as we can be.* Maybe we might someday look like a regular couple—out on a date, arguing about a movie.

"You hear how dismissive and reductive your language is, right?" I smile as I say this. "'Nutjob' really isn't a useful term."

"You're right. 'Psychopath' is better. There's another director, though, who I want you to check out. Billy Wilder. He was Jewish and escaped Nazi Germany, arrived here not speaking any English, and by 1942, he was already making movies. He's famous for all these comedies, like *Some Like It Hot*, and meanwhile, his mother died in a concentration camp."

Is he saying what I think he is? We all have dark stories; we all have to do what we can and live in spite of them.

Eileen wakes up when we get off the highway and asks if David will drop her off first. "I assume you're taking

335

Jamie home, right? I have stuff I need to do at home. I'm trying not to get a D in math."

After dropping her off, David drives over to my apartment and parks in one of the few spots that doesn't face the dumpster or a pile of trash. Now that we're alone, I feel more scared. We're not holding hands anymore. I don't know how this is supposed to go.

"Thank you for coming tonight and for all your help. I'm sorry for what I said in the art room—that being friends with you again wouldn't be good for me. Depression makes me very risk-averse. I think, if I don't take any risks, maybe I won't feel shitty again. But then I remember that taking risks is pretty much the only way to surprise myself. And surprising myself feels good."

I've been thinking about this ever since he came over to spend the afternoon folding birds. I surprised myself by entering the competition, but also by including him in the process. And it didn't feel scary. It felt right.

He nods and says, "I want to say something that we've never gotten to talk about, is that okay?"

"Okay."

He looks serious—so much so that he stares at his hands, not me. "I know what happened with your dad. I found out from one of the nurses, mostly because I was prying and asking questions about you. I never knew how to tell you or say how sorry I was."

For a long time, we're both quiet. "It's hard to talk about," I finally say.

"Yeah."

"The dad I knew for most of my life wasn't suicidal. Mostly, he was a great dad who gave me a good education. Different, but good. I wish you could have known him."

"It's strange, being old enough to see the mistakes our parents make, isn't it?"

"Do you feel that way about yours?"

"Not so much anymore. They finally listened when I told them I didn't want to go away to college. That helped. But who knows? Maybe a year from now I'll change my mind. Then I'll have to admit they were right all along. That'll be embarrassing."

"No, it won't. I've changed my mind about a few things."

He turns and looks at me. "You have? About what?"

"You, for one."

"Really? Me talking about old movies did that?"

"The movies, plus everything else. Helping me on my project, being here tonight. It makes me think maybe I should keep an open mind."

His smile widens. "An open mind is a good thing."

"Do you want to come inside?"

"Sure. Except your mom will be there, right?"

"Yes."

"So that might be awkward."

"She likes you, David. She thought I shouldn't write you because you needed to concentrate on getting well."

"So if I try to kiss you, is she going to worry about germs?"

I laugh. "She might, actually."

"So what should we do?"

We look at each other. My chest squeezes. "Maybe we should kiss out here and then go in," I say. "If you think it's safe."

He looks at me, serious again. "Nothing's totally safe."

"I know."

"Doing anything is risky for me."

"Me too."

"So we'll take it slow."

I'm surprised. For the first time, it occurs to me: He might be more nervous than I am. I lean toward him and whisper: "You might not remember, but we've done this before."

I kiss him softly.

"How did it go?" he whispers.

"It was very nice," I say, kissing him again.

"Like this?"

"Just like this."